STAG LINE

Stories by Men

STAG LINE

Stories by Men

SELECTED BY

Bonnie Burnard

Coteau Books

Edited by Bonnie Burnard

Cover painting, "Lady's Choice I," Ink and acrylic on paper, by Karen Schoonover, 1994. Courtesy of the artist.
Cover design by Coteau Books.
Book design and typesetting by Val Jakubowski.
Printed and bound in Canada.

The publisher gratefully acknowledges the financial assistance of the Saskatchewan Arts Board, the Canada Council, the Department of Canadian Heritage, and the City of Regina Arts Commission.

Excerpts from THE DEATH OF ADOLF HITLER: UNKNOWN DOCUMENTS FROM SOVIET ARCHIVES by Lev Bezymenski, copyright © 1968 by Christian Wegner Verlag, Hamburg, English translation copyright © 1968 by Harcourt Brace & Company, reprinted by permission of Harcourt Brace & Company.

Canadian Cataloguing in Publication Data

Main entry under title:

Stag Line

ISBN 1-55050-061-9

1. Canadian fiction (English) - Men authors.*
2. Canadian fiction (English) - 20th century.*
3. Men - fiction. I. Burnard, Bonnie.

PS8321.S72 1995   C813'.0108   C95-920031-2
PR9197.32.S72   1995

COTEAU BOOKS
401-2206 Dewdney Ave.
Regina, SK   S4R 1H3

Contents

Introduction

A STAG LINE, it seems to me, is a group of men thinking it over.

THE CONCEPT: DECEMBER 1992

The impetus for this anthology is curiosity: I want to explore what an anthology of stories written by men might hold. But there's a sub-text. I do have (at least) two overriding resistances. I am not receptive to writing which observes male violence in a way which is suspiciously enthusiastic or, conversely, to writing which attempts to apologize for the masculinity of men. Some would say this limits me. Perhaps the answer is that an editor is always limited in one way or another and that the best thing about books is that there are lots of them. I want to read an anthology of stories written by men about good men, I want to know how they are good and, perhaps, why they are good. If goodness is absent, I want that absence to resound. I want to be unequivocally repulsed.

All I can do is claim that in any anthology there is usually a plan, and this one is mine. Nothing definitive here: an approach, that's all.

Last Sunday was the third anniversary of the massacre of the fourteen young women in Montreal. Although when I was young I studied and have since read or heard every day of my life about wars and slaughter, both massive and singular, Marc Lepine's actions and the ongoing conjecture about his motivations may finally have made redundant (for me) fiction which showcases male violence, as if it is something undiscovered. Perhaps the simple banality of evil has ruined my taste for such fiction, made it too often predictable, without challenge. Perhaps modern journalism, with its sometimes clear-eyed focus and commentary on the actual day-by-day obscenities of human interaction, has made such fiction unnecessary. As for the masculinity of men, it still seems to me to be preferable to the alternatives. I don't take masculinity to be synonymous with violence and even if masculinity could be obliterated, with social or scientific engineering, who knows what we'd get in its place.

I did nothing on Sunday to commemorate the murder of those

fourteen young women in Montreal, nothing except think about them off and on all day long. I thought about them deliberately, both as individual women dying individually and as representatives of the particular miseries perpetrated by some men.

In the evening, I was distracted briefly from these thoughts while listening to my daughter's high school *a cappella* choir sing carols to a crowd of fifteen hundred at the Centre of the Arts here in Regina. When they sang "Silent Night," they sang the first few bars in full harmony, then there was a female soloist, who was followed by harmony again, then a male duet, and finally, to finish, full harmony. It was quite beautiful.

GOING TO PRESS: DECEMBER 1994

I like fiction anthologies for the same reason I like the occasional unpredictable party. Most of the time I prefer to be with one person, talking or listening, but once in a while I want the chaotic juxtaposition of different voices in one place. I like the potential. I like the sound of both the loners and the groupings, the familiar voices and the strange ones. I like the noise.

In fiction, for me, content is to form what presence is to style in an individual (the people who stay in my mind have what I think of as presence; their style is irrelevant). Or, what a story tells matters more to me than how it's told (as long as it's well told). And I am extremely interested in the authenticity of narrative voice. That's what I trust in a story; that's why I listen.

In what passes for real life it is not possible to know another human heart, to read another mind; one can only speculate. Reading authentic fiction is like being invisible at the party, floating from room to room, seeing and hearing things that would be missed otherwise. But it offers something more. The pull of authentic fiction is that sometimes the reader can know another imagined heart, can read another imagined mind. It's the only chance extant to see someone else, truly, if only briefly and not necessarily definitively, from the inside.

Fiction anthologies usually have some justification. Often, in Canada, they are regional, either showcases for work that would otherwise be ignored, or explorations of the importance of place in our literature. Sometimes, anthologies have themes: travel, erotica, love. Sometimes editors will gather work which is, in their critical judgement, the best from a period of time, or the best being written "now," or the best work by new, unknown writers.

Sometimes anthologies are deliberately political – issues explored through the imagination.

Regional anthologies seem to me to be necessary and healthy, given the usual concentration of literary energy in what's called central Canada (perhaps this bent can be attributed to my own years writing and editing in the West and the way my ears lock hard on the snide, disparaging comments occasionally made by literary commentators who apparently believe that North Bay is actually in the north). Perhaps my attitude is becoming less defensible; thanks largely to the Canada Council, to Morningside, the Gabereau Show and The Arts Tonight, to Imprint, to literary awards, to sophisticated teachers, librarians and bookstore owners, potential Canadian readers have been exposed to at least some writers from across the country.

Theme anthologies are almost always interesting, almost always a good read. And "best" anthologies are admittedly and happily, enthusiastically, subjective, more like showcases than definitive bits of canon. Political anthologies, issue anthologies are more difficult; they can seem preordained, the writers like witnesses for a church.

Justfication for this anthology is personal. I wanted to read a book such as this, and I wanted a woman to choose what would be in it.

Bonnie Burnard,
December, 1994

Machinery of Night

Craig Piprell

Auntie joy cuffed me in the head when she caught me squeezing Harry's hard-on. We were four or five at the time. It must have felt like I'd been sideswiped by a van.

Soon it became clear that Harry wasn't getting any older, and we stopped being pals. Mom ravelled it out for me: "Harry is special," she said. I left him behind in the sandbox, playing with kid brothers and cast metal dumptrucks, when we boarded the bus that autumn for school.

I woke up this morning in the nocturnal tideline with a big fat stiffy. Constancy in a world of change. Encumbered with such flotsam you cannot pee, so I rubbed it like a magic lamp until it went away. You could plant stony worlds with the seed I slough off in a week.

In Grade One Harry's twin sister showed me her bum in the cloak room and told me about Santa Claus. After school I ran to the teacher, who confirmed the news about old Saint Nick. I became her accomplice; promised not to tell kid brother.

I move to the crapper, hungover with sleep, where I squeeze through the entrails of the local daily. The news is a small but important indulgence: continuing education; a ritual against impending chaos.

According to the Associated Press, dozens of motorists claim

to have seen the face of Jesus Christ, shrouded in spaghetti and
tomato sauce, on a Pizza Hut billboard....

In Grade Two we learned to cut out the middleman and create our
own mythologies:

> When you're going to have babies you have to put it up
> her bum. But you're only allowed if the doctor says so,
> and then he makes you do it in his office in an L-Shaped
> Room.

One recalcitrant Cub insisted that hospital babies are carved
from the belly with a knife. He was hooted down. One or two
others held that the belly button is the orifice of the species – an
intriguing idea, reluctantly discarded after much speculative
consideration. In the end, however, it was agreed that there must
be a hole, and the bum faction won.

Early one morning my Grade Three teacher summoned me to do
multiplication problems with an excruciating hard-on. I made it to
the blackboard in a tittering squall. Harry's twin sister laughed and
pointed at my impossible corduroy trousers in front of the class.

So rub-a-dub-dub, and thanks for the tree of life, which sends
runners out in all directions. Answering a call we have no ears to
hear, these runners thrust up through flagstone and asphalt. They
grow very fast – our *eyes* are too slow. This is the law in the land of
the unclean dog. He hungers; he eats anything. He tires; he sleeps
anywhere. Nothing short of extinction can stop him from growing
as he will.

GRADE FOUR

IF: a) The prescribed hemlines of the school uniform were
     off-limits in the playground, but fair game on the stairs, and
     b) Some of the boys snatched-and-raised them, displaying
     dumb underwear

THEN: Some of the girls would squeal or blush, and not breathe a
     word.

Every day on the way home I pounded the arm of my schoolbus
seatmate black and blue. The alternative was implied but forbidden.
She had an unspeakable crush on me. We laughed as if it were funny.

My best friend Sean and I talked Harry, a year before he died, into pooping in the sandbox. He claimed he needed to go. He accepted our gracious, insistent permissions. We towered over the land of toys while he squatted among his dumptrucks. We met each other's eyes and felt manhood upon us.

Mrs. Merrivale brought the news about Harry to her Grade Five class. Harry, she said, was special. Solemnity was called for; of course we provided it. But many of us had already lost relatives, or pets. And kids grow fast. Soon there wouldn't be a boy left among us.

Mrs. M. shellacked her hair and sported an enormous derriere. I fell in love with it immediately. Her husband died too, half way through the school year, and I would lie in bed at night with a painful erection, dreaming of somehow offering succour.

Thousands of years later, I can still recite all the anthems and hymns: "I pledge allegiance to the Flag, and to the Commonwealth for which It stands." But most of what we learn in school has little to do with formalities, and knowledge is decanted retro-teleologically, subject by subject. Teaching is merely good daycare. We learn as we breath, like the unclean dog.

For example: it will take millenia to climb the tree of life. Who would believe it if you told them in class? What could children be expected to take away from such claims – that conception will recede as quickly as they scale the lower branches? We may say that first come the centuries, well spaced and worthy of youthful aspiration; that these soon provide access to handier limbs, memorable decades and years of accomplishment. We make our way quickly now, month by week. We may intimate that we tire as the going gets easier – that what was fun to begin becomes mighty hard work. We may share the secret that we assuage our weariness with dreams of abdication. But our children cluster at the base of this strongly rooted monster, old as the amoeba. "Go on! Climb higher!" they cry. Lost beyond the foliage is the pinnacle, where we measure what's left with the rulers of odd hours, slim moments. But we are far too terrified and ashamed to quit climbing. The crown of the ancient being draws everything up into flame.

The unclean dog burns, once or twice, for a heavenly connection to the starry dynamo, then wanders lonely as a cloud, into the machinery of night.

The next year I learned what a hard-on was for, courtesy of an

unpopular little gomer named Malcolm McGuirk. He had premature pimples, enough profanity to hint at the miraculous, and
questionable amounts of dubious knowledge gleaned mostly, he
said, from routine experiments on his four-year-old sister.

I was skeptical when he told me about jerking off – I couldn't
imagine I was that out of touch with my own body. But I also
couldn't wait to get home and find out.

The first seizure was best, hiccoughing up like a sudden,
unheralded reversal of the poles. I sat at my desk, bare bum stuck
to the hot wooden chair, stark flaccid with amazement. "Holy
Jesus," I thought, corduroys puddled at my knees. "The little
bugger was right!"

It was a wonderful secret, jealously guarded. Santa was back,
grinning like a madman. And every day from now to forever was
going to be Christmas, signed, sealed and delivered by me.

After a couple of inaugural sessions, spunk came out, and I
prepared one last slide for my microscope. I found it in a box of junk
when my father died. I'd cleverly labelled it "(S)" and filed it in my
specimen case, all those years ago, between "Hair (Dad's Beard)"
and "Missilaneus Protozoa."

Furtive ecstacy quickly became a daily ritual, driven by unlikely
fantasies generated by anything: an *Archie* comic; an Eaton's flyer.
The escalating frenzy was well recognized by my mother, of course,
who laundered all sheets. I didn't find out until much too late.

And so I say unto you who must learn and know: Behold the
unclean dog, who humps, from time to time, just to keep his leg
in. He has no balls. He doesn't hump dogs. Some are too embarrassed to say anything. Some don't seem to mind, or think it's cute.
The unclean dog neither knows nor cares. He squints off into an
impossible doggy future, and humps himself out of his flea-bitten
skin.

We are a small race of unruly toddlers. Most of us still pee in
our pants.

None of this has ever been set down in class.

Grade Seven brought Boy Scout dances, a thicket of pubic
hair, and a comb in each pocket. Every Thursday you had to sneak
up on a hapless peer, thwack him in the balls, and yell "Happy
National Fruits Day!" Hilarity was the key element – unjocular

boys suffered ignominious puberty; fearless boys told filthy jokes:

> … So he's taking his clothes off, and she goes in her bag
> and pulls out this special nightgown. But her panties are
> all wadded up in the bottom, eh? So she yells out: "Oh
> no – they're all pink and wrinkly!" And the guy's stripped
> down to his balls and he yells back : "Jesus Christ! I told
> you not to look!"

Boners were as secret and as frequent as lies. I slid a girlie magazine under my sweater and reeled robotically past the check-out clerk with dozens of flat, naked women stuck to my chest. It must have felt like congestive heart failure.

I had my first French kiss at an Elvis Presley matinee. It was better than anything. The earth opened wide and I floated above the abyss for hours, blood thundering in my ears. She was so fat I thought I was stroking her waist.

"Stop it right now," she hissed through my teeth, "or I'm going to go home."

Our parents and teachers prevaricated and made arbitrary, ambiguous pronouncements. By Grade Eight there had been no talk of princes, fairies or elves for some time.

Our home room teacher, Mr. Rigby, had gum disease and wore coke-bottle glasses. He presided over the national anthem and morning prayer. And one day a week he taught sex education.

"Now," he concluded. "After everything I've told you about venereal disease, abortion and unwanted pregnancy, how many of you would be crazy enough to want to try sex before marriage?"

We knew the drill. We knew how to successfully negotiate the pass. We were already scrambling to not raise a single, rhetorical hand when one of our quieter classmates said "me."

She dated a boy at high school. Every eye pendulumed, first toward Sherry, then back to Mr. Rigby, whose face had turned to claret and chalk. "I've already tried it," she said, and smiled. "It was nice."

Now. What we learn is greater than what we know. Harry is special. This we know. Perhaps he was grounded by angels. Time stood still, back there in his sandbox.

London (Reuter's) – A Danish study has found a

significant reduction in men's average sperm count over
the last 50 years.

And we have learned that there are heavy metals and fluoride
and unnamed, unfilterable polychlorinated compounds in our
drinking water. We are awash in UVs, microwaves, fluorescent
lights, electric fields. There's toxic crap leaking out of the broad-
loom and upholstery.

> The worldwide study, published this week in the *British
> Medical Journal*, said sperm density has nearly halved
> and semen quantity has decreased by roughly 25 per
> cent.

But everything we learn and know adds up to paragraphs, not
a story. The unclean dog whimpers and snivels for a scratch,
teeming with fleas. His head itches, under his collar. His ass itches,
over his tail. His crotch itches, *in medias res*. He cannot chatter
over enough furry territory to feel doggy about himself for more
than small moments at a time.

> Professor Niels Skakkebaek, of Copenhagen University,
> said, "It must be something in the environment,
> although we don't know what it is."

Our elders linger in the crown of the tree, waiting for grand-
children. Canada holds a special place in the tax base for those who
come after. The unclean dog squats, defeated, at his doggy
prayers. But the scratch is mine to withhold. I have been cuffed
for countless hard-ons, over the centuries.

I cut these teeth chattering from the belly of my unclean dog.

North, East, West, South: Malthusian biopsies; benign tubers.
Behold, here on the back page, Father Albert of Christ Church
Cathedral, cradling a potato he says looks just like the Virgin and
Child.

I have grown to rival the six-storied demigods of infancy. I own
a three-bedroom bungalow in Olympic Heights. I can stay up all
night and eat as much chocolate cake as I want. But I've learned
that sugar goes straight to my butt. The spectre of potential
unemployment tucks me in at a reasonable hour. And I've scrambled over so many buttocks and breasts they remind me of pillows.

Realism, responsibility, perspective: the rewards of maturity.

Far below, aerobics are just another word for breathing and walking around. Up here the air is thin. But once upon a time, a skinny girl invited me to the Sadie Hawkins dance.

Lotta Ruhl had earned minor notoriety by having her period in class. It stained the back of her skirt. Someone snickered when she stood up; the snickering spread, and the whole class was held in detention through recess.

We kissed even though she had a terrible cold. Two dates later Lotta allowed my hand to linger on one of her A-cups. I was hooked like a pike. For two months I laid seige to those taut Teutonic thighs. Then, following a spirited but uneven defence, the gates flew open. Hot one late afternoon, I eagerly insinuated a squirming handful of fingers.

Nothing I knew or had learned prepared me for the slipperyish heat; the divine cologne of freshly conjured juices at my fingertips. I moonwalked home, a thousand miles in the dark. But when I got there I felt I had arrived not at some inevitably disappointing final destination, but at the border of unbounded opportunity. I had tickled the lock at the door to the womb. The darkness between streetlamps receded, oasis by aromatic oasis of light, where the anointed eagerly waited to welcome me to all the glittering secrets and jewelled joy of earth.

Behind the Beach

David W. Henderson

THE COWS WERE down again on the long, narrow meadow between the summer cottages and the beach, grazing on wild grass. Michael, who had been sent protesting on an errand by his mother, threaded his way among them, keeping clear of their horns. The cows belonged to the year-rounders who lived in decrepit cabins and run-down farmhouses well back of the summer settlement on the edge of the sound. Michael had often heard the summer people, including his parents, complain about the wandering cows, but the meadow was common property, as were the area's roads and paths, so there wasn't much the summer people could do to keep the cows away.

Once past the herd, Michael went down on the beach and walked along the weathered logs stranded above the high tide mark, hopping from one to another, trying not to step off onto the pebbles. Behind him, he could hear the clink of cowbells, and, farther off, the cries of boys as they took turns waterskiing. Friends of his. A wave of irritation washed over him. By the time he got back from his errand, the skiing would probably be over.

At the edge of the settlement, just before the rocky point jutting out into the sound, he took a path leading up from the beach. The path was steep and stony, eroded by the rains. It led to the Lower Road, and, beyond that, climbed through the woods to the Gibsons Road.

When he got to the Lower Road, he looked cautiously about before crossing it and continuing on. He didn't want to run into Billy Whip. Billy was a year-rounder, five or six years older, rough and unpredictable.

A half-mile along the Gibsons Road, Michael found three men working to clear an acre of forest. He approached the one who best fitted the second-hand description his mother had given him. The man was cutting limbs off a fallen cedar with a blue-handled Swedish saw. He was old and lean, had a tangled beard. Unwashed grey hair stuck out from under a narrow-brimmed hat. Sawdust clung to his flannel shirt and canvas trousers.

When he became aware of Michael, he stopped sawing and looked up with rheumy eyes. "What do you want, boy?" he asked. His voice was full of phlegm.

"Are you Mr. Cranshaw?" Michael asked. The air was heavy with the scent of cedar laced with sour sweat.

"Why you asking?" The old man put the saw aside and straightened slowly, rubbing the small of his back. He coughed harshly, spat, and shot a look at the other two men who had stopped nearby to listen.

"My mother sent me. We're the Andrews. She'd like to speak to you about looking after our cottage this winter."

"Which one is it?"

"The old MacPherson place, right next to the Gordons'."

The old man nodded. "I know it."

"You be careful, boy," the taller of the two men listening said. "Don't matter to old Clarence here where he pokes it. Squaws, sheep, pigs, boys – it's all the same to him. Horny old bastard!" The shorter man laughed. Michael put his hands in his pockets and kicked at some wood chips.

"Shut your mouths!" Cranshaw said. The men chuckled. "Guess I could come by your place," he said to Michael, "later today or tomorrow." He coughed again.

"That'll be fine," Michael said. He turned to go.

"That'll be fine," the taller man mimicked. "Shit!" The two men laughed. "La-dee-da," the shorter one said. They laughed again. Michael felt his face go hot, sensed their eyes on him all the way down to the dusty road. Stupid year-rounders.

The old man didn't show up at the Andrews' cottage that day or the next.

"I wonder what happened to Mr. Cranshaw," Michael's mother said to him at breakfast two days after his errand. Her voice was deceptively soft. She sipped her orange juice, eyes probing him, as if searching for some nascent quality or quantity she'd somehow overlooked. Eyes grave from disappointments.

"He told me he'd be down by yesterday," Michael said.

"Did he, dear? Perhaps you misunderstood him."

"I didn't." His father glanced up briefly from his newspaper, shot a warning look at Michael and went back to his reading. He spoke sparingly these days, and Michael was conscious of an awkwardness between his parents, something to do with the business and money, or so he gathered from fragmentary comments overheard by chance, or stealth.

"It doesn't matter, really," his mother said. "The bother is, he hasn't come."

Ava, the young year-rounder who worked for them in the summertime, brought in a steaming serving platter of pancakes and bacon, and set it down firmly on the teak dining table. Michael's mother looked up sharply. "Gently, Ava."

"Cranshaw," Ava said, "is a no-account." And she returned to the kitchen, black braid bobbing on her back.

"Well...!" Michael's mother looked at the doorway through which Ava had disappeared. "Whatever's come over her?" Then she turned, and said, "Michael, I'd like you to go and speak to Mr. Cranshaw again. Tell him it's essential I see him today."

"Do I have to?" He didn't care to encounter Cranshaw or the others a second time, hear their taunts.

"Yes, dear, I want you to. It's important you learn how to deal with people while you're still young. If you don't, it opens the door to problems. It can become an impediment." She glanced towards his father, who kept his eyes on the paper. "Besides, I need to have Mr. Cranshaw's answer quickly," she continued. "The Wilsons suggested he might do the job, but if he's not available, then I'll have to look for someone else."

She began to serve from the platter. "One pancake or two, Edmund?" she asked her husband.

It was past midmorning, the sea gulls crying overhead, when Michael set out once more along the narrow meadow above the beach. Too late, he saw Billy Whip ahead, sitting on his palomino, talking to a bunch of boys from the summer cottages. Billy was squat and muscular, his face round, his hair black and straight. Everyone knew he wanted to be a jockey. He was leaning nonchalantly on the saddle horn, smoking a cigarette while he soaked up adulation and threw out comments, jibes. A raggedly dressed boy about Michael's age stood silently by the horse, holding onto a stirrup. There was no way to avoid going past them. He couldn't turn back. They'd seen him.

"Well, if it isn't little Mickey," Billy said, as Michael approached. Only Billy called him Mickey. He hoped the others wouldn't pick up on it. "What's the word?" Some of the boys giggled in anticipation. Friends Michael ran around with all summer. Michael said nothing, just kept walking, hoping Billy would leave off.

"Hold it, Mickey," Billy demanded. "Stop right there."

Michael stopped. He knew better than to get Billy riled.

"That's more like it," Billy said. "So, tell us where you're going in such a hurry, Mickey Mouse."

Laughs and titters.

"To see Mr. Cranshaw," Michael said, his voice tight.

"Old Clarence? What do want him for?" The year-rounders all seemed to know each other.

"My mom wants to speak to him."

"Is that a fact?" Billy said. "Well, I got news for you. You're not going anywhere till you fight my brother Jimmy here." He pointed a lazy finger down at the boy standing by his stirrup. "I'm betting he can beat the shit out of you."

Michael's stomach bunched up and his hands went sticky. He glanced warily at Jimmy, who was shorter, but wiry. "I'm not going to fight. Why should I?"

"Because Jimmy's not going to give you any choice. Are you, Jimmy?"

Jimmy muttered unintelligibly.

"Fight, fight," the boys chanted, relieved that Billy hadn't picked on one of them. Michael wished them dead.

Billy nudged his brother with a foot. "Go on, Jimmy! Go get him!"

Jimmy resisted the foot, stayed by the horse. But Billy and the boys jeered and encouraged him until he finally stepped towards Michael, his fists clenched. The others quickly formed a circle around them. "I don't want to fight you," Michael said to Jimmy. The boys booed.

Jimmy didn't reply. He hit Michael a tentative blow to the shoulder. "Harder!" the boys yelled. Michael backed away, but hands pushed him towards Jimmy who threw a hook that caught him on the mouth, split his lip. Surprised, Michael probed the wound with his tongue, the taste of blood filling his mouth.

"Hey, why'd you do that?" he asked. He couldn't believe what was happening.

"Chicken!" one of the boys shouted. Michael could feel his face redden. He blocked a couple of Jimmy's punches, and then tried to grab the slighter boy and wrestle him to the ground. End the fight that way. But Jimmy proved elusive. He was dancing around now, caught up in it, flicking out jabs. Anger flaring, Michael began punching back as he circled away from Jimmy's left, watching for the right. He noticed that Jimmy didn't like taking head blows, kept his defenses high. After dodging a wild swing, Michael feinted a punch to the head, then drove a right-handed blow just below the ribs, putting all his weight behind it. The air whooshed out of Jimmy as he doubled over. Michael jumped on him and brought him face down on the ground. He held him there, twisting an arm up behind his back. "You give up?" Michael asked.

Jimmy was silent.

Michael twisted the arm up as high as it would go without breaking or dislocating something. "Say uncle!" he demanded. There was no response.

After a moment, he released Jimmy and got up. "I'm going," he said to Billy, and started off. The boys moved back silently and let him pass. His heart was racing and his lip hurt. He felt nauseous.

"I didn't give up," Michael heard Jimmy say to his brother. "I didn't give up."

"But you let a summer kid beat you. A summer kid...."

Cranshaw was clearing out some alders with a double-bit axe when Michael found him. The other two were cutting down a large spruce at the far end of the lot.

The old man stopped and studied Michael. "Someone sure

gave you a whack," he said, pushing the narrow-brimmed hat back on his head.

Michael touched his swollen lip gingerly. "You were supposed to come and see my mother."

"Yeah, well, I was busy." He coughed several times. Deep, wracking coughs.

"Can you come today?"

"I'll come this evening. Before dark."

"Because, if not, she'll have to get somebody else."

"I'll come, I said."

An hour after the sun had disappeared behind the hills back of the beach, although it still shone on the top of Bowen Island and the mountains across the sound, Cranshaw knocked at the back door of the cottage. Michael watched from the porch as his mother walked the old man about the property, telling him what she wanted attended to in the autumn after the family went back to Vancouver, and what had to be done over the winter and in the spring before they returned. She showed him the bushes to be trimmed, the beds to be weeded and turned, the grass to be cut, and the creek to be kept free of debris so that it would not clog up. Through all this, the old man nodded, but said little.

At the end, they fixed a price. Cranshaw insisted on being paid half up front. Michael's mother hesitated, but finally wrote out a cheque. With the cheque, she gave him a list of the things she'd gone over with him, just to be sure, Michael heard her say, that nothing was overlooked.

The old man accepted the list with an odd smile. "I'll see to it ma'am," he said. He touched his hat, then climbed slowly through the garden and was swallowed by the cedars and gathering dark at the top.

It was early June the next year before Michael and his family returned to the cottage. They were greeted by a garden overrun with growth and trampled by the cows, which had broken through the fence. Worse, the creek's cement-lined channel had jammed and filled with branches, leaves, and gravelly soil, so that, during the spring rains, the runoff had come over the walk between the creek and the house, and inundated the basement. Michael watched as his mother and father wandered aimlessly among the scatter of paint cans, garden tools, oars and deck chairs, all sticking up out of the silt and debris. The smell of dampness and mould permeated the basement. "What negligence," his mother said. "What unspeakable negligence."

While his parents were clearly distressed, Michael noticed that Ava, who had come to help open the cottage, was amused by what she saw, even though, in the end, it would mean more work for her. A small smile, unseen by his parents, tugged at the corners of her mouth as she surveyed the scene, arms folded. Michael's previous indifference to her had changed over the winter to an awareness of the sheen of her black hair, her dark eyes, and the jut of breasts against her blouse.

"You've grown," she said to Michael.

"Yeah," he said, "six inches."

"Just six?" she asked. And she laughed, which was confusing, and he couldn't think of anything to say.

After breakfast two days later, his mother said, "Michael, I know you're not going to be happy about this, but I want you to go and find Mr. Cranshaw and tell him your father and I wish to see him. The people at the store will know where he lives."

"Why not leave a message for him at the post office?"

"Because it might be some time before he gets it, dear. I'd like to see him right away. Today, preferably."

"Wouldn't it be better if Dad went? Mr. Cranshaw's not going to pay much attention to me."

His father looked up from the newspaper, a frown forming vertical creases between his eyebrows. His mother said, "It wouldn't be right for either of us to go. That's not the way things are done. He's to come here and explain himself, and return the money he accepted, or, at least, dig out the creek and clean things up. I don't like paying out money for nothing." She looked down the table at his father, who went back to the newspaper.

Michael's annoyance broke through. "But I don't want to go."

"I know, dear," his mother said, softly but firmly, "but sometimes we just have to accept things as they come."

While he wished no part in any dispute between his parents and the year-rounder, Michael wasn't ready to pay the price of bucking his mother's will. So, after breakfast, he set out along the beach for the store, walking away from the rocky point, throwing pebbles hard out into the water and kicking angrily at pieces of driftwood.

The day was cool, and the mountains across the sound were hidden in mist. It was low tide, and seagulls cried and hunted for crabs among the barnacle-covered stones.

Halfway to the store, he spotted five or six cows grazing in the meadow above the beach and was overtaken by a sudden urge. Up onto the meadow he ran, and chased the cows in the direction of his parent's cottage, yelling and flicking a switch at them as they lumbered along, mooing. He imagined the cows breaking through the fence as they had last winter, pictured them devastating the garden while his parents stared out the window, aghast. The idea pleased him. When he stopped running, however, the cows stopped, too, and went back to grazing. He watched them for a moment, and then turned and continued on his way.

At the store, they told him Cranshaw lived up the old North Road, and gave him directions. He hung around for a while, drank a cream soda before finally setting out.

The rain the night before had left puddles in the ruts of the North Road. He walked down the centre to avoid them. The road led through thick forest, and drops fell from the branches arching overhead. Occasionally, there was a clearing with a year-rounder's ramshackle place.

With the directions, he had no trouble finding the old man's one-room shack. It stood back from the road in a clearing, with walls of weathered rough-cut planking and its one window boarded up. Smoke drifted from a stovepipe sticking up through the tarpaper roof. The whole structure leaned precariously to one side, and was shored by two-by-fours. Nearby, a rusty hand pump capped a well. It tilted in the same direction as the shack, as if both had been bowed by the same wind.

Michael followed a narrow path up through the clearing. Long grass, still heavy with rain, bent over the track and soaked the bottom half of his jeans.

The path led around behind the shack to where the door was. Near the door stood a worn chopping block with a small pile of stove-sized cedar to one side, and a heap of unsplit logs to the other. The sawdust-covered ground was littered with bottles and rusty cans. Farther back, an outhouse lay on its side.

The door to the shack hung battered and crooked in its frame. It had once been painted white, and before that, lime green. Michael had to knock three times before it opened outward to reveal the old man blinking and grimacing in the morning light. He was wearing sagging long johns and his narrow-brimmed hat. The smell of sweat, urine and mould washed over Michael. He took a step backwards.

When Cranshaw's rheumy eyes finally focused on him, Michael thought he saw a flicker of recognition, but the old man didn't say anything. Just stood there scratching himself.

"My mom and dad want you to stop by our place," Michael said. "They'd like to talk to you...." The old man snorted and started coughing. When the spasm passed, Michael added, because he didn't know what else to say, "You were supposed to look after our property last winter. We're the Andrews."

The old man leaned out the doorway and spat to one side. "I know who you are," he said, and retreated to the dark interior of the shack.

Michael hesitated, then stepped forward and stood on the threshold. Gradually, his eyes adjusted. The old man was standing behind a rickety table to Michael's left, finishing a plate of beans. At the table, over which hung an unlit coal oil lamp, sat a stout Indian woman in a faded blue shift. She was studying Michael from the corners of her eyes.

Behind the old man, a stuffed mattress lay on the floor, a couple of blankets strewn across it. A bundle of rags served as a pillow. Clothing, old newspapers and empty liquor bottles were scattered about. The blue Swedish saw, bladeless, hung on the wall beside the boarded-up window.

Opposite the table, on the other side of the shack, were a rusty tin cupboard and a potbellied stove. The stove rested on bricks, and there was a pot of water heating on it.

"Make some coffee," Cranshaw said to the woman.

"None left," she said. "You were going to bring some."

"I forgot."

She turned to Michael. "You want a glass of water? It's well water."

"No," said Michael. "Thanks."

The old man put down his plate, picked up a crumpled shirt from the floor and started to put it on.

"You coming down to see my parents?" Michael asked him.

"You got the rest of the money they owe me? I need a saw blade and some other things." He buttoned his shirt with clumsy fingers.

"They think you should give back the money you took ..."

The old man grinned at Michael, showing the rotten stumps of his teeth. "That's gone. Long gone."

"... give the money back or clean up the mess."

"Mess? What mess? I looked after your place real good." He picked up a pair of canvas trousers and pulled them on, started to button them.

"Doesn't look it."

"Rough winter. Wet spring. I was feeling poorly for a while, and things got a bit behind, that's all." He took a rumpled paper from a shelf and unfolded it. Michael recognized his mother's list. "You see this?" the old man said. "There's work for three, easy." He threw the list on the table. "I want the rest of the money. I did enough for it. You people owe me!" He coughed.

"You'd have to speak to my parents about that."

"They owe me. What's to speak about?"

"Well, they're kind of upset...."

"Are they, now." The old man pushed his hat back. "Why? What's so terrible? It's not like the place burned down or something."

"No, but the basement was flooded."

The old man raised both eyebrows. "The basement flooded." He turned to the Indian woman. "Didja hear that? The basement flooded! Now, isn't that the end of the world!" The woman said nothing. "Lucky the house didn't wash away, and all those other summer places with it. Then we wouldn't have anyone to pay us piss-all to make life easy for them. And wouldn't that be the shits!"

Michael scratched a bite on his arm. "So, what do I tell them?"

"You tell your folks if they want to see me, they can damn well come up here and bring the rest of my money. No way I'm going down there to catch hell for their troubles. You hear?"

"I hear."

"Good. You tell them all that. Now, git!" He scowled and waved both arms. "Scat!"

Michael didn't need any encouragement. He stepped down from the doorway and walked back along the path. When he reached the road, he paused for a moment and looked at the shack and the clearing with its tangle of wild grass and blackberry bushes. He tried unsuccessfully to imagine what it would be like to live there, wondered what his parents thought they could extract from such destitution. Yet he was sure they'd persist. Money was important. They'd persist until they had their way, and he'd be caught in the middle.

After a few moments, a heavy mist descended, reducing visibility to a few feet. The clop of a horse's hooves filtered through the mist. The sound was coming towards him. He moved out of the way to the side of the road. After a moment, he could see the mist-enshrouded outline of a horse and rider. At first glimpse, the horse appeared sway-backed, and the rider raggedly dressed and bent with age. A chill ran through Michael, but, as the horse drew closer, he realized that there was something familiar about the shape of the rider's head.

Michael stepped out onto the road. "Billy?"

The mist stirred, and the horse walked into a thin patch. It was Billy Whip all right, on his palomino, wearing a buckskin jacket with fringes and beading. He halted when he saw Michael. "Well, if it isn't Mickey," he said, and leaned on the saddle horn. "What you doing up here?"

"Seeing Cranshaw."

"So, what's the word? You still running messages?"

"You still pushing Jimmy into fights?"

Billy eyed him. "I should've had one of the summer kids fight you instead."

"What for?"

A grin. "For the fun of seeing two summer kids bash each other. That's all." Billy pulled out his cigarettes, lit one. "I thought Jimmy could take you. Guess I was wrong. Want a butt?"

Michael shook his head. "Thanks anyway."

Billy pocketed the package. He drew on his cigarette and squinted at Michael from behind a stream of smoke. "So, you've been talking to Clarence."

"Yeah."

"What, about the trouble you had at your place over the winter?"

"How'd you guess."

Billy chuckled. "Hear you just about got flooded out." The palomino gave the bridle a shake. "Whoa," said Billy.

"Looks worse than it is. Cranshaw said something about being 'poorly'."

"Oh, yeah? And what do you say?"

Michael considered this. "Well, he's got that cough ..."

"No kidding."

"I guess I'd say he's been sick, if that's the word going round." His parents wouldn't come after someone people said had been ill. It wouldn't look good.

Billy examined the tip of his cigarette for a long moment. "Yeah, he's had it rough," he said finally. "That's the word." Then he straightened in the saddle, stuck the cigarette in the corner of his mouth. Leather creaked. "Have fun cleaning up," he said, and flicked the reins.

Michael watched immobile as horse and rider were swallowed by the mist. Billy was right. He'd be the one now who'd have to clear out the branches and leaves and gravelly soil that jammed the creek.

Steady, Marcus, Steady

MichaelVSmith

I WAS WORKING at the store for the summer. The first time he came in I thought he must have been from out of town. He smelled of tobacco, bad, and we had Riley's plant over in Oxford Mills. A lot of the workers came in from there every other week or so. They got what they called Supplies. Beer mostly.

He walked in with green pants rolled up into cuffs too high over the ankle and wool socks. His boots were worn and his jacket didn't look new either. He'd been around, I was sure.

And I was about to pass him off cause he seemed a bit ordinary, like too many people around there were, until he stepped up to the counter and in the smoothest voice asked for *The Advance*. His voice was *so* damn smooth and calm and deep. I shivered a bit, not that he could notice, just a very little. But right after he asked for the paper he gave a quick small smile. A funny one. I thought maybe he could read right through me. And that felt good.

I handed him his *Advance* and then he just left. Just like that. I never got his name and didn't see him again till almost three weeks later. I had my eyes out for him though and mentioned him to Martha Ray but she'd hardly heard anything about him, only that he came around the mill last month with not a reference behind him. So I knew he was a drifter.

When he came in again it was a Saturday afternoon. A quiet

one. I was studying math; always did homework at the store with nothing else to do.

He came in the door, without even so much as looking over at me, then stepped up to the counter and asked for *The Advance* just like last time. And he gave that quick smile too. I looked at him a second, sure that he was playing some game, then turned and got the paper from under the counter. Bill kept them down there so no one would read them unless they paid first. Got a good look through the glass at his crotch when I bent down; no one could tell where I was looking and, besides, I couldn't resist. This was an opportunity.

So as I handed his paper over, placed it in his thick fingers, I asked him, I said. "Who are you, anyway?"

And he gave that same smirk with an irritating pause in between and answered, "No one important." Real casual.

Well hell. He turned around slow and walked right out the door. I sighed the breath that I'd been holding and sat down, couldn't believe his gall. But his ass was nice going through that door. Like I told Martha Ray when I saw her, he was real nice.

So you want to be sure the third time he came in I'll tell you I was ready. The minute he walked through that door I bet he knew he was asking for trouble. I didn't let him get off so easily. He said, "Could I have me an *Advance* please." Without even a hello. So I stood up straight and said, "Well who is this *I* you keep talking about? I don't even know him, this *I*."

And he smiled real quick. God that got me. Irritating smile. Martha Ray saw him on the street one day talking to some guy and she saw him smile like that and said it was evil. And I was starting to believe her then, for a minute I almost sent him straight out where he came.

But this time he answered me right. "Marcus," he said while practically sticking his hand in my face. I shook it. And it was firm, his grip was.

Damn. He had me good.

Well it wasn't long before I got to know this Marcus guy well enough, not that he opened up much, but out of the folks that were around, I was the one who understood him the most. Not that there was much to understand; that is, he was pretty straight-forward. No frills.

After that last meeting in the store, we spent the next weekend fishing for a couple of hours and after that it was a regular thing.

Every weekend. Never did much more than fish, neither of us had much money and there wasn't a hell of a lot to do in Kemptville, although there was one time he got his cheque and we went out for supper in Ottawa and that was kinda nice. I didn't have to pay.

Well anyway, Martha Ray didn't like him much cause he never spoke. But I'm sure she was just jealous. She was like that. Called him a fruit and said he smelled funny. Though I knew she wanted him too. I could tell by how she insulted him and then still asked questions all the time.

"Anybody that interested in caterpillars is queer," she said, referring to this hobby he had, and then she laughed at the joke she never meant. "It just ain't normal."

She wanted him alright.

"Oh shut up, Martha Ray. You loved Billy Morrison and he always picked his nose before you two kissed. And you thought it sexy."

"Did not!" She paused, looked at me with a smirk and we both started laughing. Billy Morrison was a boyfriend from four years ago and we still talked about him cause he always called her for dates. She'd refuse and hang up on him. He still picked his nose.

She deliberately sucked on her drink and then looked up, her face serious for a minute. "So you kissed him yet? Was it good?"

"No. I ain't even touched him, Martha Ray."

"Is he impotent?" she shrieked.

And I yelled back, "No!" And we laughed. "Well I hope to hell not. He's just shy, I guess."

And then she started talking instead about Miller Jenkin and his girlfriend that he got pregnant. Martha Ray was disappointed. She loved the stories about my sex life and wanted something else to shriek about. My sex was mysterious and more sinful. She loved that. Her father was a minister. But if I couldn't offer anything exciting and dirty for the conversation, she would. So it was Miller or nothing.

I didn't hear what she had to say really, something about a clotheswire and blood and stuff and her father preaching the whole suppertime about the temptation of the flesh and the sanctity of life. But I wasn't really listening. I was thinking about Marcus and his shoulders and his boots and how he hadn't even looked at me longer than five seconds the whole time we'd spent together even out on the river all alone.

So the next time I saw him I just plain asked to get it out in the open, I couldn't help myself. "You *are* queer aren't you, Marcus?" I said. I had to know. Not like I ever got much of a chance for anything, especially not with anyone from my high school. I knew that there were guys waiting down by the river and meeting by the park but that wasn't too safe considering the damn high chances of getting beat up. And most of the guys were married when I was hoping for something a little steady.

He didn't look at me, stared off at the Peterson cottage on the island and waited for a bit.

"Yeah, I am," he said. Real calm and with that small smirk that just seemed too perfect.

"And you ain't impotent or nothing, eh?"

That time he looked right at me with a quick, "Hell no! Who told you that?" But I didn't answer, I just bent straight over and kissed him. Square on the lips. Just like that. And with his hand that stretched on my lap, you want to believe it was good. My stomach spun and the boat rocked a bit and I could even see, cause I opened my eyes, Peggy Peterson looking at us from on the dock, squinting. I didn't care if that old bat was there or not. And my stomach did another somersault.

Well that's all it took. Once he got kick-started he could really go. We made love down on the bottom of the boat and all I could think, the whole time he was over me with us swinging in the water like crazy, his smooth skin tanned and full of muscle underneath, was that Peggy must still be on the dock seeing nothing but his bare ass moving over the edge of the boat. I could hardly keep from laughing except that his face was so gentle. He seemed real earnest, eager to please me. Every once in a while he looked down and gave me a little grin, different this time, sweet. "Damn," I said out loud. And he thought I meant something else.

So it was nice for the next few weeks, about a month went by and I saw Marcus real regularlike. Every weekend we still fished and fooled around before heading back at the end of the day and on a couple of nights out of the week he would visit and we'd play cards or something, sometimes just sit out on the back step and watch the neighbour's kids tease their dog.

We got nice and comfortable with each other. I liked his equipment and the muscle and the fact that I didn't have to look at magazines anymore. They were hard to get out there too. Martha Ray always bought them for me when she went to Ottawa but she fussed all the time now cause her dad caught her looking at them once. That was a whole other sermon that she preferred not to hear.

Well anyway, like I said I was comfortable with Marcus and he seemed to take to me just as much. So we got to being a little careless, more than just the first time with old Peggy looking on over the river at us. She was half-blind anyway. No, I mean we were doing it in the woods behind the cemetery sometimes, right in the daytime when we knew the school kids could be out for a nature walk. Or sometimes it was in his car at the drive-in. We counted on the windows steaming up, kept the heat off so they would.

So we never expected Martha Ray's dad to catch us after getting away with all this. We weren't even doing something behind the water mill when he did. We were just sitting there together, me lying on his lap and both of us stretching up to see the stars. Sometimes he told me the constellations and I'd tell him what I'd read of them in English class. And we were talking and laughing at some joke or another and didn't hear Reverend Banning coming down the path. He found us just like that. Me with my head on his lap.

And even though getting caught wasn't too bad and could have been a whole helluva lot worse it was still bad enough cause Reverend Banning wasn't a stupid man and he knew me and that I wasn't all right like I should be, or so he told Martha Ray, and he could figure it out easy enough. There was no amount of lying that could help us there.

Well I'm not exactly clear on everything that happened but Marcus left the next day. He stopped in for a quick goodbye at the store and I had customers so we could barely say a word. None of the people there knew anything yet but they would and that was why Marcus thought it best he'd be going. After Reverend Banning was done speaking of God's Intention and Adam and Eve and all that he and Marcus went off and had a talk. That's why there's some stuff I'm not too sure of. I wanted to go but they said no cause it was more of a man's thing. And I thought to myself, What the hell does he think I am? But I knew what he meant. Seeing as how I was still in high school Marcus could have got in a lot of trouble in that town. So at least he came the next morning to say goodbye.

"I don't stick around in one place too long anyway," he said and I knew that was just an excuse.

My throat felt funny again like when I first met him and I said, "Yeah, I know."

"I may be getting back by here some time though," he said and then with a smile added, "I could come get you and we could fish for something."

I laughed a sly little laugh, too sly cause some people looked at me weird but I didn't care. This was my first real steady man and he was going and I hated that town then anyway and couldn't wait to kick the whole goddam bunch behind me. I couldn't wait.

Well he left with me standing at the store counter and looking out the window at his car going on past the church and turning the corner. I held out as long as I could but closed up early for lunch so I could go home and have a little peace. I felt kinda glad to see Martha Ray waiting for me on the front porch. I could tell she'd been crying a bit for me too. And I felt even worse.

She said, "I'm sorry my dad's such an ass ... but at least he isn't going to let your folks know." She paused. "I missed you ... haven't seen much of you lately." And then she gave me a quick hug and made a small laughing sound. Just a small one. Trying to cheer things up.

"Yeah, I know," I said. "Sorry." We went in to the house and I made some iced tea from a mix and felt mad the whole time, mad at everyone, including her, and Marcus for actually leaving and especially Martha Ray's father.

My eyes felt hot and I was concentrating really hard on stirring the tea, trying to get the crystals to disappear. They just wouldn't dissolve. And I stirred and stirred the damn thing. Then I remembered how we thought Marcus might have been impotent and I laughed a little, made me feel better. Martha looked up when I did and I said, "Oh ... nothing." And I almost believed it was.

Princes-in-Waiting

Larry Gasper

"W HY ARE WE watching this crap?" McAllister asks. We're three beer into the evening, our fourth night in a row, and he's becoming his usual yappy self.

"Cause I'm interested in it," Brenda snaps. She's been working in the bar long enough to know how to handle McAllister's mouth.

Me, I'm watching the TV.

"And as the Queen enters her 40th year on the throne, Prince Charles is indeed a prince-in-waiting. Impatiently waiting, some palace sources say…"

"Aw, poor Chuckles," McAllister says. I frown at him. I can't say I feel sorry for Charles. Not with his money. I've got an idea how he feels, though. I've been waiting for the farm for ten years. So has McAllister.

"Shut up already!" Brenda says. I stifle a smile. Brenda's got this strange fascination with the Royal family that nobody can figure out. We just stay out of her way whenever they're on the news.

"And Edward the Seventh was sixty years old when he finally succeeded Queen Victoria…"

McAllister's laughter drowns out the rest. "Damn, I sure hope the old man don't wait that long," he says.

I laugh dutifully, but I'm wondering at the Queen's thinking. Doesn't she know what waiting does to a guy? Even a rich guy? Sitting around playing with himself for twenty years'll fuck him up even worse than he already is. But what can he do? It's what he knows. Farming's what I know, and I know Dad's thoughts on retirement all too well, though the logic always escapes me. Everyone on the Prairies knows the spiel: two-dollar wheat, the grain wars, the drought, blah, blah, blah. It's not even worth talking about anymore. Everyone ends up trotting out their favourite cliche. Dad's favourite is, "Damn Europeans are screwing up my retirement plans. Just a couple of more years, son." Sure, Dad, whatever you say. Like he'd ever give up control.

"Hey, you awake?" McAllister is looking at me, a frown on his bony face. Obviously, I missed a question. I'm saved by the door scraping open. Radinski and Hicks have arrived.

"It's the rest of the princes-in-waiting," McAllister says. They look confused, so he fills them in. Brenda brings another round and places it on the scarred table.

"Shit, I can just see it," Radinski says, taking his ball cap off, then settling it back on his head. "The shape the old man is in, I'll be sixty and he'll still be around doing all the chores saying he's good for another couple of years."

We laugh, but I notice Hicks stops before the rest of us. As if he had to worry. Partner to his dad, wife and kids, lots of land in his name, his own house.

"For sure," McAllister says. His cheeks are flushed, usually a good sign the beer is hitting him. I've seen it a lot in the last couple of months. Just like I've seen the inside of this damn bar, the ratty puke brown carpet, the big-titted women in the beer posters, the beat-up pool table. Shit, I don't even know my trailer this well.

"Should start our own club," McAllister is saying. "Secret handshakes and all that shit."

"And in every town," Ski says. I shake my head. Wish I could take things that lightly. Ski's got me thinking though and I can't get the picture out of my mind. Sixty. Grey-haired. Fat. Wrinkled. Sitting alone in an old dump of a trailer. Still waiting. Lovely thought.

"Heard from Darchuk lately?" I ask Ski. He frowns.

"Yeah, talked to him on the phone the other night. He got back from Florida last week. Said you wouldn't believe the babes down there."

"What's a babe?" McAllister asks, a puzzled look on his face. We laugh. The joke is old, but if we didn't laugh we'd cry. We all know there are only two types of women in town: high school girls and married women. Trouble either way. Every other woman got the hell out as soon as she graduated from high school. Who could blame them? It's not like there's anything out here for them. I gulp down half a beer. I told myself I wasn't going to do this anymore.

"Circle the wagons," I say to Brenda. It's Saturday night, got a couple of weeks before seeding, I'm with my buddies, we've got the bar to ourselves and the beer is cold and good. Who needs to be depressed? I say, "You see that fight on TV the other night," and we're off. No more of that serious shit. The beers flow by and we talk of the hockey playoffs, the Blue Jays' chances this year, cars, women, hunting, government incompetence. The talk keeps the picture of the lonely old man away and I relax into the groove, hoping it will last. I should know better by now.

"You see that article in the *Western Producer* about zero till?" Ski says. Damn. Would one night without this farm shit be too much to ask?

"Yeah," Hicks says. "A lot of good stuff in there. That list of all the nutrients that you keep in the land when you don't work the shit out of it. Might get some of these old farts to finally get the hint and quit burning their straw." He stops, looks at me and winces when he realizes what he's said. I look at him for a second, take a long pull from my beer.

"That would require the old farts to have a clue," I say. Or listen to their sons. I can still see the flames behind the old man as we argued. His land, his rules. Ignorant old prick. "Mostly they just want to do things like they've done them from day one."

"No doubt," Ski says. "It's like pulling teeth to get the old man to do anything."

"At least he'll listen," I say. I look at Mac. His face is tight and he's glaring down at the table. Time to change the subject. I open my mouth to speak, but Hicks butts in.

"You got to make them listen. Christ, do they think things are going to get better? Prices sure the fuck aren't going to improve and you can't depend on the government. The only thing to do is cut costs."

I grab my beer as Mac slams his fist down hard onto the table. "You fucker. Cut costs. Well Daddy's little boy, where the fuck should we cut? The extras?" He stretches his legs out so we can see the scuffed leather of his cowboy boots, the soles almost worn through. "Maybe I can get by without clothes?" He starts to stand.

Ski puts his hand on Mac's arm.

"Relax, Mac."

"Relax? That little ..."

"Shut up, Mac. We're here to have fun."

"Fun?" Mac says as he pushes himself away from the table. "Fun, my ass!" He pulls his arm out of Ski's grip, turns and stumbles to the bathroom. We're silent as he slams the door behind him. I look at Ski and shrug.

"What's biting his ass?" Hicks asks.

I look at him, at the leather jacket and three-hundred-dollar boots, and shake my head. "You didn't know about him losing the lease on that government pasture?"

"No, no I didn't. I've been busy getting my equipment ready for seeding. Haven't seen much of anybody lately."

"Yeah, well he did, so let's just lay off the farming talk for a while." I hear another slam from the can. I bite my lip and meet Ski's look. I shrug. Sounds like Mac's having a sit down. Question is, is he cooling off or working himself up for round two? Getting so none of us can read him.

"Well, looks like we've got a few minutes before Mac's back," Ski says dryly. He pushes his hat back on his head and looks at me. "Hicks is right, you know. You've got to start getting into zero till. It's going to be the only way to farm in ten years."

"Jesus, you're as bad as him," I say, waving toward Hicks. Surprised he hasn't said anything. Guess pissing off one person a night is enough for him. "They don't give the chemicals away. And the equipment sure the fuck ain't free." I lean forward. "Or maybe you figure I should cut costs too?"

Ski frowns. "No, we're all to the bone right now. You just start small. One field at a time. That's how I'm doing it. Rent or borrow the equipment. Shit, what you save in the first year in fuel will cover the chemicals. And you've got to fertilize anyway."

"And where am I supposed to get the money up front? The credit union? That'd give them a good laugh." Overextended, that prick of a manager had said. Poor credit risk. And would the old man co-sign so I could get the loan? Why waste money on a fad, he'd said. A fad. Thanks for the support, dad. It's nice to know how much you value my opinion, how equal partners we are. Must be about how Charles feels. All you get to do is wait. You don't get any control. The picture comes back. An old fat man. Waiting.

"So you'd sooner sit and watch your topsoil blow away

whenever there's a big wind?" Ski says.

"I don't have cousins to borrow equipment from," I say as sarcastically as I can. "Some of us have to do things on our own."

"I pay for anything I get," he snaps. "The old man hasn't helped me on this."

"Yeah, right."

He lifts his hat and resettles it on his head. "Maybe if you didn't spend all your time in here you might have some money. You're … " He stops as we hear the door slam in the can. "Later," he says, then jumps into a story about his Trans-Am. Later? What the fuck does that mean? I watch Mac come out of the can. Seems calm enough, not that that means anything with Mac. He drops into his chair, picks up his beer, takes a drink. I look at him. He looks back, his face blank. Damn. I feel my heart beat faster.

"That car hit eighty by the time I was at Bayne's corner," Ski says. "Gravel spraying everywhere, the whole damn thing shaking. I thought Darchuk was going to shit."

"Darchuk," McAllister says. His face is flushed deep red from the beer. I look at Ski. We both know the mood. Just what we need, over six feet of pissed-off scrapper. "Fucking lucky bastard," McAllister continues. "Shagging the bimboes in Florida." He looks at me. " Weren't you supposed to go with him?"

"Yeah, but the engine went on the tractor, remember?" As if he didn't know that.

"Oh yeah. Got it fixed yet? Been two months. Only got a couple of weeks before seeding."

"I'm getting there." I try to keep calm. Mac was always good at knowing what scabs to pick at. I don't want to think about that fucking tractor and he knows it.

"Christ, man, you forget how to use a wrench?"

"Fuck off, McAllister." My nails dig into my palms.

He frowns, then shrugs. "Just asking. Don't be so damn touchy."

"Yeah, fine. Let's just drop it," I say. "Okay?" A whole winter of grabbing whatever work I could find, busting my butt for the trip, then bye-bye money. Same old song and dance. The farm always comes first. I unclench my fists. Wouldn't solve anything anyway.

"Hey, Hicks, how come your old lady let you come out to play tonight?" Mac asks

Ski puts his hand on Hicks's arm. "For Christ Sake, Mac, quit being a dickhead," he says. Out of the corner of my eye I see Brenda moving and wave at her to stay put. McAllister and her had something going a few years ago and the split hadn't been friendly. She'd just set him off.

"Hey, I ask a few questions and I get shit on." Mac glares at Ski, who watches him silently. No reaction, no fear. Even drunk, Mac knows better. "Can't shithead talk for himself?"

"Yes, asshole, I can." Hicks lurches out of his chair, knocking it over. The beer splashes out of his glass as he bumps the table. Oh shit.

"Okay, then tell me something," McAllister says, standing up himself to tower over Hicks. "Does your wife still give good blowjobs? Best I ever had."

"Bastard!" Hicks lunges. Before I realize what I'm doing, I'm out of my chair wrestling him back. I hear Brenda yelling and McAllister swearing. I get a good grip on Hicks and risk a look. Ski has McAllister pinned against the wall, though he isn't trying to get loose. Good. Ski's almost as big as Mac but five years ago it would've taken three of us to do that. Ski is talking quietly, but all I hear is Hicks's deep breathing.

"You okay now?" I ask him.

"That motherfucker...."

"Relax. He's just had too much to drink. He doesn't know what he's talking about."

"Bastard says another thing about my wife, I'll kill him."

"Yeah, I know." I let go of him but stay between him and McAllister. "Let it go for now. Talk about it when you're sober." Not that they would, but it'll cool things off for now. "You came with Ski, right?" He nods. "Then I'll drive you home."

"But...." He looks at McAllister. Doesn't want to look like he's running away.

"It's okay. He's out of here too."

Hicks hesitates, then Brenda looks at him. She mouths the word please.

Hicks nods. We pick up our jackets and head for the door.

"Leaving, asshole," McAllister says.

"Shut up, Mac," Brenda says. "Please, Hicks, just go."

"Yeah, just go," McAllister mimics. Hicks stiffens, but I push him through the doorway and slam the door behind us. We're silent as we walk to the car.

"Beer," I say and reach into the back. I fish two out of yesterday's case and hand one to Hicks. He's silent as we open them and take a deep drink. The only sound is the Mustang's starter dragging. The beast is showing its age. I head us out of town.

"He didn't mean what he said," I say. "Shit, he was just looking for a reaction."

"A fight, you mean."

"That too." I shred the label on my beer with my thumbnail. I drain half of it. "Look, Mac's had some troubles ..."

"We've all got fucking troubles. That's no excuse for what he said."

"No, but ..." Hicks is right, but I want him to see McAllister's frustration. How can I get him to understand, though? "Look, Mac's hurting right now. There's the land, and then no work ..."

"Maybe if he didn't always get in fights and tell the boss to fuck off, he could get a job."

"Yeah, but ... Look, he's a good worker. Sitting on his ass bugs him."

"Doesn't seem to mind sitting in the bar."

I bite back my reply. Fuck this. Waste of my time. "You know Mac. Too much booze, he gets stupid."

"Then why does he drink?" Hicks asks. I shrug, draining my beer. Why do any of us? I turn into his driveway. He finishes his beer and hands me the bottle.

"Thanks for the ride." He gets out and slams the door. I watch him walk over the neatly trimmed lawn, past the swing set to the big split level. He goes inside and I shake my head. Daddy's little boy. I put the bottle away, then look around the yard. Big barn, big new equipment, the whole nine yards. Shit, some of my equipment is older than I am. I look at the zero tillage equipment neatly lined up by the shop. Wonder if Charles feels like this when he sees Buckingham Palace. I shake my head. Starting to lose it. I back the Mustang out, hoping McAllister will be gone when I get back. I open another beer.

I get lucky. Radinski's truck is gone when I pull up in front of the bar. Brenda is washing glasses when I walk in.

"Still open?" I ask.

She shrugs. "Why not? Beer?"

"Make it a double rye and coke. And get yourself one." I sit and watch her pour the drinks with quick, jerky movements.

"Ski said to wait," she says. "He'll be back as soon as he settles Mac down." She sits, handing me my drink. The warmth of the rye flows down my throat. Two more gulps and it's gone. Brenda sips her drink and points at the bar. I get up and pour another one.

"Could be hours before Mac settles down," I say.

"Maybe." She frowns as I push the glass under the dispenser a second time. "Little heavy, isn't that?"

"I'm too old for this shit," I say.

"That's tonight. What about the last couple of months?"

"I don't want a fucking lecture." I try a smile. It's weak but it's the best I can do. "Can we just change the subject?"

"Like every other time?" she says. "I give up." We sip our drinks silently for a minute before she says, "You know, I saw another documentary on Charles last week. They talked about his role as Prince of Wales and all the good he's done on the land he got with the title. I guess he's really careful with his own land."

"What the hell is that supposed to mean?" I glare at her. She just smiles softly as she looks into her drink.

"Not a damn thing." Her smile widens. "It was kind of neat though, seeing Charles driving a tractor around all dressed up in his tweeds." She chuckles, then frowns when I don't laugh too. She shrugs. "Look, it's your life, your choice, but I think you're making a mistake. You're carrying this poor misunderstood farmboy who don't get no respect crap too far." With that she swings into a story about her daughter's piano lessons. I try to listen but can't keep track. Have I been that bad? That obvious? I still don't have an answer when Ski walks in half an hour later.

I clench the handrail tightly as I try to get down the bar's outside steps without stumbling. Radinski's ahead of me with a case of beer. He flings it onto the seat in his truck, then turns to look at me.

"I'll drive," he says. I want to argue, but I find myself swaying. He's right so I get in.

"Your place, my place or cruising?" he asks.

"Home," I say, opening a beer. "Gotta work on the tractor tomorrow." He looks at me and raises an eyebrow.

"I do," I say, but I don't even sound convincing to myself. He shrugs and starts the truck.

"How about a little cruise," he says. "I see enough of my place during the week."

"Home," I say. Out of the corner of my eye I see him look at me. I keep staring out the windshield. He shakes his head.

"Christ, I don't know which is worse, McAllister flipping out or you sulking."

"I'm not sulking."

"Right." He opens a beer for himself. "At least I know where I stand with Mac."

"Mind your own business."

"Fine." He drives silently for a minute. He pulls his cap off and resettles it. "You know, Mac talked on the way home. A lot of it didn't make much sense, but he talked."

"I don't wanna talk and I don't need you playing shrink."

"Jesus H. fucking Christ!" I grab the dash as he slams on the brakes. Beer splashes out of my bottle. He rams the truck into park and swings to face me.

"It was one fucking trip!" he says. "Get over it already. You can't brood forever."

"It's not the fucking trip," I say. Son of a bitch thinks he knows me.

"Then what? You haven't done bugger all for the last two months but sit around and whine. Fuck, quit looking at the shitty side of things and do something for once. Your tractor...."

"Fuck the tractor," I say. "This isn't about the trip, it isn't about the tractor and it isn't about the zero till."

"What is it then?" Ski asks. I shrug. It's none of his business. I'll take care of things on my own. I'll get the old man to see things my way. Probably about the time Charles gets the throne.

"Look if it's about that zero till crap," Ski says, "we can work something out. I'll talk to Hicks and my cousins, see about working some sort of rent thing out."

"I told you I don't have the money."

"So work it back. Fuck, you want me to do all your thinking for you?"

"No, I want you to mind your own fucking business."

"Fine," he says, and starts the truck moving. "Brood away then. I tried." I want to say something, to tell him I appreciate the concern, but nothing comes out. We drive in silence until we reach my place. The old man plays on my mind. Two more years. Two more years. No respect. No control.

"Thanks for the ride," I say, opening the door when Ski stops in front of the trailer.

"Yeah. See you." He looks at me. "Call if you need a hand with the tractor."

"Sure." I get out, close the door and watch him drive away.

The trailer is dark. I stumble in, heading for the fridge. I grab a beer, take a sip. Doesn't taste as good as before. I wander into the living room, shovel the clothes off the couch so I can sit down, and look out the picture window. There's enough of a moon so I can see the coffee table in front of it. My graduation picture is just a shape, but I've got it memorized anyway. All us kids, tuxes and too much hair, gowns and acne. Kids that turned into a couple of teachers, businessmen, and a geologist. And farmers, housewives, and labourers. And a borderline drunk. "Our great and unlimited future," Darchuk had said. Uh-huh.

I look out the window. A barn, a garage, some granaries, and my land. Not enough of a farm, not now, not in this economy, but mine anyway. It should be enough, has been enough, but the picture keeps on playing. An old fat man, waiting. Then another picture. Charles bouncing across a field on a tractor, tweed jacket, elbow patches, the whole nine yards.

Digs

Warren Cariou

Too bad i'm not majoring in archaeology, with a place like this to study. There's decades worth of filth in here. The floor is carpeted with a mixture of grease and dust that looks like wet velour. The light patches on the tile show where the furniture was, before the fumigators came in and dragged every bed, chair and couch off to the dump. The fridge, which we've only opened once, is webbed inside with purple and orange spore clusters, some of which were sucked into the room during the five seconds the door was open.

I heard about an archaeologist who did a study of American garbage dumps. I should give him a call. I've been keeping a list of artifacts, the way they do at real excavations. So far I've found six Bandaids (all used, one with a black scab stuck to it), countless semicircles of fingernails (both bitten and clipped), hair from all bodily regions, mucous in several forms, and a half-empty tube of cream marked "for yeast infection."

With a decent lab you could find out a lot about the people who lived here. Their genetic makeup, their diet, daily habits, relationships. It's all a matter of how hard you look.

The only benefit of this job is, when I'm scraping sludge out of a stove or repainting a ceiling or cleaning a toilet, I'm free to think about whatever I want. Lately I've been thinking about the woman who works in the confectionery down the street. For some reason, all this filth and grime makes me want to be with her. I don't even know her name, but I make one up – maybe today she'll be Alice or June or Yvonne.

I don't fantasize about my ex-girlfriend Stacy, even though I saw her yesterday in a pair of cutoffs that barely qualified as clothing. Her legs were the colour of smoked salmon, her hair was oppressively blonde. My throat dropped, like something heavy was sliding into my stomach, and I think I made a little grunting noise when I saw her. I don't know if anyone heard. I was too busy watching the fringes of denim dangling between her thighs. She was walking to her new boyfriend's house, which is just across the street from here, and she didn't even see me standing at the window, scrubbing the oven rack with steel wool.

The former tenants of this house just up and left. Didn't even bother to take the food out of the cupboards. They were gone for two months before the rental agency realized they weren't coming back.

The neighbours, if they know anything, aren't talking. I've been trying to figure out the disappearance for more than a week now, but all I've got to go on is the archaeological remnants and a handful of bills than came in the mail, addressed to Terrance Dixon.

Our foreman Randy is not impressed with my research. He told me people disappear all the time in this neighbourhood. We get paid to clean houses, he said, not play detective.

Alex, the pre-law student who in my estimation will never be able to drop the "pre" from his title, is cleaning the kitchen window again. This despite orders that we do the windows only when everything else is finished. His behaviour confirms my suspicions about the relationship between dirt and sex. His nose, chin, and hands are smeared with grime, yet he's signalling out the window to his girlfriend Irene. He sprays the vinegar bottle once, then dabs at the glass with a clump of paper towel and smiles at her.

I can't see Irene, but I know she's hanging around in the back alley. She's in high school and gets a spare class at 2:30, so she's usually here before coffee. Then, when the rest of us go back to the shop for donuts, the two of them walk to her aunt's place and do whatever there's time for.

I chew on my own fingernails, comb my own hair, pick my own nose, and dispose of the evidence without a grimace. You do it too,

I suppose, and so did the Dixons. But you don't know what it's like to pry off a baseboard and find somebody else's fingernail, or blood-encrusted Bandaid, or other bodily excretion, waiting there for you. It's not the same when it's not your own.

Alex and Irene are in the basement. Randy took the afternoon off and left Alex in charge. I can't hear anything right now, but a few minutes ago I heard a flurry of giggles. He's giving her the scenic tour, showing her the pile of dead beetles we found behind the furnace.

Benny and I are in the living room trying to think of something to do besides clean the fridge. I offer him a cigarette and he takes it. We stare out the window and bounce our smoke off the glass in long breaths. Stacy's new boyfriend is out cutting his lawn. She'll likely be over to see him soon.

I tell Benny my thoughts about the confectionery woman, but I'm careful to leave out any mention of dirt.

"She's married," he says flatly. "Had twins last year." Two oscillating cones of smoke extend from his nostrils.

"Nice body, considering," I say.

"Yeah."

"I just said I'd like to, anyway. Not that I'd be able to. Just imagining, you know."

"Yeah."

Benny squints across the street at Stacy's boyfriend, who's putting his lawnmower back in the shed. This new boyfriend is always arranging, cleaning, fixing. I, according to Stacy, am quite different: I am a disorderly person who thinks too much. This must mean the new boyfriend is an orderly person who thinks just the right amount.

It's quiet downstairs, too quiet to make it prudent to check what Alex and Irene are doing. I switch on the radio so we won't have to hear anything.

We're peeling tiles off the floor – me, Alex, and Benny. I've got the tiger torch, which is really a flame-thrower that's been brought into civilian usage. Yellow and blue flames shoot from the nozzle like from the throat of a dragon. The whole assembly is connected by a ten-foot rubber hose to a propane tank in the middle of the room.

I open the valve, and the tiger torch hisses fiendishly. I aim it at a tile in front of me and the flames spread out. Little pieces of paper, dead bugs, and other small flammables ignite and disintegrate almost instantly. When the tile starts to bubble, I move on, and Alex pries it away with a flat-ended crowbar.

Under the tiles is a tar that's so black it looks clean. No dirt could be this dark. Our feet stick to the tar, and it sounds like we've got Velcro on the bottoms of our shoes.

"Check it out!" Alex says, pointing at something outside the living room window.

We look out and see Stacy stepping out of her newly-painted white Chevette. She's wearing the bikini I bought her almost a year ago, a pink and purple one that's cut high on the thighs. She has a shirt on over the top, but we can see as much of her ass as decency would permit.

Alex walks to the master bedroom and yells out the window, "Nice ass!"

She's going up the front steps when she hears this, and she stops with one foot above the other. She turns around with half a smile on her lips and looks through the living room window, directly at me. I'm standing here with tar on my face, flames snorting out in front of me, and the torch hose curling like a tail behind me. A vision straight from hell.

She recognizes me. She's not as frightened as you'd expect, considering she already thinks of me as her own personal demon. Nor, though, is she amused. Her face crumples into disdain – a mass of creases and white lips. She turns away, pulls the shirt down over her ass, and opens the screen door. It slams like a guillotine behind her.

"Hey, Jerkoff," Benny says to Alex. "That used to be Eldon's girlfriend."

"Really?" Alex comes out of the bedroom, ripping his shoes from the floor, and puts his hand on my shoulder. "Is she really as hot as she looks?"

I point the flames back at the floor, close to Alex's feet. "I don't remember," I say. I smile at the particles exploding like tiny fireworks on the tile.

Detritus is a word for dirt. It's what we get when our bodies wear down. The stuff that rubs off has to go somewhere.

Did you know that seventy percent of household dust is

composed of dead human skin? Right now you're inhaling someone
else's body.

Dirt is death.

I go in to buy a pack of cigarettes and there she is, right where I
expected her. She's sitting on a stool behind the counter, fenced
in by a collage of multicoloured junk food packages. She's wearing
a navy blue sweatshirt and baggy grey shorts. Her dark hair is pulled
back in a barrette today, and this allows a better view of her pale
green eyes.

"I'll have a pack of Viscount Kings," I say.

She doesn't reach for the cigarettes, she's busy picking at a
piece of dry skin on her arm. She looks like the type that sunburns
easily.

"You should use sunblock lotion," I say. She realizes I'm
watching her, and she stops picking. She gets up from the stool. As
she reaches above her head for the cigarettes, her sweatshirt
hitches up, and I catch a glimpse of the loose, waxy skin around her
navel.

She tosses the pack on the counter, and I flick a rolled-up ten
toward her. She rings it in, unrolls the bill and tugs on it to keep it
flat, then puts it in the cash register.

"So how come you're always around here?" she says, while
handing back my change.

I point. "Working over in the rental units. Cleaning them
out."

"Oh, yeah." She sounds almost interested. I hope she'll ask me
about the dirt so I can have something to tell her about.

"Student?" she asks.

"Yep."

"What're you taking?"

I should lie. What's a good lie? Pre-law?

"Philosophy," I say.

She's looking at me like I said "cannibalism." I should have
lied.

"Oh, yeah ..." She moves a box of green licorice shoelaces back
into place, then pulls out one long strand and swings it around in
front of her. It whizzes by, almost grazing her lips.

"So what do you philosothize about?"

Philosothize. Philoso-thighs? Was that a hint? She's uncrossed her legs now, and I notice that her thighs are uncommonly thin.

"Oh, things-in-general," I say. "Sex. Dirt. You know. Theories about everything."

I roll my eyes and she smiles, sceptically.

"Sounds pretty weird to me," she says. "What're you gonna do when you're done?"

I take time to pull out a cigarette and light it while I think about his.

"Clean rental units," I say.

She smiles and nods, but I can tell she feels like shaking her head. She makes herself busy again, shuffling and reshuffling the junk food like a Vegas dealer.

"Oh, shit, I'm late," I say, before I can even look at my watch. And I am late, it's after three-thirty. "See you!"

"Yeah," she says.

I'm going down the steps taking a final drag of my cigarette before I have to start running back to work. I've failed again. I still haven't got her name.

We've wiped out the Dixons. This house is completely renovated, just waiting for the next tenants to come in and wreck it. The only thing left to do is remove the tiles from one downstairs bedroom, which we forgot about because it was covered with the canvas drop sheets we use for painting. I, being the only volunteer, get to do the tiles all by myself.

When I've finally dragged all the equipment down to the bedroom, I spot a daddy-longlegs spider in the corner. I light the torch as quickly as I can. It's cruel, I know, but the way these little buggers ignite is fascinating. All eight legs burn from the outside in, then they curl into a tiny fist and poof! they explode like popcorn.

He's running along the side of the wall, and I think I can get him. Shit. I miss, and somehow manage to scorch the wall. The new paint is blistered and smoked in a foot-long stripe. And now the spider disappears into a space between the wall and the floor. I go over to see if I can flush him out, but he's long gone. There's a triangle of tile broken away where he escaped, and something circular is wedged into the black space. I aim the torch at the object for a few seconds, but it doesn't burn. I move the torch away and pry at the floor with a key. The object pops out and I see that it's a coin, a penny, with a hole stamped in the middle.

And I thought every last trace of the Dixons was gone. Here's a real treasure they left behind. I pick it up and try to wipe it off on my pants. It's almost too hot to touch. Most of the tar on the back comes off, but there's still too much junk on it to make the date visible. Around the hole I can see a profile view of George V. The drill, or punch, or whatever it was, brained him neatly.

I put the coin in my front pocket and get back to work on the tiles. The metal feels warm against my leg for a long time. I wonder what I'm going to do about that mark on the wall. To hell with it. This house could use some character.

I knew my mother would come into this somewhere. I'm thinking of her when the coin touches my tongue, remembering the way she used to warn me about money. It's the filthiest thing, she used to say. You never know where it's been, who's been touching it. Diseases get transmitted on money.

I turn the coin over in my mouth, push the tip of my tongue through the hole. The tast is bitter, metallic of course but with a smorgasbord of other elements too. Tar, dust, Mr. Clean. And something else – sweat? I must be imagining this. How could I possibly distinguish all these things?

Irene says she knew one of the girls who lived in the Dixon house, the eldest daughter. She was a tangled beauty with thick black hair and russett skin. Her eyes were the colour of tar. Irene can't remember the name but that's okay. I've smelled this woman for weeks, tasted her presence, inhaled her. I should be able to uncover any sign she's left, track her by odour if I have to.

She wore a perforated coin, tied around her neck with a leather cord. It nestled between her breasts, absorbed her body's warmth, wore itself smooth against her skin.

Her sisters believed the coin was the sign of a witch. Her peculiar beauty, which continued to increase even when she didn't wash herself or brush her hair, made them sure. They blamed her for every misfortune – their colds, stubbed toes, lost pencils. They plotted ways to get rid of that coin.

When their father told them one evening that they'd have to move away early the next morning, they knew the coin was responsible. That night, the second-oldest took a pair of scissors to bed. When her sister was asleep, she padded across the room and snipped the leather cord. But as she eased the coin away from her sister's throat, it slipped out of her fingers. It chimed on the tile and rattled into its place.

There must be other signs, and I'll find them. They'll lead to another basement room, littered with crumpled garments, paper, bits of food. Dusty light will stream through the window onto her bed. She's asleep, dreaming of her talisman.

A rust-coloured arm is sprawled outside the sheets. I place the coin in her palm, close the fingers around it. I brush my lips against her face. She wakes up, shifts her head to look at me. Black hair unravels on the pillow.

She's a darkness moving beneath me, around me, inside me. I purse my eyes nearly shut. Things dissolve.

Badlands

Curtis Gillespie

WHEN I WAS sixteen my father's younger brother was in jail, and my father and I used to visit him together. "No one," my father said on the drive there one time, "is all good or all bad. Don't forget that."

I was driving, having just gotten my licence, and he kept his eyes fixed on the highway, No. 9 to Drumheller. It was a lonely tarmac line that went east like a bridge to the horizon. "Any man can change his life around," he went on.

I remember wondering if he'd forgotten that Carla, Ivan's fiancée, was in the back seat. If he'd forgotten, or if he just didn't care what she thought. We didn't know her too well, but well enough for my mother and father to think that Ivan could do better. They thought Carla was a whore. A real one. This was the first time, eight months after he'd been sent up, that Carla had come with us from Calgary to Drumheller to visit Ivan in jail.

"So don't say anything that might hurt him," my father concluded.

He took his eye off the road and sort of looked over my way, though he might have been trying to sneak a look back at Carla, who sniffed when he finished. I glanced at her in the mirror and she flipped some loose blonde curls back off her forehead and stared out at the prairie, which was taking on shape and depth now that the sun had come up. She lit a cigarette and ignored us.

"Okay?" my father said. He wanted somebody to say something.

I didn't answer because I figured he was talking to Carla,

though I still wasn't sure why he would think that would need saying. Carla was Ivan's fiancée, after all. They had planned the wedding for two years March, right after he got out. Ivan was my favourite uncle, still is, and he had asked me to be his best man, though I would only be eighteen by the time of the wedding. Ivan was twenty-six and Carla couldn't have been more than a few years older than me.

In any case, I didn't have much to say to Ivan, hurtful or otherwise. What could I possibly have to say that would interest him? I'd come with Dad once every few weeks and had probably said a hundred words total, hellos and goodbyes included.

It was fully light when we passed through the badlands and pulled into Drumheller. The town lay in a valley, in a slash on the prairie, and at the bottom of the hill, at the entrance to the town, there was a big concrete dinosaur, standing on its hind legs. It was green and there was red paint dripping off its fangs. There were no people on the streets. The only sign of life was a coyote that limped in front of us at a light and then disappeared into an abandoned grocery store. We had passed the jail on the way in, but Dad wanted to rent a motel room first, so that we would have a home base. Ivan had a day pass.

The lady at the Dine-O-Saur Cafe and Motel wrote up a check-in card. "Just one night?" she asked.

"We'll actually be checking out around five o'clock today," my father said.

The lady looked at us in turn. She had pins in her hair and deeply yellow-stained fingers. "I'm still going to have to charge you for a full night." Her voice was flat but strained, like she was making an effort to not give away what she was thinking.

"No problem!" Carla blurted out. She licked her lips, then tousled my hair. "Is it, boys?"

The motel lady stopped and looked at Carla, and my father took a deep breath, pursing his lips when he exhaled. I thought it was funny but didn't laugh.

"Your business is your business," the lady said. She looked at us again. "That'll be cash."

We headed to the jail, which was only five minutes back along the highway we'd come in on. It was a bitterly cold morning and even from the town you could see the plumes of steam rising from the stacks of the penitentiary grounds, though you couldn't see the jail proper because of the valley walls.

We always met Ivan at the Visitor Centre, but today, because of the day pass, we were to pick him up at the South Door. We waited for about ten minutes before he finally appeared with a guard. He wore his prison clothes but had a shopping bag with him. They stopped at some desk behind a half-wall, and spoke. Actually all Ivan did was nod his head. He looked our way once but didn't express any kind of emotion other than a quick smile. We stood nervously waiting.

The guard came right up to us with him. "He's all yours for today."

"Thank you," my father said. "Thank you."

"My pleasure," the guard said. He stood there with arms folded across his chest and his hands in his armpits. "Less work for us, get these guys out of here for awhile."

"Do they ever let *you* fellas out?" Carla said.

"Don't, Carla," said Ivan. His voice was calm.

The guard looked at Carla, then Ivan, and he nodded slowly, as if he were allowing something to register fully. Then he turned and walked back into the jail. We heard a door close and lock somewhere not too far away.

Ivan turned on Carla. "Do you know how hard it is to get a day pass? Don't fuck it up with your little attitude."

"I've missed you, too, Hon." She made a sarcastic face, but then softened and kissed Ivan. They hugged for a minute, then my father spoke.

"We got a room in town, Ivan. It'll be nice to catch up and chat somewhere other than here for a change."

"That's a fact," he said. He looked at me as if he'd seen me for the first time. "And how's Robby?"

"Fine," I said.

"We're all fine," said my father. "How about some breakfast?"

After breakfast we got our stuff out of the car and went up to the motel room. There still weren't many people in the streets. It was a cold bright day and our breath leapt steaming out of our throats.

Inside the dingy little room were two double beds, and two chairs and a table. Carla turned on the TV as soon as we got in.

"Might as well watch Donahue," she said. "What are we gonna do all day? Talk?"

"That's what we usually do," my father said.

Ivan smiled at Carla, then looked over at us. "Pretty boring, eh, Carla. Maybe we can talk these two into going out for lunch on their own, then you and I can have our own visit."

Carla let out a cackle and my father pasted on the same smile he used at church. "Lunch," she said. "Yeah."

Ivan and my father sat in the chairs at the table, so I sat on the bed farthest from the TV. They talked about family things for the whole of the Donahue show. Carla was glued to the show and didn't even pretend to be interested in the family news that my father had to pass on to Ivan. I listened to them but watched Carla. She was on her stomach facing the TV.

We passed the whole of the morning that way, Carla watching TV, my father and uncle talking. Ivan seemed to feed off of him, hunching forward with every piece of interesting news, nodding a lot, smiling knowing smiles. He appeared so gentle, Ivan, it was hard to believe he would hurt another person. But he had.

I was sent at one point to get coffee and donuts for everybody. It was still cold but the streets had some life now. The people seemed like other people. I always expected to see obviously criminal people in Drumheller, but I never could tell if they were criminal or not. It never occurred to me that escapees would likely go somewhere else.

At noon my father said, "Robby. Why don't you and I go pick up lunch for the four of us." He asked Ivan and Carla what they wanted, and said we would be about an hour. Carla was grinning the whole time. As we walked out the door Ivan said something under his breath that made her snort with laughter.

When we came back with the food, exactly an hour later, Ivan was watching the TV and Carla was in the shower. He took his burger and fries and started on it with obvious pleasure.

"Food," he said, "has taste out here. Inside, you turn off your senses. Everything shuts down, except how to survive."

"That bad?" my father said.

"Everything," he said between mouthfuls, "is measured on only one scale. Will this get me out quicker and make my stay more bearable, or will it keep me here longer and make it tougher. That's it."

"You've got to find a way."

"That's right," he said. "It's hard, knowing what I'm missing."
He nodded towards the bathroom. "Thanks."

"You miss that?" my father said. "Her?"

"Yes."

"I don't think I'd miss a whore," my father said.

Much to my surprise, Ivan did not get upset. He seemed to
become patient with my father. "Don't be so hard on her. She's
done bad things before, but who hasn't? She told me she only ever
gave blow jobs, nothing worse. Is that so bad on the scale of things?
What I did was worse."

"I don't think so."

After Ivan finished eating he turned to me. "How's your
mother?"

"She's okay, I guess." I looked at him from the bed. He always
asked me how she was, and had never asked my father. At the
time I was aware there was a tension between Ivan and my mother.
At family dinners, Christmas, Easter, it was Ivan who would argue
with anybody. He was a smart guy, and what always seemed to
bother my mother was that she didn't think Ivan believed in
anything, that he just took any side of an argument so that he
could provoke somebody. Usually teasing, sometimes not.

My mother was someone who staked out where she stood on
any issue. She was careful, and she always complained to my
father, who tried to stay out of it, that careful was exactly what
Ivan was not. Him ending up in jail was proof, and made it easier
for her to say that he didn't care about anything, though I didn't
agree with her. I don't think my father did, either. My mother's
problem was just that she took Ivan too seriously. Ivan was my
favourite uncle and that scared her, which may have partly
explained why he continued to be my favourite.

"Is she ever going to come visit me?" Ivan said. He was still
looking at me, though I knew the question wasn't directed at me.
I looked at my father. He sat still and watched me answer.

"I don't know," I said. "Maybe."

"Why don't you write her," my father said. "And ask her to."

Ivan pulled on the skin under his chin. "I just might one of
these days."

"She'd read it," my father said.

"Or frame it," said Ivan.

They both laughed, so I did, too. Carla came out of the
bathroom at that moment.

"What's so funny?" she said. She had her jeans on but the top button was undone, and her shirt was tied in a knot under her breasts. She was rubbing a towel over her head. I was on the bed nearest the bathroom and I could smell the damp flowery scent that came out of the bathroom with her, and I could see how small her feet were. I was struck by her feet. They looked small enough to hold in my hands.

Ivan looked over. "Nothing, Hon."

She instantly pouted. "Sure," she said. She sat down on the edge of the bed I was on and put the towel completely over her head.

Ivan got up and came over beside her. "Carla," he said gently. He rubbed the outline of her head through the towel. "It was something else we were laughing about. Not you. Really." He looked at me and had a strange look in his eyes, as if we all needed to be understanding for some reason. "We were laughing at nothing. At me. Really." He kissed the towel where he thought her mouth might be. We could hear a muffled giggle from inside.

"Good," she said. There seemed to be less tension between them since lunch. For obvious reasons, I supposed.

Carla finished drying her hair and then tucked her shirt in haphazardly. She sat on the edge of the bed and listened to Ivan and my father talk about whatever subject happened to come up. I never talked anyway but she wouldn't have known that, and every now and then she would look over at me as if she was expecting something from me. Once she caught me looking at her.

"Well," said Ivan after about an hour. "I need some fresh air. I want a walk. Around a real street. Now that will be a pleasure for me." He stood up and stretched. I started to get off the bed. "No," he said. "Just me and your Dad." I looked at Dad and he looked a little surprised himself.

"I had an hour with Carla alone," said Ivan. "Now I want an hour with my brother. Maybe you and I will do something alone next time, Robby."

Carla didn't seem bothered by it, so Ivan and my father put on their boots and coats, Ivan making jokes the whole while about making a run for it. Then they left saying they'd be back in an hour.

I was left alone with Carla and that wasn't all bad. She was at least nice to look at, though there was something about her that wasn't quite right. She called to mind something that required delicate handling and had instead been roughly treated, like a bruised piece of fruit. Maybe that was part of her appeal to men, who like to hurt the things that are susceptible to being hurt. I didn't want to hurt her, but I didn't particularly like her either.

She pulled out a cigarette and sat on one of the double beds, her back against the wall, one leg up to her chest, the other straight out. I sat in a chair by the TV at the foot of the bed, holding a TV guide.

"So," she said after a couple of minutes. "You like your Uncle Ivan? A lot?" She flashed out blue wisps of smoke between her teeth.

I shrugged and nodded. "Don't you?"

She took another drag, then stubbed it out. She leaned over to the far side of the bed, stretching to reach her purse on the bedside table. Her shirt had come untucked in the back and I saw white skin and her backbone snaking down into her jeans.

She rolled back over with her purse and pulled out a joint.

"I was going to have this with Ivan, but your Dad's going to stick by him all day just because I'm here." She lit it up. "Your Dad's a fucking drag." She looked at me for a response and offered me the joint by holding it at arm's length. I shook my head no.

"Are you and Ivan going to get married?" I said.

She took a long drag on the joint and closed her eyes as she held the smoke in her lungs. When she exhaled she tipped her head back and just let it filter out with a deep groan. She dropped her head back to look at me.

"What do you care?"

"Well," I said. "I am supposed to be the best man." It was all I could think to say.

She laughed out loud. "You're cute," she said. She looked at me for a long time and had another drag on the joint. She didn't offer me any this time. "How old are you?"

"How old are *you*?" I said back.

"Well," she said slowly. "You *are* old enough to drive." She stubbed out the joint after taking a last toke, and held the smoke for a moment before making an O with her lips and blowing it in a line right at me. "And I am, too. That's old enough. Isn't it?"

I could really smell the dope. I shifted in my seat.

Carla slid down a bit on the bed so that she wasn't sitting so upright, and she put one hand behind her head, letting the other rest on her stomach. "I came out with you and your Dad today so that I could call it off with your Uncle Ivan. I figured he'd take it better with some family around."

"What!"

"That's right. It was practically over anyway."

"But you promised him you'd marry him."

"I know. I feel bad. I want to still be friends with him, though. Do you think he'll still be friends with me?"

"But why?"

"I just can't wait for him to get out. That's all. That's a long time."

"He'll wait," I said.

"Like he has a choice."

"That's not fair, Carla," I said. "That's just not fair."

"I'm too young to wait. I can't." She paused for a minute but kept her eyes on me. "And I can't not have any sex for two years. That I cannot do."

"Well," I said. "Maybe he would understand. You know."

She fixed a peculiar gaze at me. "Think so?" She took her arm from behind her head and put it on her lap with her other hand. "Who do you think Ivan would let me fuck for the next two years?"

I stared at her for a minute. "You're a slut," I said.

"That's a bad thing to call someone, Robby." She stayed still for a moment. "And it's not true, either. That's a horrible thing to call me."

I didn't move or say anything, but she slipped off the bed onto her knees. She stayed there for a few seconds like she was praying. Then she took steps on her knees over to where I was. She stopped in front of me, without touching me. Her arms were dangling at her sides.

"Do you think," she said, lifting her hands to her breasts and nipples, which I could see through her shirt. "Do you think he'd let me fuck *you* for the next two years?" She put her hands on my kneecaps and squeezed, then sent her hands nearer, tracing the inseam of my jeans upwards, her thumbs digging hard. "That'd be alright, wouldn't it?"

I said no, or at least tried to say it, and I tried to move my legs out of her hands, but her chest was between my knees. Her hands met in the middle and she rubbed against me with them, like she was kneading dough. One hand moved to my belt and fly, the other kept circling against me. I thought she might look up, but she didn't. She seemed to be concentrating, and then she had me in her mouth.

I straightened my legs out and slouched a bit in the chair. After

I came she kept her head down and her body hunched over. I could feel her hot breath and I left my hands on her head, still clutching her blonde hair. Then she drew herself up again, so that she was on her knees facing me. She looked at me and asked me if I liked that. I didn't answer, just stared at her.

"I knew you would," she said. "I could tell." She drew herself closer to me and I could smell my semen on her breath. She ran her hand through my hair, and then dropped it down and took me in her hand. I got hard again. "Let's do it. Come on, Robby. I want you to fuck me! Come on!"

I took her hand off me without looking.

"Come on," she said. She started to undo her shirt and checked her watch. "Those guys won't be back for half an hour."

I stood up. "No," I said. For some reason I wanted to put my shoes on.

Carla stood up. Her shirt was undone and she tried to press against me.

"Don't," I said. "No!" I tried to back up and hit the chair. My knees gave a little and I half-fell into the chair I had just risen out of. I looked off to avoid her stare and saw the table with Ivan's empty cigarette package on it.

"No?" she said, standing over me. She nodded and half-smiled. "I was right."

I looked up at her. "What?"

She didn't answer me at first so I kept looking at her.

"I told Ivan you wouldn't," she said.

I blinked at her.

"You're cute," she said. "It might have been fun to do it. But what you know is the square root of fuck-all."

She turned and did up her shirt. I sat for a minute and then put on my shoes. I had no particular desire to go out into the cold, but I wanted to be away from her. She had lit up a cigarette and was watching me. She wasn't anxious in the least, didn't say anything, just seemed to be enjoying her cigarette. I left.

I tried to time it so that I would arrive back just after my father and Ivan returned, but I lost track of time. When I walked back into the room Ivan and my father stopped talking.

"Jesus," said Ivan. "He decided to come back."

My father put down his drink and made a steeple with his hands. "Nice of you to join us. We were thinking we might have to leave you here."

"With all the criminals," said Ivan. They both grinned, and I glanced over at Carla. Ivan followed my look. She was sprawled on the bed reading a magazine, paying no attention to us. Ivan looked back at me but kept the same easy smile on his face.

"Well," said my father. "I hate to say it, but now that our intrepid traveller has returned I think we must depart."

Ivan's face went long, but he tried to keep up his humour. "That's for sure," he said. "Never stay here after sundown. Trust me." He went over to the track bag my father had brought. "Time to pack my own little suitcase." He took out a balloon and a jar of Vaseline. My father reached into his wallet and pulled out a number of bills. Carla also reached into her back pocket and pried some money from it. They handed the bills to him and he went into the bathroom and returned a couple of minutes later with no money and no balloon.

"Okay," he said. "Let's do it. I can only take so much of this freedom stuff."

I sat in the back all the way to Calgary. I made Carla sit in the front because I didn't want her looking at the back of my head for two hours. We passed through the badlands in the gaunt light of dusk, and you could see the ancient formations, stark and barren, looking as if nothing had lived in them for millions of years. The massive ridges of sandstone carved out of the land looked like the ribs of the earth. I sat thinking about what had happened. How could Ivan tell Carla to do those things to me? What reason would she have had to say what she did if it wasn't true? Just to be cruel? To make me feel better for letting her do it? I don't know.

We had a letter from Ivan a couple of months later, in which he explained that he and Carla had broken it off by mutual agreement and that they were still friends. He didn't say when or how they had split up. Just that she didn't want to wait for and then marry a con.

I didn't go with my father the next time he visited Ivan, but I did the time after, and things didn't seem different to me. Every visit for the next two years I looked at Ivan to see if Carla was telling the truth.

I was still his best man. Four years after he got out he married a nutritionist and moved to Red Deer, where he has lived a peaceful life ever since. Seven years after his marriage he was my best man. And not since his jail time has Carla's name come up. He has not spoken about her and no one, not my father, not my mother, not me, has asked about her. I haven't returned to the badlands, either, even though they're so close. But I remember them well, the lunar terrain, so bleak, so deeply indifferent to me and my world. I remember that with great clarity.

Driving Through Denver

William Robertson

W E'RE A DAY-and-a-half south of the border and I can't get a thing out of him. His lips are pursed like a trumpeter's. I know he's got something on his mind but I can't read whether he wants me to dig it out or leave him alone. If he wants me to leave him alone this should be a fun trip. I'll stare at maps and comment on the scenery. All the while I'll watch the money blow out the exhaust pipe and splash down the drains in barrooms like the ones we were in last night.

Three bars in one little oil town and he wouldn't say a word, not even his round or my turn to rack up the balls. And we did well at that. We were hot on the stick with some local boys. One of them put his cowboy hat on my head and offered me a Marlboro. I took it. I quit smoking four years ago but I'd had enough to drink that it didn't kill me. I had a cigarette in my mouth, a big hat on my head, and I was knocking down balls like maybe I knew the game. Well enough to be on the way to five games in a row at a dollar a game, anyway. Still no response.

I'd heard some rumours. His business could have been better, but by the look of the money he was bankrolling us with, it could have been worse. I'd told him this was a bad time for me to take a holiday, but he'd held me to an old promise. I guess I'm what friends are for.

I knew he was tired of the old home town too. He'd told me over the years that the place just might kill him. Once it walked all over him good and hard, that is. But now he was a part of the town,

Chamber of Commerce and all.

I'd also heard about somebody's wife. No names, just some-body. Either that or somebody's sister who was on her way to becoming somebody's wife. A lot of somebodies who didn't appear to have made him any happier. Nothing he wanted to get me this far from home to tell me about, anyway.

This morning I came out of the shower and was saying some-thing and he waved me quiet. The man on *Good Morning America* was talking about John Lennon. Why all the sombre faces? Then I heard. We listened for an hour, got breakfast, and hit the road. I picked up the local papers as we drove south and I read all the Lennon stories to him. Sometime in late morning President Reagan said on the radio that he didn't see the killing required a tightening of gun control.

Around one they played "Tomorrow Never Knows" from the *Revolver* album. He was still driving. I was just sitting there listening and staring straight ahead. Half-way through the song the tears started. I just let them run. I'd never felt like this about anybody's death.

He knew what I was doing and didn't say a word. I felt like turning on him and saying "This isn't an act, you fucker, just talk to me." I kept my mouth shut and went on listening to Beatles' songs.

Just south of Cheyenne we stopped for hamburgers. It was about three o'clock. After that he let me take the wheel and I kept on down I-25. "Look at all this traffic," I said. "What town are we near?" The map showed nothing straight through to Denver. I noticed I had to keep picking up the pace, and every now and then another lane tacked on. Now three, now four, now five, What was this? Well, it was Denver, of course. We hadn't realized how big the place was.

By now we could see the skyscrapers and he'd picked up a Denver station. Traffic was seven lanes per side, bumper to bumper, and everyone driving like crazy. I couldn't see how we'd ever get off this thing into Denver. Montreal's's no picnic, what with the maps in English and the signs in French, but this was pure tension.

Then everything goes haywire. Traffic on the other side crowds down to four lanes and almost stops and police are flying by at full speed, lights and sirens going. Naturally, half our side slows up to rubber in on the cops' situation. Then a helicopter goes over low.

One of those high-efficiency women's voices breaks in on "Norwegian Wood" and tells us there's a man holed up in his boarding house with a high-power rifle, two handguns, a couple sticks of dynamite, for God's sake, and an employee of the power company who'd come to read the meter. He's already shot his neighbour, dead, killed one person on the street, wounded two others, and killed the first policeman on the scene. He says he's going to kill everything that comes near him, then his hostage, then himself. He doesn't care about anything. Police, the woman tells us, are trying to get an ID on this man so as to determine the nature of his provocation.

I'm so wound up my hands feel like they're part of the wheel. Cops and ambulances are still screaming by and my good friend says, "All this commotion and it probably started with one little woman."

Duets In the Dust

Laurie Block

Do not forsake me O my darling. The finale of a nickel western. There, waiting for me, all the great ones. Coop, the Duke, Paw Cartwright and the boys. Nary a woman. Only men with leather faces and eyes of steel, men who tamed the wilderness and laid down the law, who bracketed the open range between their legs, shooting first and asking later, if at all. That's only natural. It's the end of the reel. Sun at high noon, gun still smoking, the saloon doors swing into the amazed hush of the street. The good die young and the camera bites the dust on a pair of stained boots twitching in red ochre.

If you're gonna do it, you gotta do it quick. It's a plunge in the river, a roll in the snow, it's four ounces rotgut neat. Hang on to your hats, ladies and gents. I'm talking one for the Gipper, I'm talking a far far better thang, I'm talking vasectomy.

Speaking with circumspection it's the male equivalent of gynecology, of stirrups and specula, the stainless steel finger of science. I'm not even naked. They've got me laid out on the cot with my pants down to my ankles, my shirt riding up on my belly. I lift my head and look down. One of my socks has a hole in it and my big toe sticks out, pink but shameless. With more nerve than that pathetic noodle nesting on my scrotum. We're both looking up into two friendly faces who know their business. Take no prisoners.

The doctor, a silver-haired Irishman named Murphy, beams with an earthy elegance but I know him for what he is. An angel with a sword, riding shotgun over the words of the Almighty, *be fruitful and multiply*. Cocking the syringe between his eye and the merciless light he dispenses heartless consolation with a wink. *Sure and you'll only be feeling a tiny prick my boy*. The nurse at his side is young and efficient, butter wouldn't melt. This is routine procedure, nothing to it. Snip/snap off the old vas deferens, a quick half-hitch and it's over. They send me home with simple instructions. Take it easy, stay off your feet and continue to use birth control until the sperm count settles. The next day I go for groceries and come home with grapefruit, bruised and swollen. Mama was right. It will turn black and fall off.

> A man's gotta do what a man's gotta do but I ask myself,
> could the Duke have done it, bitten the bullet, laid his
> pistol on the table and studied war no more.

Naw, he stuck to the script. You never saw him run up the white flag, limp out unarmed into no man's land. But that's exactly what I did. After all those years of pills, coils and condoms, spermicidal jellies and little rubber yarmulkes, I'd gone one on one with the goddess.

> Just your ordinary hero ridin out bareback across a
> savage land and into the purple sunset, my own true love
> behind me. That's how the west was won, with a free
> rein to desire.

Didn't ask for much. Lay back on the soft bed of virtue, closed my eyes to its own reward. Fellatio. Six weeks of the most glorious head, wreathed by her grateful lips. After the sperm count came in it was back to business as usual.

Should have learned to live with latex. After the separation she finally spit it out, how I overwhelmed her, how I never gave her time. Sonofabitch, she wanted more babies. This is news to me. I used to be her hero, now I can't hold a candle. Got myself fixed but she liked me better broken. And I'm thinking, sure, if you had those babies, by now you'd be old and fat and stuck with me or flat broke and chained to a dead-end job, and which is worse.

Long ago, time was a river and I was the kid with a worm and a hook. The past was retrievable, my future rounding the bend, the world ran by my feet. I was a true believer in freight trains and sidewalks and the logic of spiders, in the rain and the ruin that followed when I stepped on a crack. Things counted so I counted them, religiously, in multiples of three. Pennies, footsteps, fence-posts, blue Chevrolets. The ringing of the telephone as I hung back, waiting to hear my name. Readiness was everything. My theory of grace, the way wishes come true. To this day I'll drive under a bridge with a train rumbling overhead and, if I think I can make it, I'll close my eyes, take my feet off the pedals, my hands from the wheel and give myself up to the crossing.

Think about that kinda stuff all the time – time and love, surgery and healing. Hobble down memory lane and look over my shoulder at the future, closing fast. It's like a toothache, coming to terms with extraction. First the bargain with pain, what I wouldn't give for local anaesthesia, for a quick filling and an afternoon of numbness, but I can't stop exloring the cavity with the tip of my tongue. I rest my case. When it comes to love count me in. Hook, line and sinker. Might even take a chance and get married again. Love. One thing's sure, I'll fall and fall again. On my hands, my knees, in the arms of that special someone, I'll surrender to its irony, sacred and treacherous.

Another voice, a fresh arrangement but the same old song. The ticking of the biological clock. Go figure, now *she* wants a baby. And where does that leave me? Handing her a tissue while she sobs and snuffles and stops her mouth with the pillow. *Darling be reasonable. Isn't it enough we have each other, no strings, no measly fevers or hunger in the night. Think of the up side. Early retirement, that dream house by the sea. A waltz across New Mexico. A garden, poetry, tai-chi.*

Nights are the worst, wrestling with memory's knife, coming to morning naked and erect. I run a finger along the incision, picture myself repenting at leisure beside my one and only. Beautiful music fills the room. Drums thump between our ribs, the clock talks electric and the fan turns its face away and sighs at so much heat, at her naked back, at the jewelled movement as she leans through the window to touch the moon. If I were the Buddha I would stop the beast with my heart in the palm of my hand, I would pluck the pearl from my belly and embed it in her hair. Fill our changepurse and seal it with a golden clasp. There's talk of regeneration, a chance the process is reversible, but that's all behind me now. I belong to last year's crop, all juice and no seed, like an orange bursting at the skin, I am what I am. Sunkist. Sterile, stitched and complete.

In a couple years maybe the dust settles on the streets of a sun-bleached town. Peace will come, or at least stillness, except for the dust, dancing in the light of the window. Then, with the slightest commotion of the wind the curtain lifts its hem. Wherever I set my foot, how the dust dances.

Rose Cottage

Greg Hollingshead

IN THE AUTUMN Alex moved to Vancouver and got a job driving a cab, because a woman he had fallen in love with was taking classes at Simon Fraser, but in the spring she grew tired of him and asked him to move out. One day, weeping over some little thing, he answered in his neat hand an ad in the *Province* and ten days later was offered, for a small rent, a home on Vancouver Island.

Rose Cottage was a single-storey frame building with a concrete floor and white plaster walls and ceilings. Seventy years earlier it had been built against the east wall of Rose House for the use of the groundskeeper and his daughter, a servant in the main residence. Rose House was a stone mansion with a view of the ocean. It was now owned by a trust company in the name of a beautiful raw-faced widow of seventy-two named Lady Beatrice Cooper, who at some time before a succession of small strokes had damaged her brain specified that Rose Cottage should always be rented to a Canadian writer. Alex became the latest in a shabby line. He was not a writer but said he was when he answered the ad because he had always enjoyed the confidence that he could be. Who was to gainsay him?

Supported on the arm of Nurse Cheam – an ex-British-army matron fitted with a globular auburn hairpiece – Lady Cooper would yearn towards Alex and say, "Now ... sun ... go! ... solla solla ... so ... heh heh heh!"

And smiling and gentlemanly Alex would take her hand and

address her with a smiling courtly complaisance and a sort of mock obsequiousness, which though kind enough was overbearing and left him feeling like a bully. Other people's realities had always been too much for Alex, and it seemed to him logical in an unfair way that when the damaged eyes of Lady Cooper came to rest upon his face he should respond with a reality that was too much. In fact Lady Cooper's eyes were not damaged. It was the wrongness of such desolation in such proximity to that simpering mouth, the way her eyes seemed, so immediately, from a place so wrecked, to beseech him. With Lady Cooper, Alex was as much at a loss as with anyone how to behave in a way he could live with afterwards, but in her case it galled him more because with her his behaviour felt callous and wrong and not merely, as usual, half invisible.

And then one Sunday in July, six weeks after Alex had moved to Rose Cottage, he planned a day's walk through the forest that stretched from the back gate of Rose House for miles and miles along the sea. In anticipation of this adventure he ate magic mushrooms, an entire handful of the shrivelled leathery bitter gorge-heaving tiny fungi from a Ziploc bag that a sixty-year-old hippy with a yellowing ponytail had given him the previous Christmas Eve instead of cab fare. The idea was a day-long forest walk by the sea, on mushrooms. The idea was, like Wordsworth, to travel out and at the same time to travel in. Alex was not a writer, but he did sometimes feel liable to his own lies. But he was even more a novice at mushrooms than he was at Wordsworth, he didn't understand that the poisons released in his brain would take the straightforward thing he planned to do and deck it with obstacles.

The first was getting out the door of Rose Cottage. What happened was, Alex's preparations for that sea walk crumbled and the pieces multiplied. One stack of pieces toppled the next as beyond the rapidly unthinkable threshold that walk by the sea loomed ever larger and more daunting, with Alex now in one room of the little cottage and now in another.

After that came a long stretch of getting out the door but missing actually doing it. Alex would look down at the flagstone walk then back around behind him and remember the click of the door. Nothing more. An inauspicious beginning, it would seem to him, to have passed unwitnessed like that. And so he would go back inside and try again. Maybe that time notice he had forgotten to, say, wear a hat. A hat? What did he want with a hat? Well, what if it rained? Another complicated issue, with much searching, many stages, no hat to be found, did he own a hat? had he ever owned a hat? and with nothing resolved or accomplished, the minute hand sweeping, he would turn to something completely different and in the middle of that, fall into abstraction *sea walk looming* from which he would rouse himself as from a century of sleep in order to set about a new inconclusive task and suddenly be outside looking down at the flagstone walk beneath his feet and back at the door, the click having sounded behind him – until he thought, "I'll be here all day," and with a brutal focus of will *sea walk looming* shouldered aside all misgivings and moved out through the gate in the hedge of caragana onto the crushed white gravel of the courtyard, by now in a state similar to the adrenalization of one who knows that in the next instant he will be in a terrible car accident, crossing the bounding white gravel walk *sea walk looming* against an anxious seething canvas of slow-motion detail, out of which, with the astonishment that only utter predictability, as in a dream, can provide, there emerged the eyes, grey-blue, of Lady Beatrice Cooper, bobbing alongside the spherical peruke of Nurse Cheam, and from the back of Alex's head he could feel the spectra go peeling as too swiftly, apparently, *sea walk looming* he bowed to kiss Lady Cooper's ancient princess cheek and to tuck her other arm into his. Sea walk looming.

"Well, well ... san ... mol ... *tuh*! ... heh heh ... what ... ah! ... now now now ... tel!

"Good morning, Alex!" Nurse Cheam shouted. "You look like the cat that swallowed the canary this morning!"

Alex had never thought of himself as a cat before. He did now.

"Isn't it lovely!" Nurse Cheam cried. "You haven't come to take away my little girl, have you?"

He missed the next part.

And then Nurse Cheam was telling him, as she often did, about the young men interested in herself when she was "a slip of a girl."

But Alex must have missed the next part as well, because all of a sudden he heard, "... and when you come back I'll give you a lovely soft, fresh scone and a big tumbler of ice-cold whole milk!"

"Goodbye, Nurse Cheam. Goodbye Lady..."

"No, no! Take her arm! You must take her arm! Promise me you won't go far!"

"... yes."

Nurse Cheam was returning to the house.

"Where would you like to go, Lady Cooper?" Alex's voice asked as the hairs that grew from his skull passing again and again through his fingers seemed to be cilia that had bolted and died.

"Wa ... wa ... heh heh!"

"Yes," Alex said. "We'll do that." He drew himself up.

Immediately then, Alex and Lady Cooper were among roses, gazing together as if at a piece of statuary at Leadbeater, the gardener, a lean, toothless, small man with eyebrows like hanging gardens neglected and dessicant. Leadbeater stood hoe in hand gazing off at forty-five degrees, as he always did when being addressed, and Alex caught a fading trace of his own voice saying, "Nice day, Leadbeater."

"Yup," Leadbeater replied, darkly, and scowled at the heavens. "And we'll pay fer it."

Leadbeater's retributionist view of the weather seemed to tickle Lady Cooper. "Pay!" she cried. "Pay! Pay! Heh *heh*!"

Next, she and Alex were standing at the foot of the red pine by the gate to the forest. A whispering from above. Alex looked up to see each needle on that tree stir green against the sky. The clouds were three-dimensional and white and moving very fast. Dizzy, Alex lowered his eyes to Lady Cooper's, which were pleading.

"What," Lady Cooper said. "What ... what ... "

"What, what," Alex replied. Again he looked up. One thing, anyway, was trees: their size, the stubborn alien familiarity of their unutterable strangeness.

"Who," said Lady Cooper.

Alex looked at her. It was a beautiful old face that had been infantilized by cataclysms of blood.

"Who?"

"Who, *heh*!"

"Who! Who made this tree? Did you make this tree, Lady Cooper?"

"Oh no no!" she cried with alarm. "*No, no, no!*"

But Alex had stepped away from her to reach his arms around the trunk. "Isn't it beautiful?" he said. "Isn't it ... *great?*"

"What," said Lady Cooper. "What ... what will ..."

"What will," Alex said, and he gazed at her over his shoulder as he squeezed the tree with his cheek pressed foolishly against the curling, pinkish bark.

"What," said Lady Cooper. "What will ... what what ... "

"Tree, Lady Cooper!" Alex cried. *"Tree!"*

He gazed at her, but her eyes in their monkey sadness were averted down the garden towards Rose House as her fingers knotted and unknotted the air at her waist.

"What will," she said.

Alex let go of the tree. In the same instant that sea walk was right there, all around them, looming, shadowing everything, and Alex understood the depth and extent of his error, that he should ever have allowed this walk with Lady Cooper to eclipse, to preempt, that sea walk, which was now back. Not amused. Not in the least amused. How could he have forgotten?

"What will," Lady Cooper said.

"What will," Alex sighed.

One stream of Alex's thinking was saying that he really should return her to Rose House and get on with what this was supposed to be about. Another stream of his thinking was busy with a more abstract debate, one side arguing that a person needs to stick to what he intends because what else can he do? the other side arguing that if there is a single common denominator of human stupidity it is inflexibility. At some point during this debate Alex glanced at his watch without taking in the time, not that he would have known what time it was supposed to be. As he did so he caught sight of a third stream of thinking, to the effect that there is not only what you have to do, there is when you have to do it.

"What will," Lady Cooper said.

Alex turned to her. "Lady Cooper," he said. "I have to take you back now. I ..."

"No no! No no!"

"Oh yes ..."

But even as he was turning her to face the house, Alex understood that he had already missed the necessary time of setting out on his sea walk. It was now behind them, it had passed.

"Damn," Alex said quietly, and louder, "Damn," and he watched himself from above as like some generic mammal he shot frustrated little downward glances to the left and to the right.

"Damn!" said Lady Cooper. *"Heh."*

Alex continued to live at Rose Cottage through the fall. As the days became darker and autumn turned to winter, he spent more and more time walking, on the forest paths among the great estates and under the old trees where the park authorities had placed benches for the views of the sea and where the undergrowth was criss-crossed with hundreds of footpaths and bridlepaths. Many girls and women rode there, and when a footpath intersected a bridlepath, or when Alex strayed onto a bridlepath, the girls and young women would gallop past pretending not to see him, while the older women would sing "Glorious morning!" from their high English saddles, and he would fall in love with them all.

Sometimes Alex would be crossing the courtyard of Rose House, headed for the ancient trees and the paths along the sea, and all would be quiet in the great stone residence. But as often a window – usually on the second floor – would swing open on the back of Nurse Cheam's arm, and she would lean out and call Alex inside for a nice tumbler of "icy-fresh whole milk!"

Sometimes Alex, not wanting to refuse every time, would accept Nurse Cheam's invitation, and then he would stand on the front step until she opened the door and told him to go through into the sitting room, and there in the chill of the morning he would find Lady Cooper strapped into her big metal chair with the tray, dozing, and he would stand by the window and look down the lawn and the cypress walk at the weather until Nurse Cheam came in with a tray of milk and biscuits to talk to him in her loud lonely voice, the first sound of which would startle Lady Cooper into a soft babble against the din of it.

Sometimes from an upper window of Rose House as he was crossing the courtyard Alex would hear Nurse Cheam shout at Lady Cooper. Usually the sound was muffled, but sometimes he would hear *"Bad girl!"* or *"Don't you dare!"* Once he heard what sounded like slaps. Sometimes when Nurse Cheam had him in for milk and biscuits, she would refer cheerily to their "little boxing matches."

And then one morning, as Alex was eating breakfast, Nurse Cheam came to the door of Rose Cottage to ask for his help. She sometimes did this when she needed a chore done that she could not do herself or that she considered man's work, such as climbing a stepladder or tightening a hinge. Normally she used Leadbeater for these purposes, but when Leadbeater was not around or when Alex's height was an advantage she came to him. It wasn't often – no more than once every couple of weeks – and Alex hardly minded. He could see that she was very lonely.

On this morning, Alex didn't even think to ask what it was, though there was something odd about Nurse Cheam's manner, a kind of suppressed excitement. But he followed her obediently out into a cold drizzle, through the gate in the caragana hedge, along the perimeter of the courtyard into the darkness of Rose House, and up the oak staircase from the main hall. It was Alex's first visit to the second floor. By the time they reached the landing he could hear Nurse Cheam breathing hard. But along the hallway her pace did not diminish, and when she reached the far door, she pushed it open and stood back and waited significantly. Thinking now that Lady Cooper must have fallen, Alex entered a dim room where the smell of urine was thick and stale, and where, at the head of an enormous bed, he saw her white hair, whiter than her sheets, her rosy face, so small against the enormous pillow, watching him as he came towards her. She was making sounds, but it wasn't her soft gabble, it was a kind of whimpering, and he could see that her eyes were terrified.

"Good morning, Lady Cooper," Alex said as he came alongside the bed. "Are you all right?"

"There's nothing wrong with her," said Nurse Cheam, and coming up the other side of the bed she reached for a corner of the bedclothes and in one movement pulled them entirely clear of the old woman. "She refuses to get out of bed," Nurse Cheam said, as Lady Cooper writhed in an anguish of humiliation and confusion. "You'd think she was waiting for a handsome young man to put his thing in her."

In the time it took Nurse Cheam to say this, Alex's eyes consumed Lady Cooper's nakedness, from her pubic tuft to her lolling breasts to her wrists and neck, where an old woman's creased brown and exposed flesh paled suddenly to a smoothness that time and light had hardly damaged. It was not a young woman's body with an old woman's hands and face, it was an old woman's beautiful body plumped for slaughter, too ripe, too right for exactly this and still more terrible violation.

"Cover her up," Alex muttered as one hand reached back blindly for the bedclothes at the foot of the bed, and when he looked to Nurse Cheam he saw the expression on her face and knew that she knew, and he could see the grim, righteous pleasure she took in the shame that she had so easily brought upon them both.

One warm, sunny morning not many days later, Alex knocked at the front door of Rose House. When Nurse Cheam saw who it was she cried in something like relief, "Good morning, Alex! Won't you come in and have tea with us?"

So Alex took tea with Nurse Cheam and Lady Cooper, who was slumped in her chair with the tray, near a low fire in the high-ceilinged, chilly sitting room of Rose House, with a grey light coming through the lead-paned window that faced west down the cypress walk. And after tea Alex took Lady Cooper outside for her morning turn in the garden, except that at the gate to the woods he said, "Where would you like to go, Lady Cooper?"

"Walla. Walla. *Heh!*"

"The woods? Shall we walk in the woods?"

Always when Alex walked with Lady Cooper in the grounds of Rose House there would come a point when she wanted to keep on, to circle the rose bushes one more time, and he would have to say No, they really must go back to the house. But this time he had called on her because he had decided to let her lead him where she wanted, for as long as she wanted. Before her strokes she must have known this forest better than he did now. Alex's idea was that she would communicate with him by the paths she would choose.

And so the two of them set out, and at every junction of the paths, Lady Cooper knew exactly which one she wanted. They crossed a road and another road and still they continued on. But they were moving away from the sea into recent suburban developments, and Alex understood that the old woman was walking in a straight line away from Rose House towards the city, that she did not intend to diverge, that these were not her favourite paths, had nothing to do with memory or the woman she once was, this was now, this was escape.

Not long after he realized this, Alex knew they had to turn back. He could tell from the weight on his arm that Lady Cooper was tired. They had come so far that even he was tired. But she refused to stop.

"I think we'd better ..." he said.

"Oh no no no no no no ..."

"But we're so tired!" Alex said. "We have to!" And he halted and would not let her go on.

Lady Cooper turned her head away a moment, and when it swung back and she was looking at him she said, "What will, what will, what will ..."

"What will?" Alex replied impatiently. "What will what?"

"Become of me?"

"Oh dear," and Alex just stood there, gazing ahead, waiting for her eyes to leave the side of his face. When they did, he steered her in the direction of Rose House.

Keeping his own eyes fixed before him, he said, finally, "I don't know."

Lady Cooper laughed softly and at that moment Alex recognized that the emotion he was feeling was hatred, that a part of him had always believed she was laughing at him, or perhaps at the futility of looking to one such as him.

Neither spoke again until they reached the first road they had crossed. By then they had been walking so long that Alex knew they would have to take that road directly to Rose House rather than go by way of the paths through the forest. It was a narrow, paved road, a winding downhill grade, with eight-foot root-impacted banks instead of shoulders, and there was enough traffic going fast enough to make the walk dangerous. Twice women in Jeep Wagoneers, who assumed that Lady Cooper had escaped and Alex was leading her back, risked accidents to stop and offer lifts.

"No, thank you," he told them and made a little barrier with his smile. He did not want to return to Rose House by car, so visible an admission of irresponsibility. But when the police car stopped, the officer who held the door would not hear Alex's refusal, simply continued to block the way by holding the open door against the embankment until Alex helped Lady Cooper in.

As they pulled away, the one driving said, "The nurse is worried about her."

"I'm sorry," Alex said. "I guess we went too far."

"Don't walk her on the road again."

When they pulled up to the door of Rose House, Nurse Cheam bustled forth with cries of alarm to open Lady Cooper's door and tug at her arm and chastise her for being a naughty girl. Alex got out on the other side.

Stoically the policemen accepted Nurse Cheam's gratitude, declining her offers of hot scones and ice-cold whole milk. After they had pulled away, Nurse Cheam refused Alex's offer to help with Lady Cooper, who was stumbling with fatigue.

One day not a month later, just before Christmas, two men in dark suits from the trust company that administered Lady Cooper's estate came by appointment to see how the Rose Cottage tenant was keeping up the property. The younger man was sparse-bearded with red eyes, the elder somewhat aquiline, a Senior Director with burst-blood-vessel British cheeks. Both seemed embarrassed to have to look at how Alex lived. As he was shown through, the Senior Director commented that he had been to school in England with Lord Cooper, had known him rather well, as a matter of fact.

"How's the writing coming?" he asked Alex.

"Oh, pretty well."

As they were leaving, Alex said, "I wonder if you saw my letter."

"Letter?" replied the Senior Director, almost eagerly. "Why? Are you giving notice?"

Awkwardly Alex explained no, he'd written to say he was worried that Nurse Cheam was physically abusing Lady Cooper.

To the knowledge of the Senior Director no such letter had been received. "What evidence do you have?" he wanted to know.

Alex told them about the shouts and the "boxing matches." He did not tell them about Nurse Cheam's throwing off Lady Cooper's bedclothes for her own pleasure.

The younger man glanced shyly at Alex. "These are serious charges," he said.

Alex agreed that they were.

The Senior Director took out his card and wrote something on the back. "You had best write another letter," he said, "to this gentleman."

"I will," Alex said.

And so he wrote again, this time to the indicated gentleman at the trust company.

Towards the end of March he received a letter from the trust company saying that his lease would not be renewed.

Over the next few weeks Alex made visits to health authorities and tenants' rights organizations in an attempt to do something for Lady Cooper and for himself. In the meantime the trust company arranged for two local doctors to examine Lady Cooper. The doctors signed statements declaring no evidence of mistreatment. A legal aid lawyer in a nearby town told Alex that he could do nothing for Lady Cooper, and he took a moment to direct Alex's attention to the wall behind him and the important truth, done by his father in needlepoint, that was framed there: *It's a great life if you don't falter.* But he was willing to help Alex fight his eviction – until he saw the details of the lease. The trust company was pleading something called "discretionary refurbishment," and there was indeed such a clause. Meanwhile Alex's complaint to the trust company must have reached Nurse Cheam, for the offers of icy whole milk ceased. No longer did Nurse Cheam walk Lady Cooper late mornings in the courtyard or the upper garden, only in the lower garden and on the terrace at the south side of the house, where Alex would have been trespassing to go. But on the day before his return to Vancouver, he didn't come back from a walk until nearly seven one evening, and he ran into them in the courtyard.

"Goodbye, Lady Cooper," he said, taking her hand. "My lease hasn't been renewed. I'm going back to Vancouver tomorrow. Goodbye. Thank you. I'll miss you."

But Lady Cooper, whose face was bruised down the left side, only laughed softly and mumbled and did not look at him.

"You'll look after her, won't you, Nurse Cheam?" Alex said, taking her hand too.

"As well as always," Nurse Cheam replied coldly. "It's not easy for anyone. You don't know how she can be."

"No," Alex said. "I see a helpless old woman."

"You don't have to wipe her," Nurse Cheam said.

"No," Alex said. "I don't."

"You don't have to put up with her moods. Day after day. Her childishness. Her cruelty."

"And you don't have to hit her," Alex said.

Here Nurse Cheam drew herself up. "*Don't* you talk to me about what I have to do or don't have to do! How I do my job is none of your business! I am the trained expert here! I see that she gets her meals and her walks and her time on the toilet! Twenty-four hours a day she has me to look after her! I'd like to see you do my job for one week! For one day! You walk with her half an hour when the sun shines, and you think you know what it's like! But you don't! You don't know a single thing about it!"

"You don't have to hit her," Alex said.

And that's when Alex received a punch in the face so quick and hard that he didn't see it coming. But it snapped his head to the right and filled his left eye with tears, and when his vision cleared, Nurse Cheam was walking away with Lady Cooper, who looked back over her shoulder vaguely in Alex's direction, chuckling softly.

That night, Alex's last at Rose Cottage, as he was writing a letter to the Senior Director suggesting that the trust company hire a home companion to help Nurse Cheam in the afternoons and to allow her at least every other weekend off, smiling to think how these letters to the trust company were the only writing he had done at Rose Cottage, there was a kind of scrabbling at his door, like a branch, or a squirrel, that went on for some time before he went to see what it was, and what it was was Lady Cooper, in a man's green tartan dressing gown and bare feet, coming directly over the threshold, reaching to clutch Alex's hands with cold, strong fingers. Alex tried to step back, but she held him fast. He tried to laugh, he tried to be his gentlemanly self, he tried to be stern, but none of it would come. He made himself return her gaze, but it was difficult, he was afraid it would swallow him.

Her focus was beyond his eyes, on something else. Her wild red face, her murmurous gabble, her brown teeth, she knew him, and the feel of that for him was vertigo. He understood he could fall here, he could fall in. He could let himself go, and then what?

"So!" said Nurse Cheam from the doorway, startling them both. "This is where you've come, you naughty, naughty girl!"

"I think she just wanted to say goodbye," Alex said over Lady Cooper's shoulder, though he knew this was untrue.

"Whuh," Lady Cooper said. "*Whuh.*" Her eyes had left him, her fingers let go of his hands.

Nurse Cheam had not remembered to put on her wig. Her hair was thin and grey like an old man's, and her skull looked very strong.

"Well, don't encourage her. Come on, you. It'll be a wonder you haven't caught your death. I can see it's time to start tying you in. Say goodnight to your boyfriend."

"Good night, Lady Cooper," Alex said gently, with sadness and relief. "I'll come back and visit."

But he didn't.

In Vancouver Alex sank back into the person he had been before he left, as if Rose Cottage had not happened. He never seemed to have enough time, always seemed to be doing things too late, scuffling like a dog for a place to live, for enough cab work to keep off welfare but not so much the boredom would kill him. After Rose Cottage the city seemed harsh and raw. When Alex wasn't driving cab he played pickup basketball at the Y. For some reason he had the idea that if his rooms got enough light he'd have no need for furniture or pictures on the wall. A TV, a mattress, a table to eat at. No curtains. A flower in a vase.

After six months back in Vancouver, Alex was ready to crush the flower. At night he dreamed of Rose Cottage, the paths through the forest by the sea. The next summer he made the trip back. Incredibly it had been almost two years. He told himself that in her condition Lady Cooper would have little sense of the time that had passed. On the walk from the bus stop Alex's life at Rose Cottage came back in force, but the door of Rose House was opened by a small man wearing a white shirt with thick blue stripes and a polka dot bow tie.

"Does Lady Cooper live here?" Alex asked in confusion.

"No, mummy died," the man replied, looking Alex up and down. "I'm Malcom. My friends call me Mally. You must be Alex, from the cottage. I love your jacket. Of course, it's leather. I'm making myself a cup of coffee. Won't you join me? I'll catch you up."

Malcom looked like a younger, softer version of Lord Cooper, whose portrait still hung in the main hall.

"I didn't know you existed," Alex said.

"Call me Mally. I didn't. I was in Italy. You know the sitting room. I'll bring everything through."

The sitting room had been redone. There were Afghan carpets, and the walls were now pale rose. The paintings were suburban watercolours and pastel abstracts. The room was lighter and warmer. Alex crossed to the window to look down the cypress walk and was amazed to see a house not fifteen feet away.

"I *know*," said Mally, wheeling in a tea service. "I had to. Had to turn out old Leadbeater too. He's in a home now. I simply couldn't afford to live here otherwise. Still can't. And I'm a shitty gardener. Cream?"

Mally was an art dealer. Lady Cooper had died six months after Alex returned to Vancouver.

"I appreciate tremendously what you tried to do for mummy," Mally said. "As soon as I found out, through my spies at the trust co., I had Cheam pensioned off. Looked after mummy myself. It was horrible. I only did it because I fully expect to be in the same condition one day and I want to be justified when I'm pissed off, and I promise you I will be, because no one's going to lift a fucking finger for me. I mean, mummy could afford a nurse. Would you mind if I sketched while we talk? You do have the most magnificent mouth …"

Alex did mind, but he said he didn't.

"Just fifteen minutes," Mally promised, moving onto his knees. "It's the line of that marvellous lower lip ..."

And so Alex had himself sketched by Mally. The sketching was meant to be preliminary to fellatio. Mally was a good talker, and without saying a thing about it he succeeded in conveying to Alex that there was nothing reciprocal expected, that this would be a forthright no-strings gesture of gratitude for what Alex had tried to do for his mother, and besides, what could be nicer than to return a favour in so delightful a way? Alex would hardly need to put down his cup.

Now, Alex had a long way to go before he could have enjoyed being fellated by a stranger, but mostly his problem was feeling that he hadn't done all that much for Lady Cooper, he should have done more. He felt confused about accepting this favour he neither wanted nor deserved nor considered a favour. Fellatio was something he had allowed women only so that they would indulge his surely incomparably greater desire to witness the fragrance between their legs. But whatever he said as Mally wedged one narrow shoulder and then two between his knees sounded not so much like false modesty as like a running-down conversation in a seduction, when the love-making has already started and the meaning is draining out of the words. Really what Alex wanted to do was jump up.

"Mm, I just love 501s," Mally murmured, his fingers at work on the buttons. The hair on Mally's head was very straight and fine and going a little thin at the top.

Alex could tell that Mally was a gentleman, quite able to chat them through any awkwardness, so that afterwards there would hardly have been an awkwardness at all, whether it was a sudden clamour by Alex to his feet or an uncontrollable bucking of his hips or the tight quick hug and peck on the cheek that he would receive at the door when leaving too quickly (though never quickly enough), and before he knew it he would be on his way across the courtyard and passing through what was left of the roses to step beyond the upper gate and into the forest. Feeling like a pushover, feeling foolish and dismissed and implicated in an unconsidered act of abasement and undoing but otherwise feeling pretty much the way he always felt, except for an old small amazement to be so effortlessly, so unaccountably free, once again. Except for an old, small, cautionary feeling that no one, not even he, could so prevail forever.

Blurred Edges

Edward O. Phillips

CRAWFORD AND MARGARET were not romantically involved, nor had they ever been. His wife of twenty-five years had recently died, leaving him a widower at fifty-six. Margaret, on the other hand, now lived with her third husband, the first two marriages having ended in divorce. She confessed to being fiftyish, meaning she was about the same age as Crawford. They met at a dinner party given by a mutual friend who believed Crawford "ought to get out more." In effect his newly found condition of widower and single man made him an asset in the eyes of fiftyish hostesses. Just imagine a single man who wasn't, well – you know.

Crawford had noticed Margaret the second she came into the drawing room. As if reading the prompt book for a light summer comedy she entered laughing, then headed for the most comfortable wing chair in the room, ignoring the half-finished highball resting on a cocktail napkin on the occasional table beside it. "I've taken your chair, haven't I," she announced to the male guest re-entering the room to claim his place.

"That's all right," he replied, as Crawford knew he would.

Dinner itself found Margaret seated on Crawford's right; her own husband sat across and down the long refectory table. She set out to charm, drawing on a seemingly endless supply of inconsequential chatter. He learned in some detail of the inconveniences she had undergone as her street had been torn up to permit the laying of a natural gas pipeline. Nobody had any idea of what she'd been through.

"May I try one of your cigarettes?" she inquired after soup. "They look interesting."

"They're not really interesting, just American," he replied, flicking a gold lighter, an anniversary present from his wife.

"Thanks." For just a moment her hand rested on his holding the lighter, a fleeting moment of familiarity.

Crawford was more given to listening than talking, especially in public and more especially when the flow of talk neither expected nor merited a reply. He ate his way silently through the Beef Wellington, then reached for a cigarette from the package in his right-hand pocket.

"May I?" she said, plucking the cigarette from his fingers. He nodded. She waited expectantly until, after only a moment's hesitation, he again flicked his lighter and held it to the cigarette. She also used his tiny ash tray even though the hostess had provided one at every place.

Over salad the current of conversation began to flow across the table. Launching herself into a tirade against the proposed reorganization of Quebec school boards, Margaret reached almost casually into Crawford's jacket pocket. Flashing him a quick smile she took the package, talking with animation as she tapped out a cigarette. Then she put the package down beside his place mat. He appeared not to notice. Gradually growing aware that the cigarette remained unlit she reached for the sconce holding two candles, which sat in front of her place, dropping gobs of hot wax onto the highly polished surface of the table. After dinner Crawford sat beside someone else.

He met Margaret a few more times, casually, here and there: at cocktail parties, during intermissions, once at a *vernissage*. Sometimes she was with her husband, a computer wizard who travelled a good deal. Other times she turned up with a female companion in tow, or else a man, obviously homosexual. She never went out in public alone, and it fell to whomever she was with to stand, three deep, at the bar during intermissions, procuring drinks, and also to feed her cigarettes which she always claimed loudly to have just given up.

Late one afternoon Crawford met Margaret at a wine and cheese party. Crawford did not much care for wine and cheese parties; the wine was generally warm and the cheese cold, but solitude weighed upon him. The pattern of his adult life had been profoundly altered, old habits broken off short. And although attentive, his children were both married with families of their own. Crawford did not wish to intrude on their autonomy. But sometimes he wanted to be around other people, to spend an hour or so listening to the hum of other human beings.

Over a glass of Chablis Margaret begged a cigarette and asked him what he had been up to.

"Nothing much out of the ordinary," he replied. "And you?"

"I've been helping Isobel to pack. Isn't it a shame she and Harry are moving to Vancouver. But they both so dislike the winter."

"Harry and Isobel who?"

"You don't know Harry and Isobel – Norman? They live just across the street from me. He's an engineer – brilliant; and she paints. Heaps of talent. You've never met them?"

"No, I haven't."

"I guess Westmount isn't as small as I thought. Anyhow, Harry's soon to retire and his daughter lives in West Vancouver, and...." Margaret went on at some length to explain why Harry and Isobel were leaving Quebec, about how Isobel longed for the light of the West Coast. The grandchild, it appeared, had a learning disability; and they had been obliged to cut the price of their house because of the slack market. Moving was dreadfully expensive, and they had decided not to take the dining room furniture.

Crawford listened politely to a story about people he did not know, all the time thinking that nothing really interesting or unusual coloured their daily problems.

After a while Margaret drifted away and Crawford fell into conversation with a lawyer he had known for many years. The talk turned from cheese to vacations, of how expensive it had become to visit the American seashore when paying in weak Canadian dollars.

"I know," said Crawford. "I have to drive down to Boston on business next week. I'm budgeting for my trip plus twenty-five per cent surcharge."

"Did I hear you say you were driving to Boston?" asked Margaret from the fringes of the conversation. Having found nobody to whom she wished to attach herself, she had returned to the general vicinity of Crawford, who at least had cigarettes.

"Hi, I'm Margaret Drake," she said by way of introduction to

Crawford's lawyer friend before turning her full attention back to Crawford. "Are you really driving down to Boston?"

"Yes, I am."

"How marvelous! I happen to be going to Boston myself next week. I don't suppose I could come along."

"It's not a pleasure trip," replied Crawford. "Strictly business. The only reason I'm taking my car is that I have to deliver a large box of china which is too fragile to ship. Otherwise I'd fly." He glanced at his watch. "Time to run along, for me at least." Crawford said his goodbyes and peeled himself away before the subject of Boston could be pursued further.

The following morning found Crawford as usual at his desk when his secretary announced a Mrs. Drake on the telephone. Mrs. Drake? It took him a few seconds to make the connection between the woman on the line and the dinner partner who purloined cigarettes. Warily he picked up the telephone. "Yes?"

"Crawford. Darling; it's Margaret."

His neck stiffened. Neither he nor his wife had been given to easy endearments, and in Crawford's experience women only called you "darling" when they wanted something.

"Yes, Margaret, what can I do for you?"

"Crawford, about Boston. It really would be heaven if I could drive down with you. I'm going to Cape Cod for a visit and I have to take so many clothes. It would be marvelous to have a drive."

"I'm only staying two nights. How will you get home?"

"No problem. My husband is driving down for a long weekend. I'll drive back with him. Wouldn't you like to have company for the trip?"

Crawford did not want company for the trip. His own thoughts unrolling against a background of FM radio were more than enough companionship. Moreover, since the death of his wife he found himself less and less inclined to be around people for long periods of time, and even more reluctant to be trapped in a car for a long drive with a woman he hardly knew and did not particularly like.

But Crawford was a product of the codes: of society, of the gentleman, of good manners. Short of being rude he could not come up with an excuse why she should not come along. "Very well. But I insist on two conditions. First, I like, rather I intend to be on the road early – well beyond the city limits before the morning rush hour. Second, you will bring and smoke your own cigarettes."

Margaret laughed. "Point taken. I'll be ready. I'll have a carton of cigarettes, and matches."

"Wednesday morning then. Eight o'clock sharp!"

Almost to Crawford's surprise Margaret was ready and waiting when he pulled up in front of her large house in upper Westmount. A carton of cigarettes lay in full view on top of a woven straw beach bag. The day promised to be fine, and they were soon outside the city limits on their way to the United States border. If one thing could have bothered Crawford it was Margaret's obvious conviction that she must be entertaining. They had not even reached the bridge across the St. Lawrence River when she launched into a story about David and Sheila and how they had decided to separate after all these years and wasn't it a shame they couldn't seem to work things out.

"David and Sheila who?" inquired Crawford.

"David and Sheila Young. I thought you knew them. They're great friends of Harry and Isobel."

"I don't know Harry and Isobel."

"Oh," she said at a loss, but only for a moment. Abandoning the topic of David and Sheila, Margaret took off on the subject of her own daughter, by her first husband. It seems the girl, now a young woman, had decided to give up her law practice and go for an M.B.A.

"What's wrong with that?" asked Crawford.

Margaret did not really have an answer beyond that which arose from a free-wheeling sense of parental disapproval and a mistrust of change. Crawford let her run down. While she was engaged in lighting a cigarette – she did really intend to give them up but one more can't hurt – he reached over and switched on the radio. "*Dove sono,*" sang the Countess, "*i bei momenti?*"

"*The Marriage of Figaro!*" exclaimed Margaret. "My favourite Mozart opera. We saw it last time we were in Vienna. Tickets were all sold out but the hall porter managed to come up with two, for a large tip you may be sure. We tried to get into the Imperial Hotel but it was booked solid, so we stayed at the Sacher. Quite charming really. And that cake! Suicide if you're on a diet...." And off she went, offering random reminiscences about Vienna, unmatched beads on a knotted string, and making it totally impossible for Crawford to concentrate on the music.

Shortly, however, his full attention was drawn to the red light on the dashboard which warned the motor had overheated.

Margaret suggested they stop for coffee while the motor cooled. Coffee turned into a full-scale breakfast after which Margaret excused herself to use the ladies room, leaving Crawford to pay the bill. When he unlocked the car she climbed into the passenger seat. "You wouldn't believe that bathroom," she said, wrenching the rearview mirror around so she could put on fresh lipstick. Scarcely had they pulled away from the restaurant when the red light again began to blink ominously. At thirty-five miles an hour Crawford drove to the next town on the Vermont-New Hampshire border and pulled into the sole garage.

What followed was the kind of day which made Crawford deeply regret his scant knowledge of the internal combustion engine. A short length of hose needed replacing; however, the piece could not be found in the jumble of spare parts, chaotic to all but the laconic mechanic. Several telephone calls located the necessary part in another town some twenty-five miles distant. But the truck was presently out on call. When it did arrive back at the garage it was dispatched to pick up the necessary part. The truck and lunch time arrived at the same moment. Not until early afternoon did the unfailingly pleasant but slow mechanic get down to work on Crawford's car, interrupting his task periodically as cronies dropped by to chat.

Crawford bought Margaret some lunch and listened politely to her chatter. In no particular hurry and possessed of a captive audience she seemed not to mind the delay in the least. She was on holiday, and one diversion proved as amusing as the next. After lunch they strolled idly through a town offering little in the way of distraction. In the general store Crawford bought a newspaper, then went to sit on a bench in a small square dominated by a monument to the dead of both world wars. Margaret fidgeted, lit a cigarette, then came to stand behind him as he read.

"I'll bet you just hate people reading over your shoulder."

"As a matter of fact I do."

"I'll just take a piece of the paper and read quietly." Riffling through the pages and causing Crawford to lose his place, she yanked out the entertainment section and sat on the bench beside him. Crossly he teased his newspaper back into shape and found his place. Whenever he used to travel with his wife they bought two newspapers. Friends thought them a bit eccentric, but Crawford considered the extra paper a sound thirty-cent investment in marital harmony.

"Do you suppose they'll be much longer working on the car?" she asked after about one minute and forty seconds.

"I have no way of knowing." Turning the page he continued to read.

"I brought along some jam for my hostess. I hope it will be all right."

"I see no reason why it shouldn't be," replied Crawford without lifting his eyes from the page. He read gamely on.

"Who is the box of china for?"

"A friend of my wife's. She has always admired the service and I wanted her to have it. Now do you have any more questions before I read my paper?" By way of reply Margaret made a show of fishing a paperback novel from her shoulder bag and resigned herself to reading.

The afternoon was already well advanced by the time they pulled away from the garage. Crawford fretted because he knew they would be unable to reach Boston by dinner time. He did not relish the idea of arriving late, tired, hungry, dying for a drink, yet obliged to fulfill the duties of civilized house guest. But he had little choice.

"I have a marvelous idea," said Margaret in the breathy tone of voice certain women use to get their own way. "About forty miles from here there is a darling little inn. Marvelous dining room. We could stop for the night and get off early tomorrow morning."

"Sounds good," agreed Crawford. "But I am expected in Boston tonight."

"There's no way we can reach Boston in time for dinner. And I do so hate to barge in on people late in the evening."

She echoed Crawford's sentiments. But he who hesitates is lost. Crawford paused to reflect just a moment. He felt cranky, and they still had a good two hundred miles to drive. His better judgement urged him to press on, but the siren song of a drink and a good meal sounded sweetly in his ear.

"I guess I can be swayed," he replied after some seconds. "Either we can drive straight through, or we can stop. Which would you prefer?"

"Oh, please; let's stop!" she cried, her enthusiasm contagious. "It's really adorable. I know you'll love it."

Crawford had to admit the white clapboard building circled by an ivy-covered porch and facing onto the manicured village green was indeed pleasant. As luck would have it two rooms were available. Crawford took his one suitcase up to his room, then made two trips for Margaret who seemed to need all five pieces of luggage in order to dress for dinner.

"I'd give you a hand," she said, making her voice caressing and confidential, "but I just spent a fortune on my manicure."

Crawford telephoned his Boston hostess to explain the delay; he took a shower and dressed for dinner. On his way to the bar he paused to hold open the front door for a handsome woman in her late forties carrying two suitcases.

"Thank you," she smiled at Crawford.

"You're quite welcome. Those suction arms on screen doors have a life of their own."

The front desk being temporarily deserted, the woman put down her bags. "I'm supposed to meet my son," she explained. "He's coming up from Dartmouth. He looks quite disreputable but he's really awfully nice." She laughed; so did Crawford, who liked her on sight.

"Let me see if I can't scare up somebody to check you in." He looked around.

"Please don't bother. I am sure whoever is on duty will show up momentarily."

"Oh, there you are, Darling," cooed Margaret, sailing up to slide her arm under Crawford's. She acknowledged the woman with a nod. "Time for that drink!" And she bore Crawford off to the pine-panelled bar.

Concealing his real annoyance – how dare she be so presumptuous? – he ordered drinks, vodka-tonic for Margaret, a dry rob roy for himself. When the drinks arrived Margaret looked quizzically at his glass.

"What's a dry rob roy?"

"Scotch and white vermouth, a scotch martini in effect."

"Sounds interesting. I'd love to try it."

Crawford shrugged but did not speak. Margaret reached across the table for his glass, took a large sip which she rolled around thoughtfully in her mouth like someone trying a fine vintage, then swallowed. "Not bad," she murmured, raising her eyebrows in appreciation. Then, as if to convince herself beyond all reasonable doubt, she took another swallow, repeating the performance before pronouncing the drink "yummy." Crawford said nothing; he considered his drink inviolate, just like his newspaper. And she had drunk roughly one quarter of his cocktail.

But by now Margaret had taken off on another chronicle, this time about Pete and Lizabeth and how they were having trouble making ends meet what with the house in the Eastern Townships and the condominium in Sarasota, not to mention the large city house, way too big since the children moved out but impossible to sell. Crawford did not know Pete and Lizabeth, nor did he ask for a glossary. He agreed times were hard.

Over the good but not outstanding meal they shared a bottle of wine. Thirsty, Crawford ordered a beer on the side. It arrived in a tall glass misted with condensation.

"Doesn't that look good! I don't suppose I could have a sip."

Crawford did not answer; he did not have time since the tall glass was already en route to her mouth which then went on to reel off another tale about Harry and Isobel and how they had been robbed when they went to Mexico and forgot to turn on the burglar alarm.

Crawford listened impassively. He did not feel impelled to speak. And he realized that Margaret had little or no interest in what he had to say. What she demanded, even compelled, was his full attention. Around her one could not even woolgather, much less read. "You aren't listening," followed by a bright, mirthless laugh, got Crawford back into line.

Totally uninterested in the items, enumerated one by one, which had been stolen from Harry and Isobel, Crawford had been trying to figure out how Margaret thought of herself in relation to him, to other men in general. What were the guidelines, if any, which governed her conduct around men other than her husband? She did not flirt with Crawford except to try to control him. Her "darlings" were proprietary, not sexual. In fact she would probably have been astonished, perhaps even offended, had Crawford suggested they spend the night together. Nor did he want to. Not that she wasn't attractive. She had not slid into weight; her jawline was clean. (Anyone who talked that much ought to have a firm jaw, thought Crawford.) Whoever had tinted her hair had done so with skill and artifice, and she dressed with the care that only an idle woman with plenty of money can lavish on her wardrobe.

But sex is more a quality of mind than of body, and Crawford found Margaret totally without feminine appeal. Even her perfume, musky and sweet, did not so much proclaim her femininity as stake out the area where she expected to be in charge. Nor could he regard her simply as a friend. His friends did not call him darling and smoke his cigarettes. They paid their own way. They did not invade his consciousness and turn his own code of good manners into a fulcrum on which he could be levered into position. His friends did not manipulate nor intrude. Margaret, however, belonged to that generation of women, somewhere between fifty and sixty-five, who had remained untouched by the egalitarian principles of feminism. They were female chauvinists, women who believed men should pay for drinks and meals and hand out endless cigarettes simply because they were men. Those who were neither husbands nor lovers inhabited a kind of limbo where edges blurred, categories shifted at will, and the view was obscured by an opaque film of sex, present but unspoken.

Margaret was a taker; her hand was always outstretched to receive a drink, but never to pour. Her batteries recharged themselves from the current of other people's energy, but she offered little energy in exchange. If only she would shut up, thought Crawford, and allow him to enjoy his dinner in peace. Her constant chatter eroded his patience. He found her both tiring and tiresome.

"Oh, Darling, I just ran out of cigarettes and the others are upstairs in my room. I don't suppose ..."

Crawford handed her the package, at the same time tempted to suggest she go upstairs and fetch her own cigarettes. A book of matches advertising the inn lay beside the ashtray; Crawford did not reach for his lighter.

He signed the check so it would be added to the room account, then suggested having a liqueur in the bar. It was still too early for bed and the early retirement he had promised himself. Margaret ordered herself a Cointreau; Crawford ordered a rusty nail.

"What's that?" inquired Margaret, obviously not a drinker of scotch.

"Scotch and Drambuie; the scotch cuts the sweetness in the liqueur."

"May I?"

"No, you may not. If you want one, order one." The asperity in his tone surprised even Crawford himself. "Look," he said to change the subject. "There's the woman I spoke to briefly at the front desk. She seems to be alone. Shall I ask her to join us for a drink?"

"Are you bored with me?"

"Not in the least," lied Crawford. "I just thought it might be courteous."

"She looks awfully dreary – hair in a braid, and those rubber-soled shoes. I'll bet she carries tracts in her purse. Besides, I'm going to have to give you up tomorrow morning."

"I'm afraid you're going to have to give me up right now," answered Crawford. "I want to be on the road at six tomorrow and it's been a long day."

"But you haven't even finished your drink."

"I don't really want it. Here, keep these." He put the package holding four cigarettes onto the table. "They will save you a trip upstairs. Sleep well."

"But it's still early. And there's no TV in the room."

"I have work to do. Goodnight." Before she could protest further he left the bar and climbed the stairs to his room. And although he carried nothing of real value, and even though he was quite certain both guests and staff were above reproach, Crawford locked his bedroom door.

It was six forty-five the following morning before Crawford started his engine and turned the car towards Boston. Margaret's luggage had to be ferried down from her room, and she couldn't even breathe without three cups of coffee and several cigarettes. She sat in the car while Crawford paid the bill at the front desk.

He had slept well, country air and quiet; and his room seemed like a haven once he entered it and shut Margaret outside. She on the other hand had slept badly; the bed was too soft; the faucet dripped; early morning birds had made a racket. For the first time since they had left Montreal, she felt disinclined to talk, and Crawford was able to pick up bit of news on the car radio.

The drive passed totally with incident; they reached the out-skirts of Boston just as the worst morning traffic was beginning to thin out. However, Margaret expected to be delivered to Newton, almost directly across the city from Charlestown, Crawford's final destination. They drove at random, Margaret fairly certain but not quite positive about her hostess's street. Finally Crawford con-sulted his map of Boston in the glove compartment, and located the avenue.

"Won't you come in for coffee? I'm sure Lois would love to meet you," said Margaret as Crawford lifted her bags once more from the car and placed them neatly on the sidewalk.

"No thanks. I'm late as it is."

"Well, it was lovely. Thanks again. I'll call when I get back to Montreal." She gave him a quick peck on either cheek and turned towards the house.

Crawford spoke. "Margaret?"

"Yes?"

"How do you intend to pay me?"

"Pay you?"

"For your share of the hotel bill and dinner. I don't expect you to pay for gas as I had intended to take the car anyway. But I put the other tab on my credit card."

She stood dumbfounded. "Well, I really didn't ..."

"Didn't think you would have to pay your way? Stopping at the inn was your idea, if you remember."

"If your car hadn't broken down we wouldn't have had to stop."

"I have been just as inconvenienced as you, more so perhaps. And I had wanted to push on last night. You made the choice."

"I'm really rather short of cash."

"Then give me a cheque."

"A cheque?"

"Yes a cheque. You have a chequebook in your handbag. I saw it when you were fishing around for a cigarette." He slid the credit card receipt from his wallet, made a quick calculation, and quoted a figure. Clad in an air of injured dignity, Margaret took the chequebook from her bag. Crawford was ready with a pen. Wordlessly she wrote out a cheque, using the hood of the car as escritoire. Tearing out the slip of paper she handed it to him.

"Thanks," he said, tucking the blue rectangle of paper into his wallet. "Now I really have to go." Without further ceremony he climbed into his car and drove away, leaving Margaret standing on the sidewalk surrounded by luggage. She had not said goodbye; she did not wave.

Some time passed before Crawford saw Margaret again. It was during an intermission at the opera. Crawford had gone with his daughter. Margaret was escorted by two willowy young men, one of whom stood in line at the bar. She caught Crawford's eye and nodded without smiling, but they did not speak.

The Girl Next Door

Don Kerr

IT'S NOT EASY being in this room, not easy at all. The room itself is okay, four walls and a roof, a firm mattress, no aching back though an ache is there. It's not my room. It's Mr. Hilton's room. This time. Nothing wrong with the room, a chair and a table to write letters at, a window with a view of another building and another building over that, and clouds over that and blue sky on top. Very comfortable, with a television and a shower and a thermostat.

The problem is next door, which is a room just like mine only it's inhabited by the imagined lady. Have you one of those? You know what that can mean? The imagined lady in the next bedroom, only she's for real. We've never been this close in a strange city before. Maybe Toronto's not all that strange but it's not home either and at home close don't count. Wives, husbands, friends, children, uncles, cousins, eyes, all over the city. You could be very close, like a hello kiss or dancing together, playing cards, talking, but you were always in a web of people, a web of eyes like in a dream sequence in an old movie, a web of things to do, of deadlines, of expectations, and you don't want to break things if you can help it. If you can help it.

Sex is like one of those insects with the long tongues that snap out and gobble up another insect, only sex is invisible and it doesn't actually swallow you and make you disappear. But it touches you, stirs you, mixes you. It's a very ordinary day, quotidian, as the French would say, trying to make something out of nothing. You've been to the office, talking to clients and staff, of both sexes, some of the women extraordinarily beautiful, yet you're at work and they're a few words and nothing else, sometimes quite amusing words, yours and theirs, but quotidian all the way. Then you get home and your wife says Maureen's invited us over for supper and that tongue's all over you. And if the name can do it think of the person herself.

She gave me a kiss at a party once, a private kiss, a real one, in a back hall, after we'd been drinking. It went right through me. Her lips were so warm, wet, active. I felt her ass as the kiss went on and on and thought, what should I feel next? As an adequate response to that kiss? But we heard someone coming so she said bye everyone and went home. It's still in my head.

My dilemma is whether to keep her in the next room, permanently, close enough so that I could, if I decided to, but just out of sight, out of touch. Never out of mind. You can decide what she wears each day, every flavour, every nuance, every twist and turn. That's a pleasure not to be sneezed at.

Her first husband told me in a bar many years ago how fantastic it had been the first time. He didn't know it could be that great. Know what I mean? Etc., etc. Yeh, sure, right, of course, good, sure, yeh yeh yeh. He was now in hell because they were breaking up. She had someone else, he said. He hated her. He could remember what it was like and now it wasn't there. He was in the next room so to speak and it drove him crazy, out of his mind and into ten years of medical treatment, perpetual hatred because she was, well, you know, Jesus, I never ever, I couldn't believe, she is, god, she is …. Right pal, she is. I'll take your word for it. Now shut your face. At least you had it. And it took him a decade to get over it and the next time he married he married cool, he married an ice cream cone. She was attractive, slender, lovely, appetizing, but she was cool, the kind you dance with and can never get hold of, like dancing with a stick or a ghost or a nightgown. They make all the turns you do but at the far end of your arm. Is she actually there, you wonder? But he was right. He couldn't go through the hell of passion again. He needed a clipped lawn and an automated kitchen. From hot to cool. Out of the frying pan into the refrigerator. You've only one life. Why throw it away on someone else? It's your life not hers. Only if she's so deep you have to cut her out of you, then there's no way out, is there? Can you amputate a heart? He lived with hatred for so long he can't do without it. He doesn't hate her now, and is on tenterhooks with the new cool wife, who can't stand scenes, but the anger is always there, on the edge, ready to spill out. I think that's why he became so dedicated a right-winger. He hates the poor, the lazy, goddam etc. The girl next door can be dangerous, like the smoking ads say, for your health.

I don't want you to get the idea she's perfect in any way, not even in looks. But in my life she is the one in the next room, has been for years, maybe since her first husband talked to me. She's the one in my head. I take her with me on trips. She turns up on streets I've never been on before, on airplanes, buses, when I'm sliding off to sleep and there she is. The world and the mind are filled with beautiful women, but she's the one my fancy's been true to. For years and years. She's not perfect but she is perfectly passionate. That kiss is still in me, knocking around in there. I've been faithful to her in my way. My imagination takes many trips but it always comes home to her. That's fidelity, right?

So now she really is next door, curled in a bed or sitting on a chair, and Toronto is outside, all of it, stretching for miles, and full of nothing but strangers, whole neighborhoods where we wouldn't know a soul. It's a test. I either do or do not say anything. I'm assuming she would say yes. That certainly makes the dilemma a more interesting one. If I say hello and she says so do I, then I step over the invisible line and can't come back again. Without a passport to my name I enter a foreign country and learn to speak a new language. If I say hello the other way and she says hello and that's it, knives and spoons conversation, king and queen of the quotidian, then I cross no invisible line, enter no new country, stay home, remain comfortable, true to my wife. And am plagued with a sense of my own timidity, restraint, cowardice. Plagued for years perhaps. Frank Ashurst in *The Apple Tree*. He chose the cool lady and missed forever the apple tree, the singing and the gold. Passion, story, whatever it was, he missed it. But Maureen is resolutely not Megan, poor passionate young Megan. Megan's mother maybe, and no Treasure House of Atreus untapped, un-visited for years. She's had her own royal succession, of husbands, two more, and lovers, some number or other, and for me one kiss. She's been faithful to me in her way, never upsetting the precise disequilibrium in which we stand towards each other. Or fall. A university friend from long ago, friend of the family, professional woman in no uncertain terms. And at the end of all, of all the years and words, touches and goodbye and hello kisses, I shall be her last male confidant. Here's what my life amounted to and I'm so sad, she says. Here too is my life, I say, the summation of my life. Of course we're sad. The bloody thing is all over and there is nothing now, as the poet says, but the inescapable lousiness of growing old. Shit. But not yet, not yet. There's still today and all of Toronto and it's May, sunshine, and so on and so on.

What's the time? Turn on the hotel TV, community channel keeping you up to date with Canadian content. It is in central Canada 8:30 AM. One hour till the conference starts up its engines again and drones implacably forward. I don't have to go. I could skip out. From a conference entitled Canadian Book and Periodical Publishing and the American Presence. I made a speech yesterday at the first general session on the name of the conference itself. I said why would we use, and thus consolidate, the word American, the name that they've given to themselves. We're all of us Americans, whether we come from Canada, Mexico, Nicaragua, Chile, Argentina. Why should we let our neighbour govern our terminology to its benefit? It can be called the States or the USA, and if we want a shorthand I suggest USam for the country and USer for the people. The conference should therefore be entitled Canadian Book and Periodical Publishing and the USam Presence. Linguistic imperialism as well as economic and cultural imperialism. A few people thought I was terrific. Most people thought I was a real shit. I'd cribbed the speech from a friend back home. Maureen squeezed my hand when I sat down beside her. She's an editor of a woman's mag called Lady Pluck, aimed at the middle management women, of whom she is a prime example, suited and tied on the job, and on her own after. Her own woman. After the session I invited her for a drink, martinis like in days of yore, in a place that was mostly brown and dark. And we talked. We talked of a regional strategy against central Canada.

And then I said, I said, then I said, shall we go to a movie? And we did, talking in the dark, *Letter to Breshnev*. Well, we're a tasty group, well-educated, sympathetic to the plight of the poor, the Kirkby girls. Then I said, I said, supper and a nightcap? Absolutely. So the four of us, yes four of us, Maureen, myself and two women from Waterloo who publish *The New Monthly* or *The Last Echo* or some other bloody little lit mag, tucked into a small cafe that served Ecuadorian food and North American liquor. We were very amusing. The young women were such a good audience that I did talk a lot. As did we all. I kept one eye on the present, the

ephemeral, the joke the youngest one was telling about cannibalism.
And one eye on the eternal, the unchanging, Maureen's sexual
attributes, undimmed by these beautiful skinny young things. Her
every shift, taking a drink, napkinning, spooning, forking, buttering
up, breading. It's a disease, a bloody disease, the sexual appetite,
though I continued to defend Canada with ferocious rhetoric. You
must not allow your private desires to infect your public life. Who
would want to be Antony, all for love or the world well lost? Who'd
want that?

Maureen has eyes as black as the queen of spades, or do you
play hearts? Going for power or playing it safe. I hand on the king
of spades and two small diamonds. Black eyes like blow darts.
Death to the recipient. The lips I won't describe. Why should I
torment myself? Bread roll breasts. Etc. Eye glasses the size of
coasters. Well, not that large, but certainly a feature, a show, that
hides and magnifies the eyes. A body fuller than average in size, for
the years have added substance, and in Canada she's a winter
woman, a survival shelter, a wilderness kit. A voice like a late night
jazz deejay. Still life with Laurendo Almeida. She the lazy tenor
sax before and after, breathing a ballad. A mane of black hair. At
her age. Goodnight, we all said.

Now it's today. We met for breakfast in a professionally cheerful
room, blond wood, tall windows, Mondrian drapes and Mondrian
blouses on the waitresses, fluorescent lights, a fountain playing
behind the plant screen, ferns dipping into your coffee, and a
bright rug that would drive a hangover mad. I put on my dark
glasses for breakfast.

> A bit cheerful in here, I said.
> Have you a hangover? Maureen asked.
> I wanta pretend I'm not in this room.
> Let me try them.

She reached over and took off my dark glasses. The glare made
me squint. She looked like a Mexican gangster's moll. I ordered
Alpen, orange juice, tea. She ordered French toast and coffee.

> Coffee's bad for you.
> O, not ours, said the waitress.
> Maureen and I grinned at each other.
> Can you last another day?

I get so restless.

She made a little shiver with her shoulders to show that.

How could we ever have been students?
You skipped class a lot Maureen.
I know. And I feel like it again. I'd like to be a bad girl and play hookey.

The waitress brought the orange juice.

Can I have my glasses back now please? I'm dying out here Egypt.

She smiled sure, but smiles have in the eye of the beholder a way of adding things onto themselves. She peeled off the glasses and smiled, again.

So what session are you going to skip?
I thought maybe....
Hey can we join ya?

And there they were, two young guys – why is everybody else so goddam young? – a promotions editor from *Toronto Living* – hey, do you know where there's a good restaurant? – ah no, well, lemme think if, uh – so much for *Toronto Living* – and a publisher of children's fiction from Scarborough, which is even more of Toronto.

Sure, said Maureen. Love to have ya, I said. All of which helps to prove you can't trust anybody including yourself.
Listen, you know what's just happened? said *TL*.
What?
Just heard that they, the government, the bloody Conservatives, are at it again.
We heard last night at a party y'know about....
You know how important section C58 of the income tax regulations is?
Yes.
Well, they're gonna repeal it.
That's what those guys said at the party and one of them's an Ontario Arts Council officer.
So, d'ya know what we gotta do?
Yes. Order your breakfast.
Oh. Bacon and eggs for two. Coffees, toast, juice, the lot, the

special, yeh, number four for both of us. Right. Right. Thanks darling. Nice lookin little thing, eh?

A bit slender I thought, said Maureen. But a person nonetheless.

Yeh sure. Anyway, where was I?

Saving Canada for advertising.

Yeh, you understand. Right, it's on the table again at the Can-Am free trade talks. Okay?

I thought that was all settled and safe.

So did we, said kids lit, but it's out there again and we all....

We gotta get together and make a motion in support of retaining section C58. Whataya think?

Should be easy. If you think it'll do any good.

Anyway, we have to get onto the agenda and we have to appeal to book publishers and small mags to help the magazines that rely on adverts, right?

Every magazine in the country that fosters capitalism and the market economy, I said.

Well, I suppose, but it is Canadian.

Benjamin, said Maureen, don't get boring.

Okay. What do you want?

Well, we want your support.

You got it.

Sure, said Maureen, already losing interest. They explained all over again what we already understood. I got caught up in their excitement. Maureen had taken a second cup of coffee and was watching something or other at another table. Maybe a guy who wasn't talking. She wore a cerise blouse, with two buttons undone at top, as is her fashion, and a long wrap-around skirt of so many colours you couldn't count them, and if you can believe it, a bow at the back of her long black hair, like the teenagers were wearing out on Bloor. She had quit listening. I listened. I talked. I watched her. I listened, I talked. I watched her. And invented her, sitting right in front of me and I invented her, a future, our future, while I talked. The mind is capable of more than one thing at a time. What I invented I would be embarrassed to write. I am embarrassed to write. When she rose to leave I smiled at her and hung onto the conversation like a drowning man.

Being with her is like having a hangover and needing a beer. There's all kinds of things going on in the world around you. You're sitting at an outside table waiting for service. All shapes walk by, a bloke in serious blue with a frown that could crack china, a priest in a turtleneck smoking a cigarette, and maybe all the little hands in his lungs are reaching out gratefully for that smoke, desperately, all the filaments, like the miniature mouths that line your throat and stomach waiting for their share of that first beer, rising to meet it more than halfway, or there's a plain woman in a red jacket smiling to herself, a beautiful girl with a handbag on one shoulder, an umbrella on the other and reflective dark glasses in between. Etc., etc. But your real eye is looking inside at your own desperate needs. The beer arrives. Most of the time you are not hung over and are your own master, daydreaming idly or watching others on the street. But when the fit is on you are your own hangover. You are nothing else but. You are what you drink. You are what you desire. God, what a fantastic beer, and all the little voices inside you sing at once.

I spent all day at duty, listening, making notes, doodling, sorting out what I'd say to the publishing house back home, a little press, the West and bills due. Mart Kenny and his Western Gentlemen featuring the lovely vocal stylings of the lovely Norma Locke. The talk went on and on. Maureen disappeared sometime in the early afternoon. Our western group had divided the sessions among the six of us and hers was entitled Indigenous Technology. When I dropped in she'd already done a bunk and there was a slide of a sod house on one screen and a diagram of the world's most coaxial-cabled country on the other. My session was called The Cowboy Crosses the Border, and the spokesperson, as the program called Leslie Morton, told us that we now even dreamed American, or USam, so pervasive were their images. I dream Maureen much of the time, and she's one hundred per cent Canadian content, so I'm patriotic, but she was missing in action all afternoon and for the banquet too. I ate with the Waterloo girls and two USer ladies who were nice as pie, mild-mannered as Clark Kent, sweet as young Piper Laurie. We talked and talked and talked. The USers didn't know who Dizzy Gillispie or Howard Hawks or Raymond Chandler were. I'm Canadian so I know.

The banquet was filled to the brim with wine and no one else at the table drank much so I had a hell of a time, forgot about Maureen, and had a dance with a Melony, a Sam (a girl, slender as a straw and very graceful) and a Cindy. Anything to keep the world in the semblance of motion. Jived, we jived, danced with our hands touching, even if we weren't supposed to. The USers knew how to do it and innocuous Cindy from Illinois was a glory on the dancefloor. She sprang to life and stayed there.

Is it the wine wakes you up, Cindy?

I hate meetings. I just hate them specially when I haveta be somebody, not myself but somebody who's representing something. Now I can relax.

You can dance like this and you don't know who Dizzy Gillespie is?

Yep.

Amazing.

It's another one of your Marxist contradictions.

Touché.

You Canadians are so bilingual.

You wake somebody up and they start making fun of you right off. I nipped leftover wine from other tables at the tail end of the evening, said goodby to them all, as well as I was able. Cindy gave me a kiss.

You're really sweet.

I toddled off to my room. Maureen got off the elevator while I was fumbling with the key.

Hey, let me.

Hey Maureen, where ya been?

Shopping.

Til one o'clock in the morning?

Never you mind. It's open. Can you find your own way to bed?

Sure. Course I can.

Night.

She gave me a kiss, a wet one, a smooch, and was gone. Yeh, well. So was I, gone, too far gone to do anything but collapse into a sleep that took me halfway through next day's sessions. I missed one on Intellectual Reciprocity.

This story does not necessarily have an end. I failed to cross the line. Something failed me. It's too complicated to describe. It may be the way I was brought up. It may be terminal intellectualism with complications. It may be cowardice. It may be fidelity. It may be the trembling blue green of the sky, as the poet says, the uncertain hour. I failed to cross the line at that conference. But we were both elected to the steering committee to plan the next conference, on Canadian Book and Periodical Publishing and the Regional Fact. They wanted to call it "and Regionalism" but I made a speech. Another one. I said Regionalism sounded like an ideology, just one more ism in a world dying of isms, like nationalism, liberalism, socialism, and the dread monetarism, but it was not so cohesive a force as that, yet at the same time much more deeply ingrained in Canadians than any set of precepts. It is our geography; it is an economic relationship of long standing; it is indeed our ways of thinking and even our ways of dreaming, ways of defining who we are on the face of the earth. So we should say Regional Fact. Some Ontarians objected but I said that was true to their central regional sense to do that. They were living out their own deep-seated regional imperative. Regional Fact. I can do that stuff, I like winning. I like putting sentences together. Yet when it comes to Maureen I'm tongue-tied. Maureen squeezed my hand when I sat down. She was no mean speaker herself but that's not the point of the story. She was a mean lady carting all that stuff around for years in my eyes. Long live flesh and all it's heir to wherever it's been. If only.

> You did it again, she said.
> My successful public life.
> And your private life?
> Well.
> Wanta take me to another movie?
> What would you like to see?
> *My Beautiful Launderette*'s on.
> Okay.

Anything to draw out expectation, nineteen years of foreplay, and the ebbing and the flowing, the long dance, the aroma of the almost, the scent of tomorrow, of possibility, chapter two, gaining a place in the story, should there be one. Is there an award, like a long distance dance award, for a long invisible courtship?

There are two possible endings, were this story to end. Should one climb into bed with one's neighbour? Because she is almost unbearably attractive, powerful in her grip on things, rich in all matters of the flesh, its accoutrements and flavours, and the very inventor in these our latter days of the engines of desire. Can anyone do more in our sad world, assuming it to be a post-industrial well-to-do world of course, can anyone do more than increase human desire? Ought we not to climb in bed with our wild, exotic, dangerous neighbour, slip across, as the poet says, the world's longest undefended border? Into a world of advertised splendour. Look at any map and you'll see it has already begun, the great prick of Lake Michigan stuffing USam up its midwest or industrial heartland or whatever. Should we slip next door and inhabit the same bed with our neighbour filled as she is with every lump and declivity going? Should we? Should we not? Have you seen Ansel Adams' photos of the Grand Canyon? Have you seen Cindy dance?

The other ending is the abstemious one. Stay at home but always on edge, trembling. It's an exciting life, no matter which way you look at it. Maureen's coming for supper tomorrow night. Perhaps this time I'll ignore her. Go into the study and work. I'm not hung over all the time. It's one of the steps in the long distance dance. A step in continental negotiations. Face the music and sit this one out.

The Boy from Moogradi and the Woman with the Map to Kolooltopec

Leon Rooke

for Melissa and Ricardo of Melissa's Piano Bar, Santorini, Greece

"Are they crazy?"

"Yes."

"I think my officers would like to shoot these crazy people."

"Of course. But their deaths would reflect badly upon me."

A white woman and two white male companions lay unmoving on the ground, on their bellies, their hands tied behind their heads. They lay in swirling pools of mud and water, rivulets coursing about them and gushing down the mountain side. A handful of soldiers, dressed in rags, dark-skinned and solemn, armed with knives and rifles, stood guard over them, displaying only marginal interest.

"If my officers shoot you as well then your honour would be salvaged."

The speaker had given his name as Raoul; he was questioning a boy of about twelve, who had not yet been asked how he was called.

A heavy, warm rain was falling, with great monotony, as had been the case for the past several weeks.

"Tell the crazy people if they move my officers will shoot them."

"They will not move."

The man poked the woman with his rifle, lifting her hair so that he could see her burnished neck. He stood between her spread legs, his shoulders slumped under the drenching rain. Around them there existed a gnarl of twisty vines and trees, and leafy, swollen vegetation, and mountains rising another ten thousand feet, though they could not see beyond their own weary group because of the rain's steady downpour.

"What is the journey of these crazy people?"

"Their mission is to find Kolooltopec."

"But Kolooltopec does not exist."

"I agree."

"It does not matter whether you agree. I could agree also, but this would not change the matter."

"Yes," the boy said. "Because Kolooltopec still would not exist and you and I would both be as crazy as these gringos."

"Yes."

"Good. Then we are in agreement."

The man stepped from between the woman's legs and stretched his naked arm around the boy's shoulder. They remained that way for some minutes, the three on the ground silent and unmoving, their faces all but buried within the coursing water, and the swarthy officers with their rifles muttering to themselves as they watched the rain and each other and their bedraggled prisoners on the ground.

"How long have you been on this journey with the crazy people?"

"Five days."

"Along the river?"

"Two days along the river. Then we began our ascent of the mountains."

"In the rain?"

"Yes."

"Then you must be from Ooldooroo. Or Moogradi."

"Moogradi. It is the village of my people."

"Does Ooldooroo still exist? We have heard rumours."

"I do not know."

The man fell silent for a moment, as a few of the men nearby spoke nervously of the apparent destruction of Ooldooroo.

"One of my officers came from Moogradi. He spoke well of the river basin and its people."

The boy nodded.

"He is dead three years now, this man from Moogradi."

The boy made a quick, violent sign of the cross, and each of the several officers within hearing did likewise, with murmurs of pain and astonishment that lifted above the rain. One of the prisoners coughed and made to stretch his legs, but quit this when he was nudged by one of the officers' rifles.

"It is a poor place, Moogradi."

"Yes."

"An affliction. Do you agree?"

"Yes"

"Nothing stinks so much as Moogradi."

"Yes."

"The men of Moogradi do nothing all day long, while the women work. Is this true?"

"Yes."

The man laughed.

"But the women are all ugly in Moogradi, especially the young girls. That is what I have heard."

"It is very true," the boy said. "But bless them anyhow."

The man laughed harder and pounded his hand merrily on the boy's shoulder. All the officers were laughing now and passing lewd comments back and forth.

"Whereas, Ooldooroo."

All fell silent.

The three on the ground lay as though stricken and the warm rain continued to fall and the rivulets to course noisily down the mountainside.

"What is your name, boy from Moogradi?"

"Toodoo."

"Is Toodoo a good name?"

"It is my parents' good name."

"But you have ugly sisters."

"Yes."

All laughed again, including the boy, although his face was strained and he looked on the point of exhaustion. He did not believe this man standing beside him, with a hand on his shoulder, was the famous desperado Raoul.

"My dead officer from Moogradi was a Frooloo. Do you know the Frooloo family of Moogradi?"

The boy looked out into the rain. The entire Frooloo family, a long time ago, had disappeared; if the officer asking him so many questions was the famous desperado Raoul, he would know this.

The man took his hand from the boy's shoulder and once again stood between the woman's split legs. He regarded the woman's backside solemnly for a while, before kneeling and doing something with the ropes binding her hands. Rainwater coursed down his face, which was without expression.

"No? Then perhaps my dead officer lied. Perhaps he had never seen Moogradi. Or perhaps the Frooloos of Moogradi are also in journey towards Kolooltopec."

The man smiled. The boy tried to smile back, but he was too tired.

The woman lifted her shoulders somewhat and covered her face with her hands. Then she slumped down again and lay motionless.

A number of the officers slung their rifles and threaded their way carefully through the underbrush and sat down out of the rain, under a rocky precipice. The boy watched them remove some spit of stalk from their pockets and thoughtfully chew upon these.

The man leaned upon his rifle and with his free hand turned the woman's head about so that she was suddenly looking up into his face and the rain. She gave a silent moan; her face was slick with mud and ravaged by a terrible swelling. He lowered his face and said something to her. She keened softly and closed her eyes.

The boy crouched down, hands circling his knees. He was looking with fascination at the three prisoners. The isolated pools of water had now become one large pool of muddy, gushing water, eroding the soil and chewing away at the lip of this small plateau, with the result that the three bodies were ever so slowly sliding down the incline, their boots now all but touching the edge of the cliff. They would soon tumble to their deaths in the great valley below.

The man knelt by the boy, also absorbed in this phenomenon.

"Kolooltopec?" the man said to the boy.

"Yes."

"Kolooltopec, which does not exist?"

"Yes?"

"How is it that a Toodoo boy from Moogradi has come to be in the company of these crazy people in journey towards Kolooltopec?"

"I am their guide."

"Then you are not the best of guides or you would have known not to come by way of this jurisdiction."

"Yes."

"My officers are much disturbed."

"Yes."

"It has occurred to them that you and these gringos may be spies."

The boy regarded the officers in silence. They were at first few in number, now they were numerous, all assembled under the small protection of the rocky overhang, chewing on whatever dried meat or vine they had to chew upon, jabbering softly among themselves.

"Are you spies?"

The boy reached into the puddle at his feet, and pitched a small stone out over the valley.

The woman had risen to her hands and knees. They watched her hold to that position; she seemed unempowered to do more. One of her companions let out a helpless moan as water coursed about him and slid him another few inches out over the cliff.

"A Toodoo does not spy," the boy said.

"No. He only journeys towards what does not exist."

The officers under the small overhang had broken off twigs from a nearby bush, and were now comparing them for length. The longest was perhaps two inches. The shortest could barely be seen.

The man turned on his heels and made a gesture towards them. "How long before our unfortunate prisoners hurtle to their deaths?"

The officers displayed their various sticks. They were jabbering and laughing among themselves. The rain had momentarily slackened; it now drove down again in a renewed burst.

The prisoner nearest the edge gave a strangled cry.

The boy touched the officer's arm.

"They have a map," he said.

"Oh?"

"A map which purports to show where Kolooltopec may be found."

The man considered this statement. He rubbed his eyes and wiped both hands across his face. The boy noticed that the skin on the man's hands was deeply scarred and that none of his fingers were longer than his thumbs. They had been cut away, the boy thought, probably with an axe.

" 'Purports,' " the man said. "I do not know this word. What does it mean, this 'purports,' and how does it come to pass that a boy from Moogradi makes use of the unknown word?"

"School," the boy said. "I was a student."

"Ah. So the famous Moogradi village now has a school?"

"My village once had school. But the teacher vanished and the school was torched."

The man nodded.

"And did your great village have a fine clinic where the sick could come?"

"Yes."

"Which was also torched? So that now your clinic and the school and the schoolteacher, along with the Frooloo family you have never heard of, are lost to the world? Do not exist? Like our fabled Kolooltopec?"

"Yes."

"But your adventurers have a map, you say?"

"Yes."

A couple of the soldiers ventured out from their overhang and dragged the two male prisoners a few feet forward from the cliff edge.

"You have seen their map?"

"Many times. They have studied it unceasingly."

" 'Unceasingly'?"

"Yes."

"Is this map a good map?"

The boy shook his head. "It is a worthless map. It is a map to Kolooltopec."

"I wish to see this map."

"Of course."

They sat in their crouch, side by side, for some while before saying anything further.

"Which of these fine prisoners possesses the valueless document?"

The boy pointed at the woman. She sat folded over, her head drooped on her knees.

She had cropped her hair close to her skull the second day out from the village; the boy had some of this woman's shorn hair still in his pocket.

"Does this prisoner, who possesses the famous map, also possess a name?"

"They call her Emma."

"Emma. I have never known anyone purporting to possess this name."

The boy shrugged.

"Has Emma béen good to the guide from Moogradi?" asked the man. He circled one hand lazily over his groin.

The boy grinned.

"Unceasingly."

The officers under the protection of the overhang laughed merrily. Some few of them now had their shirts off. They would step out into the warm rain for a few minutes, wash themselves, and then step back into their drier environment. Then they would step out into the rain again and for a few brief seconds furiously scrub and flap their ragged shirts. The boy studied these half-naked officers. He could count their ribs. One had a filthy cloth wrapping his chest; the blood flowed red for a second, then went pinkish in the rain, before the red stain showed again. Another of these officers was a boy not much older than himself. He tried catching this one's eyes, although it was clear the young officer had no interest in one of his experience. Several of them were women. The soldiers now numbered a dozen or more, a fresh face frequently arriving, although the boy could not see how this was possible unless they had burrowed a tunnel somewhere through the mountain and its mouth was nearby.

"Where are these crazy people from?" the man asked.

"America."

The man weighed this, watching the woman. He seemed amused.

"I had a young cousin who went to live in the country of America. Perhaps I and these prisoners are related."

The boy smiled halfheartedly. "I hope your cousin in America is well," he said.

"I thank you for your good wishes. But I expect this young cousin is now dead. He returned home, you see."

"It grieves me to hear it."

"I thank you. Yes, he is dead. My village was not so fortunate as your Moogradi with its teacher and clinic and the vanished school."

The boy shut his eyes.

"But I have my officers and it is not wise to dwell upon those sorrowful deaths."

The boy was crying. But he reasoned that no one would notice in the falling rain.

The woman had moved again. She had crawled in the mud to

a spot somewhat removed from her two companions. She lay with her head between two large rocks, her muddy hands covering her head.

The rain had turned cold. The sky was darkening.

It seemed to the boy that there now were as many as twenty officers milling about the tiny encampment.

"These crazy people," asked the man. "Do they have food?"

"Yes."

"Is it good?"

"Yes. Although it is of a kind I have never tasted before. They call it hiking food."

"Hiking food? You are right. I have never heard of hiking food."

The officers were busy under their little overhang. They were on their hands and knees working with knives and sticks and an assortment of other tools. They were enlarging their little pocket in the mountainside.

"Tell me this," the man said to the boy. "In your five days' journey towards Kolooltopec did you come across soldiers wearing the uniform of our republic?"

"Yes. In their camp at the headwaters. But they let us continue when your prisoners showed them their documents, and after prolonged inquiry."

"Because you were on your way to Kolooltopec, which does not exist."

The boy shrugged.

"Which meant that our prisoners were not to be taken seriously?"

"Yes."

"Or perhaps your three friends are peacekeepers from the famous United Nations, and the soldiers of the republic did not wish to offend their benefactors."

"I do not know."

"And because the soldiers of the republic were given money."

"Yes."

"And what was the view of the soldiers of the republic as to the merits of the boy from Moogradi?"

"I do not know."

"My officers have heard there are informers in Moogradi. Some, so it is reported, express sympathy for the cause of the soldiers of the republic, while others align themselves with our movement.

The Frooloo family, for instance. Have you heard these reports?"

"I have heard whispers."

"Did these soldiers of the republic harm you?"

"Not excessively."

"What does this mean, this 'not excessively'?"

"They twisted my arms. They beat me about the head."

"But not excessively."

"No."

"Since I see no visible wounds."

"Yes. No." The boy was confused.

"No cigarettes to your skin. No finger in the electrical socket. No axe to your hand or your head in the vice. No threats to put the torch to the whole of your wonderful Moogradi as you and your family are asleep on your mats."

"No."

"Because you were the guide for these people from the country of America who are now my prisoners and not because you are a spy in the employment of these soldiers of the republic?"

"Yes."

One of the officers strode over and slapped the boy hard in the face. The boy tumbled into the mud, and lay still until the man who said he was Raoul helped him to his feet.

"You will excuse him," he said. "My officers are distrustful of boy guides from Moogradi. He thinks you have been making a count of our members."

The boy looked at the coursing ground. His shoulders were shaking.

"How many would you estimate are among us?"

"I do not know." The boy took a deep sigh and squared his shoulders. He looked into his inquisitor's eyes. "It was out of curiosity only. But your officers seem to come and go."

The man smiled sadly. He lay his hand over the backside of the boy, and said, "Yes. Yes. I agree. They come and they go."

"I am sorry," the boy said.

"Yes, we are all sorry." He held the boy's cheek in the hand with the shorn fingers, and lifted the boy's head into the rain. "Look up there," he said.

The boy squinted his eyes and looked up into the cold rain. The mountains here stretched another ten thousand feet, but the sky was all but black now and the boy could see nothing of that vast height in the blinding rain.

"We are as numerous as the raindrops," the man said. "That is how many." The man allowed him to lower his face, and affectionately tousled the boy's hair. The officers wove in and out. The boy was now convinced they had burrowed some crawl space through the mountain. But it would have taken them many years to accomplish this; perhaps the task was begun even before he was born. The war had been going on a long time.

The man and the boy watched as the two male prisoners rose and staggered over to the rocks and dropped down into a heap near where the woman was lying.

"Why are they so spiritless?" the man asked the boy. "We have not harmed them."

The boy peered at his thin ankles puddled in the muddy, streaming water. "No, you did not harm them. But they did not believe it would be so difficult as this, reaching Kolooltopec."

"Then they are crazy."

"Yes. They are crazy."

The woman seemed to be trying to scramble away from the two men, but her feet kept sliding from beneath her as rainwater sluiced its trails down the mountain. There was no place she could go, in any event.

Some of the officers were still digging into the mountainside. Others were laboriously attempting to get a fire going beneath a teepee of small, smoking sticks erected within a ring of stones.

The boy found he had fallen asleep, because when he opened his eyes the man was shaking him.

"My prisoners whom you are guiding to Kolooltopec, do they have money? How is it they are funding this elusive expedition?"

"I do no know. They are very strange on the subject."

"In what manner?"

"They bargained long hours with my family before my fee could be settled. They feared they might be cheated."

"What was the settlement, may I ask?"

"My family received one thousand moolees. A second thousand is to be paid upon my safe return."

The man's face brightened. "Two thousand? Two thousand moolees is very little. Such a sum, I believe, would amount to no more than ten or so of your friend Emma's American dollars."

"Yes. But since the Koo does not exist then the expedition to it is foolish and thus has no value. So my family did not wish to charge extravagantly for my services."

"Agreed. But there is still the issue of your time and expertise. Do you know the word, 'expertise'?"

"Yes."

"Or there might also be the extra remuneration to your family for the small informational services you are meant to provide the soldiers of the republic."

"No."

The man smiled and playfully ruffled the boy's hair. The boy shivered.

"On the other hand, you are serving your explorers as guide through a terrain totally unknown to yourself. Do you agree?"

"Yes."

"So the sum of two thousand moolees is perhaps fair."

"Yes. Such was my family's determination after long deliberation of the matter, and after much imbibing of the pulqoo."

"Ah, the pulqoo! Did your adventurers admire the pulqoo?"

"They became very merry. They could not stand up. The woman said she would return once she found Kolooltopec, and marry any handsome man in my village who could provide her with an eternal flow of the pulqoo."

"She said this!"

"Many times."

They looked admiringly over at the woman. She was holding a flat wedge of slate over her head, this slate providing shelter of a sort, under which her downcast face was hidden by multiple curtains of rain and a fine mist now steaming up from the earth.

"Yes, many times," the boy said. "But the next day she repented."

He pulled the woman's wet hair out from his pocket and showed it to this man who might or might not be the legendary figure Raoul.

The hair was examined at length although the man would not touch it.

"Did the soldiers of the republic do this to our Emma?"

"No. She clipped the hair herself because of the heat."

"It was not the best hair, to begin with."

"No. It is not the best hair."

Finally he was told to return the woman's hair to his pocket, and the boy quickly complied.

"And our other prisoners, what did they do under influence of the pulqoo?"

"They argued and shouted. They danced and sang."

"As did your own people?"

"Yes."

"And how is it your poor family in the insolvent village of Moogradi chanced to have such a wealth of the wonderful pulqoo?"

"The jugs had been hidden, along with my sisters, when the soldiers of the republic occupied our village. It did not take much pulqoo to arouse the enthusiasm of our distinguished visitors."

"My officers would give much to have this pulqoo in front of them this minute."

The officers who heard this left off their digging and fire building to shout out "Pulqoo, Pulqoo," while thrusting their arms time and time again into the air.

"But alas," the man said. "Alas, the pulqoo is all hidden away in Moogradi, side by side with its young daughters."

"Alas."

The officers had succeeded in getting a fire going. It was a high blaze now, with thick smoke pummeling above the flames and vanishing moments later within the ceaseless rain.

"Excuse me," the man said.

The woman's head was down between her bent knees, her shoulders scrunched. She looked up, startled, when his hands touched her. He said something to her and the boy, incomprehensibly, heard her laugh. The man helped her to her feet and led her over to the fire. One of the many officers milling about there dislodged a large stone and rolled it up by the fire. The man seated her upon the stone and after a moment her face lifted and she held her hands up to the fire. Several officers thrust their little spits of food upon her, but she refused.

The other two prisoners arose and staggered towards the assembly.

The man returned and stood by the boy, who had given up trying to follow the movements of the officers and could no longer even guess at their numbers.

"We will first warm them," the man said. "Perhaps then we will shoot them."

"The Toodoo family thanks you on their behalf."

"On the other hand, if my officers shoot them the Toodoo

family of Moogradi will be denied their next one thousand moolees and our adventurers will never reach Kolooltopec."

"They will not reach it in any case."

The boy's eyes snapped open. For a moment he had imagined he saw doors opening in the mountainside and a stream of officers, endless in number, entering and leaving.

The man knelt beside him.

"These soldiers of the republic, in their garrison at the head-waters, were they many?"

"No more than fifty."

"Well-armed?"

"Yes. With heavy weapons, including artillery. Many trucks, and armoured vehicles without number."

"Yes. More vehicles than they have soldiers to fill them. But such vehicles cannot scale these mountains. Are they well-fed?"

"They have much food, and more cargo arriving by the hour."

"Which cargo they will not distribute among the people for whom it is intended. Is this correct?"

The boy spat into the mud at his feet.

"These goods are stamped in what manner?"

"The usual."

The man was quiet for some time.

The boy heard some little noise from afar and thought he saw a trio of goats at graze beyond the clearing.

He closed his eyes, hugging himself against the rain.

It was a very cold rain now, and he could not stop his limbs from shaking; his buttocks were all but numb in the icy, flowing water, and a wind was whipping the rain against his face. He had his shoulders turned towards the fire and he imagined he could feel some little heat against the skin.

"And what did these heroes of the republic say to you of my officers?"

"They were contemptuous. Raoul's forces were puny, and cowardly, and beneath consideration, they said. His officers were of diminished capacity, without weaponry, the daughters of ro-dents, and were at final rot in the jungle. The insurrection would soon be terminated, they said, and your heads afloat in the river."

"Yes. Yet they are frightened and dare not venture outside their garrisons, except to pillage and burn innocent villages, and rape and maim our sisters. What is the news of the latest atrocity?"

"We saw fresh burning along the river. The villagers at the

headwaters spoke of many corpses. Some say it is the work of your officers. Most believe otherwise."

The man unslung his rifle, yanked back the bolt, and showed the boy the empty chamber. He stroked the wet stock before returning the weapon to his shoulder.

"Lamentable, yes?" he said. "But do not surmise from this deficiency that were are unempowered."

The boy did not speak of that other matter of which he had heard whispered speculation, even within the household of the Toodoo family of Moogradi: of the many villages, up and down river, largely deserted now. Of the great secret exodus of his people to a sanctuary high in these mountains.

"My teacher spoke of Raoul's cause with much reverence."

"He who has vanished."

"Yes."

"And is likely rotting in the jungle."

"Yes. Or his head afloat in the river."

"Perhaps your scholar has found bliss in Kolooltopec."

"That is doubtful."

"I agree. That is all but impossible. But your friends, you say, have with them a map."

"Yes. It is wrapped in skin inside the woman's pocket."

"In Emma's pocket. And what is in the pockets of her companions? Money? Tobacco? Beads? The pulqoo?"

"I do not know. They have a card."

"A card?"

"Yes. A gold card."

"A card made of gold? I do not believe it. For what purpose?"

"I am uncertain. They took their gold card to the bank in Foolderoo and came out with a fistful of our moolees, one thousand of which they presented to my family. I saw this with my own eyes."

"I must see this card of gold."

"Of course."

"And the map."

"Naturally."

"My officers are expert readers of maps."

"Yes."

"And we know the country."

"Precisely."

"You do not think our presence would diminish your own guide's assignment?"

"Quite the contrary."

"A thousand such maps distributed wisely along the river might prove profitable for those hidden away beside your pulqoo."

"Yes. If Kolooltopec exists."

"But it does not exist."

"No. Even so, the woman asleep by the fire has the map."

"Yes. Perhaps we should join her."

"If you are satisfied a boy from Moogradi deserves this honour."

"I cannot attest to the boy's honour. But I will extend to you our welcome."

"I am grateful."

They could see steam rising from the flesh of the three outsiders, and their wet clothes smoking. Some few other fires were alight now and the officers, some thirty or more, huddled around these, on this craggy lip of mountain.

For a moment the rain thinned and the boy thought he saw a thousand faces strung out over the hillside, and fires from a string of other such encampments carved into the mountainside; in these could be seen the stark faces of mothers nursing their babies, and old women tending the fire pots; he could see bony children of his own age and younger at kneel upon the stone shelves, and goats, and pigs, and burrows, and an ancient, bedraggled figure with hollow eyes seated upon a bird cage.

But he blinked and shook his head and when his eyes cleared they had all vanished. There was only loud, coursing water, and great sheets of rain splattering like gunshots all about them.

The boy slumbered by the fire, his body at rest among the three adventurers for whom he was guide. He was thinking of the one thousand moolees paid and of the one thousand more his family in Moogradi would likely never receive, since Kolooltopec was only a figment of the crazy imagination.

He slept. Then it was morning, and blinding sunlight, and the earth already baking, and considerable activity in their encampment.

"Onwards," the officers were shouting. "Onwards to Kolooltopec!"

Up and down the mountainside came the same cry. "Onwards. Onwards to Kolooltopec!"

The Redheaded Woman with the Black Black Heart

Birk Sproxton

A GASH OF white crackles across the top edge of the photo, breaking the white border. Framed by this (broken) border and oblivious to the white gash above their heads, three Mounties grin their glossy smiles. They are young, these three, and they wear flat tin riot helmets. They cradle Lee-Enfield rifles in their fingertips. You can feel their confidence. All three stand between the gleaming rails, their feet spread to shoulder width, chests forward, rifle butts on the gravel. Their smiles make small white slashes against a backdrop of interlacing black and grey. Their smiles, as smiles do, tell a tale. Their smiles tell a tale of glorious pursuit, of stern justice and the heart of a woman.

Since their eyes are open, we know that these three men have shaken off the cobwebs of sleep. They have dressed themselves for action: sucked up the leather belt a notch, polished their brass buttons, cocked helmets at a rakish angle. Hefted revolvers, shrugged them into the holsters. You can smell the leather.

They puff out their chests, three jolly policemen gloating at their own good fortune. The police force has been called in to quell a strike, and they have been singled out to hunt down a lone striker. They are on a woman hunt. They are after Mickey. Their brown serge uniforms glow crimson in the light of their pleasure.

Maebelle "Mickey" Marlowe. She's the one to be arrested, the only one, though she wasn't alone that day. Mickey sang and laughed with the other women. She sang and laughed when the scabs tried to walk up the staircase. She laughed when Mathilda stroked yellow chalk down a scab's back. She laughed when the Big Weird Sister slammed a rotten tomato into a scab's ear and nose, seeds and red pulp and fresh garden smell spilling down her wrists. Mickey laughed when the Middle Weird Sister hoisted her knee directly between the big toes and up (wahh) to the crotch of a writhing scab. The women laughed together when the Small Weird Sister raked sharp fingernails down a scabby back, tore off a shirt and snapped suspenders with a fleshy twang. Their laughter drowned out the sound of popping buttons and shredding under-wear. No, Mickey wasn't alone on the stairs that day. She and the others raised their voices as one: "We'll hang yellow scabbies from a rotten apple tree," they sang. Elbow to breast to backside, they all sang and laughed together: "Did you ever see a scab voting...?"

And now these smiling men have orders to arrest only her. Mickey, the ringleader, the blackhearted villain, fingered by the Law.

The corporal, he's in the centre of this photo, and he has heard stories about Mickey. He has talked with Mickey, he listened to her big speech from the flat car. You've seen that photo, too. Mickey stands on the flat car and leans forward, haranguing or seducing the crowd. She holds her left hand up to her tam, to her dark red hair. We don't see her face, but our corporal knows what she looks like. He knows, too, the slick phrases that try to capture her in words.

"A looker, she is, but red right through. Red as the curls on her head. Red red red, right down to her underwear."

"Her voice could charm the socks off a horse."

"Underwear? She doesn't bother with underwear, that girl. Lets her bum blow in the breeze."

The corporal has his own story to tell. He fingers his moustache as he talks.

"One morning the CO – yes, our man Brown, your commanding officer – he saw her sitting alone in the Bluebird so he walks over to her table, saying hello to everybody in the place, you know the way he is, he walks over thinking he might have coffee with her. He says, 'And you, Miss Mickey, do you need a boyfriend?'"

"Mickey doesn't answer. She takes her time. She stirs milk into

her coffee. Then she stops stirring, and gives him a look.
"'*And you, Sergeant Preston, do you need a dog?*'"

The smiling Mounties set out in the drizzling rain. They bang on
doors. They ask for Mickey.

Some people say she lives on North Avenue: "One of those red
light places." Others say she lives down Sipple Hill. "In the middle
of Sipple Hill, that big white house. She has a tiny basement room,
a closet really. Only space enough for a small bed and two copies of
the Communist Manifesto."

Some people laugh. "You'll never find her. She lives under-
ground, in the mine."

Or they say, "She lives with those Scandihoovians on Ross
Lake Island. Trolls guard the bridge. You'll never get over, unless
you have a big billy goat. Are you a billy goat, or just gruff?"

"She lives with the Tooth Fairy and Peter Pan."

"Mickey? Easy to find her. Listen for her singing."

The next morning, Monday, the corporal faces the mirror and
straightens his tie. Behind him, the other officers lace their boots.
A song flits and tugs at his ear, "Did you ever see a scab voting…?"
He wants to laugh but adjusts his face into a policeman's frown.
The wrinkle makes a dark pencil line between his eyes.

He frowns again when he learns that Mickey was seen on the
street. Yesterday, Sunday, she pranced down Main Street as brazen
as could be, red hair and all. Not only that, she accosted someone,
an upright citizen, who, the story goes, was on his way to church.
According to the upright man, Mickey offered to relieve him of his
shirt, his favourite blue plaid shirt.

"We want it for our collection."

She said.

He alleges.

Tuesday. The search and the rain continue.

The officers knock on Early Wakeham's door.

Over the steady patter of rain on the wooden stoop, a door
creaks open, a typical radio door creak.

Early welcomes his gentlemen callers.

"Yes, and here you are and what do you be wanting with me on
this sweet night, my fine feathered friends?" He can see the

corporal's hat drooping with water, but Early stands in the doorway, blocking it. He shapes a ring of smoke in his mouth. Early narrows his eyes.

"We want to talk to her," the corporal says. "The woman who made the Big Speech." (You can hear the capital letters in his voice.) "That Mickey Woman."

The townspeople say this visit brought out something in Early they hadn't seen before. The townspeople knew Early as the sort of man who would cheat his mother and refuse credit to his sister. Early always looked after Number One, he said, and Number One is spelled with two words: Early Wakeham. They all knew that. But in this case Early showed something different – Early took Mickey's part. He wouldn't let that young woman be pushed around by cops. No sirree.

So Early lets the cops stand in the rain, while he, Early, proposes that they, the Mounties and the bosses, should all take the primrose way to the everlasting bonfire. Early proposes that the Mounties and their bosses should have, for the betterment of their health, flying intercourse with a rolling doughnut. He proposes that they should get back on the train and pull their dinky little chains all the way home to Regina, or to Winnipeg, or to Ottawa. They could row across the effing Atlantic to England where they would find hundreds of lard-assed crooks to hassle. Starting with the King.

And then Early closes the door.

His head back, showing teeth, laughing.

No one laughs when the Mounties reach strike headquarters. Over the click of snooker balls, the corporal starts to ask his questions, the usual litany.

"Is Mickey Marlowe here?"

The Big Weird Sister wiggles her plaid shirt as she banks a red ball to the side pocket.

"Mickey Marlowe is not here."

The red ball rattles off the rail and knocks the pink into the corner.

"Have you seen her?"

The Small Weird Sister (also dressed in plaid) has been keeping score. She plants the pink ball on its spot. The Middle Sister moves forward to shoot. She tugs at the plaid kerchief around her neck, then slams a red into the corner. The cue ball draws back for a straight-in shot on the black. Middle Sister lines up the shot, extending her fingers as a bridge.

"I have not seen her."

The black ball hits both sides of the pocket and scoots down the table, the cue ball glides into the pocket, dead center. Middle mutters *damn*, almost under her breath.

"Do you know where she lives?"

The Small Weird Sister fishes out the cue ball and walks over to the corporal. He has a touch of dried blood on his chin; he nicked himself this morning. (You can't see this blood in the photo, a tiny sliver of crimson slanting across his chin.) Small holds the cue ball in front of the Mountie's face and spins it between her fingers.

"Mickey lives in her blood and her bones, like any woman. And don't you forget it, young man." She slams the cue ball on the table. "Don't you dare forget it."

Her plaid partners tattoo their cues on the floor. Big then Middle, Big then Middle.

Tuesday passes into Wednesday.

In the assay office, Mounties with revolvers on their hips shuffle papers into file folders. They have set up a temporary jail. They twirl stubby little pencils between their fingers. They are waiting for customers, inmates, prisoners, perpetrators, black-hearted villains, dastardly criminals, wicked folk.

Meanwhile the snapshot officers walk. Released from the frozen stillness of the photograph, the officers roll their fingers into fists and knock on doors. They plow through mud and muskeg. Up and down hills and rocks and stairs. Their smiles disappear. The crimson sheen fades from their brown serge. They have no luck at all.

Until Thursday afternoon, when Nick, the corporal with the tiny shaving scar on his chin, knocks on Mickey's door, or finds her nested in a tree, or catches her arm as she walks along the street, or calls her back from Kingdom Come.

"Yoo hooo. Yooo hooooooo. We know who you are. We've come to get you. We'll make you blue."

One time my friend Tom got arrested. He was painting the town red. He staggered out of a beer parlour and tilted his way over to the police cruiser. "I bet you're afraid to arrest me," he said. Tom adjusted the side mirror on the car so he could admire his own cockeyed grin, his green plaid shirt. The cop was not afraid. Tom was released in the morning but not before he tried to coax his fellow guests to join him in a riot, all the time sawing fiercely on the cell bars with his fingernail file.

Mickey played the temptress and dangled herself in front of their noses. "Aha, here I am," she said. "Do I get a rise out of you, Nick? Book any good reds lately? Do you dare arrest me? You are an armed man. Here's my hand, you wanna hold my hand? Did you ever see a scab voting?"

Corporal Nick lists the charges. Assault, and intimidation. Opening thy trap. You can hear the tut-tut in his voice. Unlawful assembly and tumultuously disturbing the peace. He aims the adverb at her, as if she should raise her hands in surrender. Too-mult-choo-us-lee. And we got you red-handed. This is a red-letter day.

For her part, Mickey throws words at him, pointed missiles.
Who are you?
Do you have identification?
Show me your badge, Big Boy.
Who is your commanding officer, Nickaloo?
Do you have paper with you? An itsy-bitsy pencil?
I think you are teasing me, Nickie. You have no evidence for such charges. How do you know I was there?
You're only pretending to be a police officer. You're too young and pretty to be a Mountie.
Your shirt is a dream, Nick-ups dear. (She fingers his collar.) *I want it for my collection.*
You want to climb the smokestack with me?

The Mounties lead Mickey through the picket lines to the big steel gate. She is surrounded by serge coats and rifles. Tin helmets and billy clubs. Someone rattles the massive lock, a chain rings its way through the steel mesh.

"Mickey Mickey Mickey," the crowd calls out.

Three women cloaked in plaid sing into the smoking barrel. "Double rubble trouble," they say between giggles. "We'll bake you a cake, we'll bake a file in the cake. A woman needs iron in her diet. We'll bake a cake. They can't keep a good woman locked up."

Painted on the door in black letters: *Assay Office.* A typewriter clacks away in the reception area. Hunched over their papers, Mounties make notes with stubby little pencils. They scribble, they scribble. At last they have caught a wicked person, a suspect, a perpetrator. A blackhearted villain.

Mickey is quiet. They usher her into an inner office, close the door, and turn the lock. They open the filing cabinet, roll out the red tape. They will test her mettle. They want to shut her up in their files, to write her into a sentence as long as they can make it. Paint the blackhearted villain with their red red tape.

Mickey bangs on the door and asks for coffee. Later, she wants a refill. She bangs a third time and demands to use the lavatory.

She parks there, powdering her nose, she spends her pennies, every red cent, until the men rap rap rap.

"You homesteading in there? Hey, woman, you fall in and drown? Do you need a rope?"

She doesn't answer.

They pace the floor. They squirm and twist their torsos into strange contortions, jig and jig and jig across the room, knees together.

Corporal Nick starts to see red. He lifts the phone, cupped hand clenched between his legs.

JULY 6. Friday. *The Northern Mail* carries a brief report. "Eight men and one woman arrested Thursday were taken today to The Pas for incarceration there over the weekend owing to the lack of jail accommodations." The newspaper identifies the woman as "Miss Nettie Kukarik, alias Peggy Marlowe, alias 'Mickey' Maebelle Marlowe, 23, Austrian, Winnipeg, secretary of the Canadian Labor Defence League." All these persons jammed into a single young body.

The next photo is an action shot. This time there are no smiles aimed at the camera, no chests puffed out. No posing. This time the blobs of grey and black take the shape of men and women, all of them moving. They are walking north along the railroad tracks. You can count the policemen – at least twelve, perhaps thirteen, bustle into the frame. Seven cluster right around a woman, who I take to be Mickey, alias Nettie, alias Peggy, alias Maebelle. Seven men try to keep her from breaking out and assuming other identities. They crowd around and squish her into a single person, a single blob of grey dots, black at the very heart. She wears the same dark coat she wore in the flat car photo. One of those seven Mounties must be her friend, Old Scarface himself, Corporal Nick. The cut on his chin will have healed by now. No doubt he hopes Mickey doesn't break loose.

There are no rifles in this photo, Lee-Enfields or otherwise, but the Mounties carry billy clubs (no *billets-doux* these) to deliver their messages. They have themselves decked out in felt hats, instead of helmets. Mickey has raised her left hand to her black tam; she covers her flaming red hair. If you look closely you find only one person without a hat. Is it a man with long hair, or a woman in pants? A female officer? Perhaps she accompanies the prisoner to the Ladies' room.

The photo deserves a title. Something like "The Mounties Get their Woman," or "Maebelle Escorted by Beaus." I wonder if that's a smile on Mickey's face. Can you see it? That small crackling sliver of white. Is that her smile?

Pancho Villa's Head

Graeme Gibson

"*T*ODO POR AMOR." As the
rancher shook his head, admiringly, highlights flashed in his eyes.
One side of his moustache appeared in meticulous detail, then
retreated into shadow. "*Su Rey*, how is it to say *Rey?*"

"King." Without looking up from her empty glass, the American woman spoke as if not speaking.

"*Si* – King *Eduardo*, she understand the love, yes?" Still watching the woman, the tourist nodded, then turned to stare into the
garden, past stunted palms wrapped in their own dead leaves. The
brandy was harsh in his throat, so he chased it with mineral water,
and heard again small bodies scuttling in the thatch above their
heads. He knew the drink would soon taste smooth, and expensive,
and he would keep at it until he went to bed.

Through the wall of vegetation he saw headlights as a car
laboured up the hill toward them. Obviously an old car, its brown
lights illuminated nothing. He watched them idly as the rancher,
collapsing back into Spanish, marveled at what Edward had for-
saken. The money, *mucho dinero, verdad?* The power. Twelve years
ago he would have understood most of what was being said, but
now only individual words and phrases made any sense. Something
about a kingdom and *su tierra*, then *todos* again. "*Todo por una
mujer, por amor.*" Everything for a woman, for love. An image of
some kind, a memory of the dead ex-king and his forbidden wife,
drifted near the surface. He concentrated on the lights, trying to
predict when they'd vanish, when they'd reappear. Wondering

why there wasn't any music, some guitars maybe, he nodded
soberly, hoping the rancher's aggressive sentiment wouldn't suddenly expect something from him.

There were four of them at the table, in a ragged garden under
the thatched roof of *El Patio Palenque*: the tourist himself, and the
rancher; the American, a well-used woman in her forties; and the
Canadian, a youth with red lips and even teeth. Since the woman
and the boy were both fluent in Spanish, and the rancher spoke
little English, the tourist only stayed in the vague hope something
might happen. It would be a relief if there were music.

Sudden laughter at the next table, where a small family had
come to celebrate: the father, a young man with limpid eyes, was
remonstrating, while his girls, their raven hair filled with blue and
red ribbons, bent their heads to giggle explosively. He smiled,
shifting his chair closer to his wife, who was pushing bread back
into the mouth of an infant. Apparently placing his hand on her
thigh, beneath the table, he poured wine into their glasses.

The rancher's strong voice, repeating itself, had risen expectantly. The tourist looked at him. A short man, fat but powerfully
built, crisply dressed in white with his sombrero tilted at a rakish
angle, he was pivoting slowly in a frozen shrug; his forearms were
raised in front of his body, the palms of his hands upturned, as if
to receive an answer. A battery of fireworks exploded in the village
below and two skyrockets drove between the hills in a shower of
sparks. Raising his glass, the tourist discovered it was empty. He
reached for a cigarette from his package among the bottles, he
reached into the rancher's grasp, and the question was repeated.
He saw delicate needlework on the shirt cuff, and the three ornate
rings; he felt them bite into the small bones at his wrist.

The grip relaxed when the American woman spoke in her
disembodied voice. "He wants to know how many of us would have
done the same." The car, in fact it was a van, crept into the circle
of light by the patio entrance, as the rancher impatiently corrected
her. "He says how many people today, in these times ..." A man
dressed in khaki, a thick man with a handgun on his hip, got out of
the van and, rapping on the door, said something to whoever
remained inside.

"Is he asking me?" And suddenly he remembered what it was.
A series of photographs in *Life* magazine. Famous people leaping
from the ground for an ambitious photographer. Richard Nixon,
before he was president, and Robert Oppenheimer. Marilyn

Monroe, caught in a self-protective hug, her legs tucked beneath her bum, sadly glorious, as if she'd never come down. And the Duke and Duchess of Windsor, their faces already dry and wrinkled, the faces of apple dolls. They had taken off their shoes for the camera. Holding hands, their fingers clenched together, they had leaped side by side in the air; incredibly vulnerable, they'd hung there startled and unsmiling. "Not many of us have the choice," he said. The woman shrugged so he turned to the rancher. It isn't important. "*No es importante.*" They didn't seem to hear him although the fingers left his wrist. He concluded mournfully that he didn't know what was going on any more. He tried to remember what the woman had said: how many people in these times could do it? Was that the question? The rancher appeared to be observing him from the corner of his eyes. Do what? "*No tenemos la posibilidad, la tentación.*" The woman glanced up from where her large hands rested on the table; it was an uncertain, defensive look, as if she feared what he might say next. Then, surprisingly, she smiled. The bruised mouth parted to reveal the tip of her tongue pressing between narrow teeth. He experienced an unexpected tremor of lust. Perhaps he would go with her. Instead of returning to his wife in the cabin, he'd follow her among the foliage by the pavilion, he'd tell her she had extraordinary cheek bones, or something, and she would open herself to him with sharp cries....

When he reached towards her for his glass, the man in khaki appeared behind the bar. Squat and powerful, he was a soldier or policeman, clearly an officer with a flash of gold in his mouth. The young family at the next table had fallen silent. Jiggling the infant nervously, the mother opened her blouse, and gave it her breast. The father, staring fixedly at his half-eaten dinner, lit a cigarette.

"*El Capitán,*" said the American woman without moving her lips. The rancher poised himself, breathing slowly, and then reached for the bottle. His three rings, each one set with coloured stones, glinted over their glasses. "He's chief cop." The tourist drank his brandy and smoked. Nodding his head vigorously, the waiter averted his face as the captain leaned over him, speaking directly into his ear. "And a real clown," she said. "A fascist clown...."

"*Chingao.*" The Canadian swore cheerfully. "Jesus, I hate those bastards. Here, give me a light will you? *Gracias.*" Clenching the filter tip between his teeth, grimacing through the smoke, he tilted his chair against the pillar and said something in Spanish.

The woman protested, but her laughter joined his, nevertheless. The rancher rapped a warning with his fist and, savagely, from the pavilion beyond the trees, guitars blared through a tinny loudspeaker. The needle jumped and screeched, there was an instant of silence, and then it started again.

From behind them a car horn blared without apparent purpose and the woman was becoming agitated: she tossed her head, rolling her eyes in mock horror at the noise. As the tourist stared at her thin, sharp mouth, the column of her throat, she ran her fingers through her hair, briefly uncovering a delicate ear. He imagined taking the lobe of it gently between his teeth.

"Like...who was it? That Idi Amin, for Chrissakes. You know who I mean?" The Canadian was trying to glare at the captain through the drifting smoke of his cigarette. The tourist wondered if the boy was so much of a fool. Was he compelled to perform for them? And for which one, the American? He wished she'd stop laughing. "People like that should be shot. Pow!" said the Canadian, jabbing his index finger at his temple.

Despite himself, the tourist felt laughter, like a sickness, high in his own belly. He crouched forward, hugging his arms across his chest, as the captain sauntered (almost in time with the music) from behind the bar. The waiter snatched a clean glass and, darting past him, pushed an empty chair among the Mexican family. The policeman didn't sit, but leaned over the young mother, as if to admire her baby. "*Buenos noches,*" he said, and then, after a pause – "*Señora.*" The Indian woman bobbed her head without raising her eyes. Her hair, the colour of gun metal, was drawn with white ribbons into a braid. Puffing lightly, without inhaling, her husband held his cigarette between thumb and forefinger, as if he didn't hear the insinuating voice.

The officer placed his hand on the baby's skull, with his fingers around it, as if he were selecting a melon. The tourist understood only *un regalo,* a gift. And *magnifico,* while the waiter, concentrating as if it was an impossible task, poured wine into the clean glass. When the captain turned the tiny head until its face appeared, a moist brown nipple slipped from its mouth. The woman moved to rearrange her blouse, but the policeman brushed her hand aside. "*La cena,*" he laughed explosively. Supper, don't interrupt its supper. The tourist desperately wanted a drink but the American had seized his arm, her nails cutting into the flesh beneath his sleeve.

Bending over the mewling child, the dark breast swelling with milk, the captain stared intently. He pursed his lips and made little sucking noises while bending closer, so the visor of his cap hovered by her shoulder. Mercifully the car remained silent. The record had ended. They could hear dogs barking from the other hill as the policeman straightened, guiding the small face until it retrieved the nipple. "*Come bien,*" he laughed again. Eat well, good supper. "*Todos,*" he said, taking his glass from the waiter and drinking it down. "*Salud, amor y pesitos.*" Health, love and money, thought the tourist, watching the man plump himself beside the young father and reach for the bottle. And time to enjoy them....

"Jesus Christ!" The Canadian propelled his chair forward with a crash. The policeman turned, as if he hadn't realized they were there. Empty as a camera, his dark face regarded them without curiosity or rancour. "Just because he's got a fucken gun...." Intricate panels decorated the grip of his automatic and, half-hidden by the hard roll of his belly, brass studs clustered in his belt. The tourist wondered if he should nod, acknowledge and maybe defuse that empty stare, but instead, he rested his hand lightly on the woman's. A solitary dog barked sporadically but there was no reply, no chorus.

"*Tío Pedro.*" Gold flashed in the captain's mouth as he spoke. "*Qué tal?*" Caught with his glass in the air, the rancher made as if to acknowledge the greeting with a toast, but changed his mind and drank.

"*Tío?*" The Canadian whistled through his teeth. "*Usted?*" The rancher's absurd sombrero nodded affirmation. Studiously he picked up the bottle, whereupon the woman, with a final squeeze, removed her hand from the tourist's arm.

"Apparently our host is the cop's uncle," she said, watching the rancher refill her glass.

"That's incredible." The Canadian grinned wolfishly. "Fantastic, eh? Wow!"

"Please most careful." Twisting his mouth, the rancher proffered the tourist's package of cigarettes. "It is a man very bad this one." He whispered unhappily, once the captain had turned his back. "Most, how do you say?" They leaned, conspiratorially, to hear. "Most ... furious."

Two days earlier, just after they boarded the train, a wiry man, immaculate in the uniform of an important officer, had bustled a plump, wide-eyed girl into the adjoining compartment. Wrestling a final bag in the narrow passage, the tourist saw her before the door closed; rummaging in her purse, she had the air of someone who had forgotten something, but can't recall what. Curled on the jamb, the man's fingers were astonishingly clean, the nails perfect as artificial flowers. Their voices, even the movement of their bodies, came so clearly through the partition that the tourist and his wife, when they finally spoke, whispered guiltily.

"Did you know," she said, looking up from her book after he'd found them some cold beer. "They stole Pancho Villa's head?"

"Who did?"

"They. Them ... you know. Nobody was ever caught."

"Pancho Villa's?" Unrolling beyond the window, day was ending on suburbs of raw concrete, on crumbling squalor, with figures crouching by open fires in the street. And in the next compartment, rising monotonously, the girl's voice went on and on, as if explaining, or apologizing. Intermittently the man made low, soothing noises, sometimes he laughed, but she scarcely paused.

"They dug him up." He noticed that wisps of hair had escaped from her bun, that her face was drawn, almost lurid in the fading light. "This one says they must have planned to sell it."

"Who'd want to buy his head, Pancho Villa's head?"

"Lots of people. Jesus, I wish they'd shut up!" Because now there were sounds of physical effort as one of their neighbours, then the other, clambered giggling into the top berth which, like theirs, ran across the compartment. Quite obviously it was right against the adjoining wall. "Oh my God," she said. She wanted him to call the guard. "Call the guard," she insisted. "Tell him to make them stop!" Crouched by the window, that now only reflected the two of them in their rattling cell, she stared with growing fury and disgust. "The stupid train's almost empty," she said. Then raising her voice, because the girl had begun to squeal, the partition to pulse, alarmingly, in time with their galloping rhythm, "He can give us another room."

"But they'll be finished before I find anyone."

"You never do anything, you know that? You never do anything at all."

"They won't be long now," he persisted, trying not to listen because, oh boy, it seemed the man was growling! "Let's go along to the buffet ..."

They did it once more in the night. Waking from some disturbing dream, he didn't know what it was at first: the interminable

squeaking and thumping, the growls again, and wrestling protes-
tations. If he hadn't feared his wife's accusations – surely she
wasn't still asleep? – he would have gone into the corridor, or out
onto the observation platform at the rear of the train. Instead, he
rested his palm on the thin wall beside his face. She had worn long
gloves and looked like someone else's wife. They might just as well
all have been in the same bed.

Leaning on the dirty rail, drinking Carta Blanca for breakfast,
he saw them descend at a freshly whitewashed station. After the
altitude of Mexico City the air seemed dense and stagnant, the
vegetation artificial, as if it were made from heavy plastic, as if it
were waiting to be shipped back to the lobbies of bank buildings in
Toronto. Before they went around a corner, he noted that she wore
the pink satin skirt; it accentuated her buttocks, and the officer
was still immaculate.

Nearby, in shade along a cracked and peeling wall, half a dozen
soldiers stared at him. Suspicious and defensive, in ill-fitting
uniforms, they cradled automatic weapons; and yet, when the
train shuddered into motion, one waved, then leaned to spit foam
between his regulation boots.

Elevated as he was, the tourist caught glimpses of rooms with
white furniture, of gardens, like other rooms, with masses of red
flowers for ceilings. Inevitably, with his wife reading, and another
town receding behind him, he tried to imagine the ruins to come,
the ravaged temples and ancient ball courts, where men had
played a deadly game. And the friezes that he'd seen in pictures –
warriors stamping on the heads of men whose screaming faces
were identical to their own.

Returning for another beer, pausing at the open door, he
noticed one of her gloves beside the unmade bed. When he picked
it up it smelled, somewhat curiously, of peaches.

What with the drink, and the language, there was much the tourist
didn't catch. The garden, it is true, had filled with fireflies, with
the monotonous noise of tree frogs; high and electric, it both
soothed and alarmed. And watching a long-tailed animal, somewhat bigger than a rat, where it shuffled at the verge of light and
dark, he became convinced that, should it turn to stare at him, its
eyes would contain an unnatural brilliance.

The captain had arrived with his chair. Inserting it between the
American woman and his uncle, he'd launched into an abrasive

tirade featuring the words *guerrilleros* and hippies. Filling his uniform with hard fat, he leaned over her hands, which glistened faintly, as if they'd been massaged with oil. He said the word again. This time he spoke directly at the Canadian who, against all wisdom, maintained his superior smile. "Hippies!" Coughing the glottal H, a small, derisive explosion, he grinned at the woman and, with a flourish that showed his gold tooth, emptied her glass.

In another age, thought the tourist, and in the right novel, he'd have made a compelling pirate, a corsair. There was that brutal grace about him, a kind of weightlessness – like the polar bear, in a TV film, effortlessly hunting seals under water, the captain knew he could do anything he pleased. And he was leading up to something, the tourist had become certain of that. Keeping his eyes on the young family, who were finally stirring at the next table, *El Capitán* was playing a game.

Silenced by his nephew's arrival, and no longer their host, the rancher, his face hidden beneath the brim of his hat, appeared to be sleeping. Crouched in his chair, the tourist smoked and drank while the Canadian, perhaps mistaking fear for adrenalin, treated the policeman as if he was some loutish fraternity brother, or a drunk on the subway. Was it because he spoke the language, and in speaking it, failed to see the danger they were in?

Democracy, for Crissakes. Human Aspirations. Poverty. While no longer interested in words, he leaned to the woman, who whispered eagerly, conveying the gist of what they said. Freedom, Discipline, Hippies, Guerrillas, always *los guerrilleros*. He stared, focusing on the way her mouth moved, her narrow teeth like an animal's. And what about Pancho Villa's head? he thought. That's the question. *La cabeza de Pancho Villa*. What's that worth? He'd have preferred her hand on his arm again. Or his leg, the blunt fingers exploring between his thighs....

After paying his bill the young father rose to his feet. The older girl, a lovely child whose hair was filled with blue ribbons, couldn't keep her eyes off them. And then, with a filter tip between his teeth, like in some goddamn Clint Eastwood movie, the Canadian said, "What if we were guerrillas?" Whereupon the captain, without using his fingers, whistled a shrill blast, then another as uniformed men tumbled from the van with automatic weapons; they closed on the Indian, who started to run but, seeing it was futile …

As the Canadian leaped to his feet, the captain's pistol hit the table, flat on its side, between them, its dark barrel menacing. "Sit down!" One of the children was shrieking a single note, continuously, as if she didn't need to breathe. The soldiers wrestled her father, getting in each other's way, upsetting chairs even though he didn't resist. He tried to stare back to his wife, his children, his mouth was open. And then they bundled him into the van.

With her infant in one arm, the mother took the hysterical child in her other, but nobody else moved. Still standing, the Canadian was pale as a moonflower; the soldiers, waiting by the van in their crumpled uniforms, puffed like grampuses. It was the older girl who screamed.

At a sign from the captain, three men scrambled into the van; the others shuffled into the dark garden and the vehicle shook into life. The brown lights flashed on and it drove away. The Indian woman gathered her children. The one was merely sobbing now. The other, who looked maybe seven or eight, held the baby with its head lolling over her shoulder like a big doll.

The captain had spoken in English. "Sit down," he said again. The Canadian lowered himself dutifully, as if his chair might splinter beneath him. Suddenly coming to life, the rancher ordered a round of drinks with coffee. The tourist caught glimpses of the van's lights where they twisted back down the hill. The small family had gone. The waiter was rearranging his chairs and the tourist felt colour returning to his face. Soon it would be as if nothing had happened.

"Ask him what he will do with the Indian." Discovering his throat was dry he poured a glass of mineral water.

"Let him go." The captain laughed because the woman remained silent. "Is, how you say? Is *precaución, solamente una precaución*." Then, after a silence, he began to speak quickly, without emphasis, and in the lowest possible voice. Bobbing his head by the woman's shoulder, the tourist wanted to understand, what's he saying? He leaned his face closer to hers and seized her arm above the elbow.

"What's he saying?"

"He says...." She didn't want to speak. He had to squeeze harder. "He comes here...." Her breath was sour, smelling of cigarettes. She no longer looked at him. "Your Canadian comes here. His fingernails are dirty, but not from work. His hands are soft like a woman's."

The captain grinned as the boy removed his hands from view –

then he lifted his own, leaving the decorated automatic on the table between them. "He whines," she reported, with difficulty, "he's outraged. He visits the ruins, he fucks the women, or the boys. He takes pictures of them. It's cheap, he says, because we have dollars."

"*Los dólares*," agreed the policeman, rubbing his thumb and fingers rapidly together. "The dollars, *verdad*?" The tourist almost said it wasn't his fault, for Chrissakes. What would he do with a bloody head? Despite his claustrophobia, it is true, he'd followed his wife, descending into the heart of the Temple of Inscriptions. There, the skeletons of six young people had once protected another, whose bones were richly decked with jade – of course the tomb was empty, a ruin. So far as he could tell there weren't even any spirits.

"He is …" The woman was trying to free her arm. "He's a boy scout, but you. He says that you're different. Perhaps you are dangerous." The captain's round, dark face, its eyes languorous now, contemplated the tourist with apparent interest. What could he mean, dangerous? How was he different? But the captain only shrugged. He knew it was absurd, that the game somehow continued, but the tourist sensed the way shadows played upon his face. It was as if his expression no longer concealed the skull beneath its flesh.

Bumping into unfamiliar objects, as he undressed in their darkened room, the tourist discovered he was grinning almost happily. Despite the night's events, the poor bloody Indian and his family, and an apprehension that the captain's men might still burst in and – and what? – despite the stupid cruelty of it all, he was excited.

Climbing into bed, he couldn't wait to tell her. He took her breast in his hand, so his elbow and forearm rested along her belly, and laid his leg over hers. But, rolling from him, she said, and the words were muffled by her pillow: "Sometimes it gets so I can't stand you crawling into the same bed with me."

"Well, that's it then," he said automatically. "That's it, isn't it." Finally, because of the silence, he appealed to her again. "That must be the end, eh?"

"Go to sleep," she said. "You're drunk."

In the Ear of the Beholder

Rudy Wiebe

On TV A WOMAN and a very stout man were explaining why John F. Kennedy, the first president of the United States born in the twentieth century, could not have been murdered in the way the Warren Commission reported he had been. Adam was, as usual, clicking through the channels to avoid boredom and himself and sometimes ads when this sudden show – so amateurish, so miserably home video with its camera fixed on two motionless people behind a table scruffed with papers, talking – stopped him in mid-click. He was already two channels past when those two plain faces twitched him back, a memory of a word, their – what was it? – their completely TV-unnatural normality?

He fumbled buttons a moment before he understood a diagram now filled the screen on that channel: a side view, a line of dots marking the necessary flight of "Magic Bullet." That was its name now, the man's voice-over explained, "Magic Bullet:" the first bullet – not the real killer bullet – from Lee Harvey Oswald's rifle which must have gone in six different directions, first through Kennedy and then through Texas Governor Connelly to end up as it apparently did in Connelly's left thigh. The dotted line showed it caroming about billiard-like, thud thud thud – off what? – political flesh so hardened by high office? And then an overhead view of the necessary trajectory: the bullet passing with inerrant destiny from president to governor and ignoring completely the proximity of presidential lady must also have shifted itself sideways at least 1.7 feet to orchestrate those wounds – seven in all, entrance and exit – bursting from the two men.

Then the screen cut to "Magic Bullet" itself. Close-up, and never shown in the Warren Commission Report. After smashing through Kennedy's neck and into Connelly – chest, ribs, arm, and finally wrist, the bullet had come to rest at last (uneasily it seemed) in the flesh of Connelly's thigh. Job done. Perhaps because of its miraculous changes in direction, it also revealed itself quite un-marked when it was found – the doctors dug nothing out of Connelly – on the Dallas Hospital floor an hour later; perhaps discovered by being stepped on, fallen from no one knew which, if any stretcher.

Quite unmarked, oh marvelous Magic Bullet! Described in the report signed by the chief justice of the Supreme Court of the United States of America Earl Warren himself, and six others: a bullet. The most adored of all American death dealers, always the infallible, instantaneous cure for every problem, especially on TV.

Lovingly as it seemed the male voice lingered over the sup-posed image of a bit of lead, a faint gleam along its right side – such blunt photographic silence – longly bald on blank paper; framed. The voice grew so deep, so profoundly large including as it did the entire century nearly completed and every trace of humanity anywhere on the globe: the greatest, the most (greater even than the World Series and the Superbowl combined?), this unfathom-able mystery of a Made in USA mail order bullet. And suddenly washed over by a long skiff of laughter.

As if he had laughed himself. Adam had dropped the book he was holding, though the TV control seemed still to be in his right hand. He could feel it.

The slender woman talked now. Sitting with calm, number confidence beside the man who had explained the bullet, and listing names, ages, home addresses of witnesses and ever more volunteer witnesses. The absolute TV evidence of numbers running in such heavy lists like accumulating weather: scrolling too fast to read but clearly and most irrefutably there. Five hundred and fifty-two in all, yes ... the numbers vanishing for Adam as he heard them explained: so many hundred and something (how many?) witnesses who had been around that corner of Houston and Elm where the motorcade turned in Dallas on November 22, 1963, and who had declared to someone or other that they wanted to testify to the Warren Commission, only (how many?) had actually been interviewed, most superficially and without notes being taken, and of those a large percentage (how many?) were in 1991 already dead. More than (how many?) percent of these dead had died of un-natural causes: single-car accidents, suicides, fires, lightning or tornadoes, plane crashes, cave-ins, dropped out (of life?) and vanished untraceably and unknown even to their nearest families. It seemed that Lloyds of London had calculated the odds of such vanishment happening in that time to that number of persons gathered fortuitously in one particular place as being in the range of 17 trillion to one, Yes! That was it! 17 trillion – statistical certainty.

Who had laughed? Had he, laughed? A TV audience, deliber-ately unrevealed by any camera?

On the hotel bed, staring along his legs stretched towards the TV in its high shelf, Adam thought: a two-inch shift of camera away from those two ordinary people talking might very well destroy the illusion of what I believe I am at this instant seeing. A shift to me sitting here, my possible cock a possible stick in my hand? As easily as the shift of his mind to the exact moment, the exact place where he had first heard of that shot.

Or those three shots as the commission claimed. Or more than four as various people, never officially believed, insisted. He was talking to a colleague in his basement office of the Illinois college where he then, briefly, taught; the colleague wanted to stage John Gay's *The Beggars' Opera* with his English students and felt that the criminals in the play, highwaymen, thieves and murderers, would not raise an eyebrow with the college board of governors but that the whores and particularly the hilarious bigamy in it would create certain problems, what did he think? – when the freckled student thrust her red head in at the door and gasped, "They have shot my president!" – just like that, "*They* have shot *my* president" – and fled, sobbing.

He must have smiled then, he still thought. Perhaps, stunned and puzzling stupidly whether this might be a new student joke, he may even have laughed. He could never forget his first clear thought: God, you Americans! You'll try to make an Abraham Lincoln out of a TV president even if you have to murder him! His American colleague had been staring at him; perhaps he had laughed – or worse, said that aloud. He must at some time have left, quickly. He knew he had stood with several hundreds in the Students' Association Lounge watching small screen history being fumbled about, summary and detail upon inadequate, inconsequential, self-important detail in inconsequential repetition and the grey voice of Walter Cronkite, whom to see remove his heavy glasses and hear, glancing up at a studio clock off screen, say " ... thirty-eight minutes ago," was to believe. No flight possible for doubt.

And the murderer, with picture and full U.S. Marine biography, announced there too within three hours. Not to miss the evening news from New York? And formally charged at 1:30 in the morning, November 23.

The book lying beside him on the bed now, unnoticed where it fell from his left hand, is A *Gun For Sale*. Adam sees it; he can pick it up again, it has remained at his fingertips. It first appeared in a box of books he pulled out from under the rummage table in the church hall, still spine-coded G 311 but stamped all over in capitals DISCARDED from The George Brown College of Applied Arts and Technology Library. Casa Loma Campus Library grey Date Due Apr 1, 1986. A dog-eared Penguin whose first words emerge out of forgotten distance like an intimate, ghostly voice:

> *Murder didn't mean much to Raven. It was just a new job.*
> *You had to be careful. You had to use your brains. It was*
> *not a question of hatred. He had only seen the Minister*
> *once, an old rather grubby man without friends, who was*
> *said to love humanity.*

The voice, presumably, of Graham Greene. Speaking to him through a re-ordered alphabet? Adam has never personally met Greene who is now very aged and may be, just recently, dead. A voice out of a past he recognizes he remembers, thirty years at least, speaking with a delicate enchantment only language can create out of fear and botched murder and luck, harelips and gas masks, of a chorus line dancer tied, gagged, and thrust up to die grotesquely in a fireplace chimney but she doesn't – a novelist foreseeing the Second World War in 1936! – the dancer apparently not traumatized by hours rammed up into sooty claustrophobia; an accumulating double hunt into the black hole of criminal and business and military and individual amorality. More than thirty years actually – fifty-five were possible if he could have heard English in 1936.

The little man behind the book table wears a name tag on his vest: "Hello my name is Arnold." Too close to mine for comfort,

Adam thinks, and it comes to him like words in his ear: there will be other books for me, here. And discovers his right hand already fondling one: *The Death of Adolf Hitler/Unknown Documents from Soviet Archives*, by Lev Bezymenski. In perfect hard-cover condition, including dust jacket, unmarked and undiscarded and available for one Canadian dollar. Between his fingers it falls open like a trap on two pictures: "Helga Goebbels after autopsy in Berlin-Buch," a black rubber apron and gloves lifting a small head, and on the opposite page, "Burned corpses of Goebbels, his wife, and two of their children." This captioned upside down, so that the charred remains of the adults are at the bottom, the smudged but un-charred children laid out in white nightclothes at the top.

Over his skin then he feels the hubbub of stragglers and book-lovers digging for rummage discoveries in the church hall shift imperceptibly into the silence. Everyone in the room is standing with him, motionless, an exploded book in each hand which has, the instant before, blown the faintest sound with itself into unexistence. And silence breathing, an animal run to ground.

"That's quite a book, eh, for Monday?"

"Wha…?"

From his open mouth it would seem Hello-my-name-is-Arnold has spoken, in a voice as small as any expectable Canadian apology. But precise, too, in the texture of his lumpy sweater – without hearing him, Adam would have understood him even if there had been another sound in the grubby hall with its grey, dappled windows grinning. The small voice clamours at him along the dusty book spines crammed in boxes, in jumbled heaps on the folding tables more accustomed to serving coffee and unsellable doughnuts to people hunching in from sleep somewhere under Toronto cardboard; Adam is standing on a book. He feels its edge slip, crunch aside under his feet, oh oh, he kicks it hopefully away. Anywhere.

"Remembrance Day, I mean, next Monday, that beast," gesturing at his book.

"Oh him, yes, that … don't insult the beasts of the field!" and he feels fine about his quick literary rejoinder but stupidly ashamed as well, closing the book softly on the gruesome pictures as if they might squash while nevertheless unable to put it aside. The little men of rummage sales should shut up and shuffle books and leave you alone, who wants to confess their ashes of words into pictures here? It was enough to walk down the north side of Bloor with November sunlight almost warm off the brick and concrete walls with the careful, heaped trash of transients buried in the corners of cemented parks and not be required to make a sound louder than breathing in a charity hall or pretend there was purpose, pattern in what you were doing in this enormous city when you were avoiding everything by doing nothing at all – where did this mouse Hello-Arnold get the gall to utter a word? He must have made the mistake of catching his eye. Not consciously, hell – and why should eye be connected to mouth, and voice, and having to listen? Could you catch someone's ear? By the mere pass of hearing?

He is at the left corner of the cashier's table – a card table – with his two books in hand, or three, and he lays them down, fumbles as if he were looking for – and discovers himself inside romances. Tender pastel chapters always ending when Eric's or whosoever hard but gentle hand just brushes Isabelle or whoever at some sensitive place oh so gently. He cannot pretend long – shit, who here would bother to watch him? – and he turns to see the belted man who may at some point have been standing beside him hand the Bezymenski book to the cashier. Are there two? He has been spared? – his own is no longer on his small pile sweet jesus gone surely he can resist going back to see if another one – yes! His heart leaps quick as if he had bolted oxygen, there is cosmic design, *all has been taken from me*, and in his hand he finds one more air-brushed woman, one Megan Farrell to be exact, being un-dressed by Ashton Hartford Chadbourne III in *Dreams on Fire* by one Kathleen O'Brien:

> *Last night, with one shattering kiss, with one endless moment of hard hands against soft skin, she had discovered that, like all steely things, she could be as weak as rubber when raised to the right temperature.*

Already, on page 15? How will you ever "she knew he must set the pace" reach page 187 "like the stab of a white-hot poker" unpenetrated? "First, tell me. Is it safe for you?"

Romance #1,267 – in the nineties even pastels must first utter safety. There is no one at the table before the oddly young cashier. And her slim hand is pushing *The Death of Adolf Hitler* aside. The man is gone, did not buy it. Perhaps he accidently picked it up together with his own worn selection and, seeing it when he paid, said, "No, I don't want *that*." The cashier girl – she is very young, so young as to be untemptable? – has pushed it behind various plastic containers of paper money rolled on edge, a huge map of coins spread at her fingertips. That's the way to treat money, he thinks with enormous weariness: stand it indistinguishably on edge in recyclable plastic, dump it in a heap in front of you, all this careful ordering, this dedicated veneration of tolling numbers, this penny-counting of taxes on every goddamn copper – throw it on a pile, pluck out whatever you need whenever, and then scrape it all, paper, coins, plastic, dirt off the table-top from too many dirty books into a sack when finally you're done with it – he puts his few books down, reaches, places Hitler on top.

"This one too."

"Great!" exclaims the girl, so inviolably cheerful. She is no Hello; unlabeled her hands fly. "One dollar for the hardback one for two paperbacks two dollars in all thank you have a nice day!"

And no tax. Trying suddenly to focus her he bobs his head, but his bifocals fuzz in both areas: to see her exactly he would have to lift his glasses and bend to within eighteen inches of her good, round face, perhaps even take her by the shoulders and lift her firmly into place so his eyes – you cannot touch a woman in public, not any more, it will always, and rightly be misunderstood, into a scream perhaps. She is not even looking at him but for one instant, it may have been at the cut between distance and close-up, it seems her focused mouth actually means what he heard. A good day: have it. Good god. He sees the third paperback he has bought, there in his left hand with an indelible clarity: big, folio size, a dark, glowering bald face, by Roderick Stewart *The Mind of Norman Bethune.*

Sitting on the hotel bed with his legs spread and glasses beside him, beside Greene, the afternoon light in blotches careening about the room and the steady TV drone of the stout man continuing until he finds the right spot at his fingertips and the sound fuzzes away too, Adam is amazed. At his thoughtless, probably stupid innocence of walking west along the north side of the street in Saturday November sunlight. Approaching the venerable brick assemblage of Bloor Street United Church, a good church presumably, a church with the goodness to overflow in a memorial service for Margaret Laurence. Goodness. Why doesn't that lurk in dark corners, under dust, behind old brick and cracked concrete, in urine-soaked corners and around peeling trees grown lopsided with the desperation of survival, why not that waiting patiently

through a January funeral to waylay you and knuckle you, over-
whelm you into purity and care and enduring tenderness and
compassion which all humanity prayed for before you are aware of
it and can set yourself against its willful seduction? Ugh, always a
coward, always such a fucked-up weakling, goodness. Hiding, if
anywhere at all, among the venerable dead.

And he has already gulped Hitler to page 51, the undigestible
brutality of DOCUMENT NO. 12:

> *Concerning the forensic examination of a male corpse ...*
> *Splinters of glass in the oral cavity, yellowish glass*
> *splinters ...The remains disfigured by fire were delivered*
> *in a wooden box ... A smell of bitter almonds developed*
> *upon dissection ... Height 165 cm. (5 ft.4.35 in.)...The*
> *corpse is severely charred ... part of the cranium is missing*
> *... Berlin-Buch, 8. V., 1945... In the upper jaw there are*
> *nine teeth connected by a bridge of yellow metal (gold) ...*
> *The heart muscle is tough and looks like boiled meat ...*
> *The lower jaw consists of fifteen teeth, ten of which are*
> *artificial ... In the scrotum, which is singed but preserved,*
> *only the right testicle is found. The left testicle could not*
> *be found in the inguinal canal ...Crushed glass ampule*
> *... A smell of bitter almonds ... The left foot is missing ...*

A male so far right as to have no left foot or testicle? No left
cranium too? That actually made sense ...

There is a knocking at the door. And again, like a memory. His
door? No one knows him, or that he is here – and the rattle of keys
with another, gentle knock makes it obvious, and he calls,

"Yes? Come in?"

Adam hears the door open, steps, the hotel maid. The skin of
her bare arms and her face is not quite so black as the stockings on
her slender legs; her hair, if possible, blacker.

"Oh, excuse me, sir. I'm here to turn down your bed."

She may have said something, who knows. He is looking at her
and after a moment she comes towards him, between the two beds
very close since the room is not that large, and places what he knows
are two rectangles of silver-wrapped chocolate beside the telephone on the table nearest his elbow. Then she turns her back to him,
lifts counterpane and blanket from the bed on which he is not
sitting, folds it back with one smooth motion to the white sheet,
the white pillow; her fingers slender and powerful, their inner skin

so pale, sharpen that edge straight at herself quick as a gesture.

She is bent to her business. Such textures of slender blacks; such tightness. There is a seam of her uniform tucked at her waist and he speaks to that,

"Would you care to make some extra money?"

Her back straightens into an instant of hesitation, then she turns – the beds are so close he could touch her – her right thumb and elegant finger offer between them at the exact point of his shortsighted focus a plastic package. A condom. Contemporary safety available, in any public washroom.

"You will have to include the 7 per cent Good Service Tax."

She could not have said that. No one would. He swings his legs off the edge of the bed and she is standing between his knees, so close his nose brushes the tuck of her uniform below her waist. The uniform, a button, it is buttoned grey up between her breasts to the dark vee at her neck, down to the middle between her long thighs, one straight line which he does not need to move his neck to know is there, five buttons for easy egress, ingress, aggress under her fingers they are opening, top to bottom, he does not need to move his head, he can hear it, and she wears nothing underneath, he can hear that too, only the stockings – pantyhose, black textures changing in the light tighter than glistening skin; her body absolutely there. As it of course always has been, somewhere.

> We carry within us the wonders we seek without us: there
> is all Africa and her prodigies in us.

The goodness of Sir Thomas theological Browne, given to silent powerless words. Adam gestures and she shifts slightly, aside, and with long fingers (the plastic still gripped between the thumb and finger of the right) widens the stockings out at her hips, slides them down over her hips, down her long legs, together with the shoes off her feet, first left then right.

"Is there anything else?"

Her endless skin laid it seems against his very eyes. But he tries to tilt back, to see her face and she is towering so valley and mountain over him that he cannot discern what he knows, what she must be – nor does it matter since she is already doing what he would certainly imagine were he still capable of it: an ineffable movement of her arms lifts both her hands to her breasts, pushes them up so that the nipples beak forward, out between her spread fingers, and it is obvious her breasts are so full and her neck so long that if she bowed her head over him she could curl her tongue around either nipple, whichever she chose, left, right, it is as if she spoke these impossible possibilities into his very eyes, numbered them in his ears.

"Everything else? Too?"

"Slow... slow..."

His senses stagger, perhaps he is tilting, but her hands continue to push at her overwhelming breasts, up, and they are completely distorted now, they are being lifted up from her ribs smoothly grotesque, she is hoisting them up past her face, over her head and she drops them both somewhere behind her without a sound, her hands quick as water everywhere flowing down her torso and stripping off her hips and buttocks, the hollowed lines and folds of her thighs, the full backs of her legs (that obscene little plastic square for safety flickering) and her hands rise to her round belly, her groin, the black centre of her curled mons which ever since she turned to him has always been right there and so he delayed looking because it was most certainly there a tongue-length from his face, and it is gone: she is become, suddenly, the thing itself. And once her dreadful hands reach the stunned beauty of her face who could say she is there at all. This poor, bare, forked, stick.

"Is there anything else I can do for you, sir?"

She stands at the door. It may be Adam shakes his head. When the door closes he recognizes she has left her breasts behind. And the long curved sheen of her legs.

On the TV the woman and the man sit motionless, still talking. Inside the electrical box with them swirl particulations: backs, faces, breasts, hands, bunched buttocks, nipples, knees, hair, thighs – all possible human parts available except cunts and cocks – presumably the TV expects the viewer to contribute what s/he can, a handful of whatever – bodies in whole or in part pumping and gasping and moaning away with relentless endurance hour after hour, the buttons and sticks for search and uncovery under the finger-tips. Coloured mist for the seeing eye, moving; not at all like these patterns of ink dots, these shades and density that shape Blondi's German shepherd corpse, the dog that belonged to the German shepherd – or leader, guide, chief, commander – god perhaps. Beside the six delicate Goebbels children: Hilde, Helmut, Holde, Hedda, Heide, Helga, all "H"s in honour of the one inexpressible "H" himself and no doubt falling into their last slender sleep with a Third Reich murmur of prayer,

> *"Haendchen fallten,*   "Fold your little hands,
> *Koepfchen senken,*   Bow your little heads,
> *Und an Adolf Hitler denken."* And remember Adolf
>   Hitler."

No rhyme nor rhythm (nor reason) in English. All the parts of the children when so carefully dissected: brain, tongue, lungs, kidneys, heart, offering up the smell of bitter almonds. Glass splinters in every mouth.

Bitter almonds. A few solitary corpses, so few among those European mountains of them. These few now seemingly as harmless as slender children. And proving nothing except what everyone already knows: that a human body will burn only roughly and in part, not at all properly unless placed, or stacked if necessary, inside a scientifically designed and fueled oven. Looking is impossibly silent: what is needed to declare this is primordial scream, a vomiting OUT that would rip OUT every feeling gut. Adam's stomach heaves, a pathetic exorcism of bile and revulsion. He is looking at the other bed, folded down to its white sheets. There is no body part there. For this moment. Though he has no hope there will not be again, and quite soon. He will make his contribution.

Pick up, clutch the glowering, almost devilish book-face of Norman Bethune: a GOOD man. Though continually and throughout his life an egotistical bastard – well, not according to Mao, but then he only met him once and never answered a single letter after. Good at least the closer he came to death, apparently better and better as his blood diligently circulated rot away from the gangrene having entered at the tip of his finger. Finger, the official record had it, though it could as easily have been the tip of his cock. If a man were in pain and dying at his farthest extremities long enough, slowly enough, did gathering goodness become a possibility? Mould you eventually into a wholeness? Not a Hitler; he came apart.

Adam cannot remember ever having a possible death pain: he laughs at the very pretentiousness of the thought sitting legs spread on a bed in the enervating comfort of a Toronto hotel where a beautiful tall woman has just turned down his bedding and left him two exquisite chocolates: he feels sick, and alone, but – unfortunately – neither is a pain unto death. Nothing possible at his fingertips in this cliché of a room will make itself or anything anywhere better.

But Bethune was a doctor involved in both the great oh great world killings of his final decade! On opposites turns of the globe he tried to cure wounded soldiers of whose languages he spoke not a word – so they would be healthy enough to kill again? From the Wu T'ai Mountains in China, August 21, 1938, he can write at last,

> *"I don't think I have been so happy in a long time. I am content. Here I have found those comrades whom one recognizes as belonging to the hierarchy of Communism – the Bolshevists. Quiet, steady, wise, patient; with an unshakeable optimism; gentle and cruel; sweet and bitter; unselfish, determined; implacable in their hate; world-embracing in their love.*

Slow, slow, Bethune. You are writing about trained killers; whose hatred and love, gentleness and cruelty conceived dreams to rule the world and all the people in it. Mao at their head. And yet, suddenly for Adam the deftness of Bethune's scalpel is so temporary, his disordering of the alphabet so masterfully enduring:

> *How beautiful the body is; how perfect its parts; with what precision it moves, how obedient; proud; and strong. How terrible when torn. (Burned?) The little flame of life goes out like a candle goes out. Quietly and gently. It makes its protest and extinction, then submits. Four Japanese prisoners. Bring them in. In this community of pain there are no enemies. Cut away that blood-stained uniform. Lay them beside the others. Why they're as alike as brothers!*
>
> *What is the cause of this cruelty, this stupidity? A million workmen come from Japan to kill or mutilate a million Chinese workmen. Will the Japanese worker benefit by the death of the Chinese? No, how can he gain? Then, in God's name, who will gain? Who will profit? How is it possible to persuade the Japanese workman to attack his brother in poverty; his companion in misery?*

The names of God and gain and profit. Even Bethune dying cannot avoid those enduring excuses. As if he already anticipated the coming horrors of Mao in control of the Chinese, his behaviour thirty years later indistinguishable from anything the Japanese ever did to them. Well, distinguishable perhaps because it would be worse, since no stranger, no matter how sadistic, can ever hurt a family – or a race – as deeply as one of its own members.

This is not my country, this is not my land, this is not my race – but of course in spirit we are all brothers, so I can come here and be good enough to die, I can come here and be good enough to watch: what is happening here is not happening to me though of course I understand and sympathize so deeply – Adam sees himself suddenly in Illinois that convulsive autumn 1963 and knows in a flick of sarcasm he is rethinking himself – but from here I am always writing somewhere else, writing home, even though when I am home I cannot endure half the silly bastards who imagine they are my friends simply because they knew me once but cannot imagine who I really am, now. If I am any more than bits and pieces, at any given time, now.

Like these two silent analysts on the TV, mouths moving without any visible emotion, still making sounds, still presumably explaining and explaining why a weak-minded man like Lee Harvey Oswald, who in a short life had been used by everyone he ever met – and by so many organizations, both illegal and official, both in the United States and in the Soviet Union and perhaps even in Cuba and Mexico – how such a feeble man could not possibly have conceived and carried out a complex assassination with such brilliant and untraceable success. The place where he happened to work on the sixth floor of the Texas Book Depository as unlikely as being able to fire, with such unbelievable accuracy at a target moving away from him, three shots from a bolt-action rifle in less than six seconds, the last shot blowing John Kennedy's head apart so that Jacqueline Kennedy's first instinctive reaction, her mouth open in unutterable scream, was to scramble onto the trunk of the Cadillac to try and collect the bloody pieces. As if they could be, somehow, smeared back on the exploded cranium and all will still be well and all will still be very well in waning Camelot. The practical question was: why would those pieces be on the trunk if the killer bullet came from *behind* the car?

The man and the woman are saying this. In ten thousand different ways. Adam does not need to hear them, their motionless bodies behind the desk a cipher of invisible words. The room he inhabits is as still as a 1990 room in the centre of an enormous city can ever be: a faint utterance of traffic, of plumbing, of heating:

the omniscient noise of twentieth century indolence. Nothing is here for tears, nothing to wail; nothing but a tremor of sad wisdom.

There is never an end to TV; there is an end to a book. A singular discreteness. A book can be held, in your hand beginning, middle, end. Adam holds them, thus.

The Death of Adolf Hitler: *"The corpse is that of a girl appearing to be about 13 years old, well nourished, dressed in a light-blue nightgown trimmed with lace. Height: 1 m. 58 cm. (5 ft., 1.6 in.) Chest measurement on the nipple line: 65 cm. (25.4 in.). No signs of violence on the body surface. In the mouth glass splinters."*

The Mind of Norman Bethune: *"'Comrade Bethune's spirit, his utter devotion to others without any thought of self, was shown in his great sense of responsibility in his work and his great warm-heartedness towards all comrades and the people. I am deeply grieved over his death. Now we are all commemorating him, which shows how profoundly his spirit inspires everyone. We must all learn the spirit of absolute selflessness from him.' – Mao Tse-tung. Yenan, December 21, 1939."*

A Gun for Sale: *"'Oh, I'm sorry,' Anne said. 'I've said it before, haven't I? What else can I ... I'd say it if I'd spilt your coffee, and I've got to say it after all these people are killed. All the same,' she said, as Raven covered her with his sack; dead Raven toucher her with his icy hand: 'I failed.' She began to cry without tears; it was as if those ducts were frozen.*

"'Failed?' Mather said. 'You've been the biggest success,' and it seemed to Anne for a few moments that this sense of failure would never die from her brain, that it would cloud a little every happiness; it was something she could never explain: her policeman lover would never understand it. Already as his face lost its gloom, she was failing again."

Adam drops the third book, gets himself stiffly up from the rumpled bed at last and walks past the silent TV with all its trapped pictures hammering for attention. Nevertheless, in it you can still occasionally discover individuals who believe in planning their lives; who believe in responsible actions; who actually believe there are people in control of the world who know what they are doing. Who can somehow believe with their feeble Greek minds in a vaguely Hebrew god.

He is at the inevitable window. All around him the stacked city burns in a kind of, as if seems, unending light.

He thinks, this is safe. Like Anne, he thinks, Oh, I'm home. Twenty-seven stories below him a shadow moves along the base of the building. It seems to Adam he can hear footsteps; there may be a knocking at the door. He stands at the window, waiting to hear the next shadow.

And prays: If only it might be possible to love others so as not to hate one's self. And touches the window with the surfaces of his ear: it is there; it is cool.

Thin Branches of Rainbow

Patrick Lane

"WELL," CHARLIE SAYS, and Gramma, because she hates being driven anywhere by Charlie says, "I think we've gone just about far enough. I think you should stop this car anywhere along here and we'll have the picnic there." She turns around then and says the same thing to Rayanne who is sitting in the back with Maddy and Charmaine, her and Charlie's two girls, who are tired and hot like everyone else. They are also bored. They're twelve and fourteen and they'd rather be anywhere but in this car and going on a picnic, but they know better than to argue about it. When Charlie gets going there's no arguing with him about doing this or doing that. Charlie just sweeps you up, Rayanne has said to them a hundred times. He just sweeps you up.

As the car grinds around a sharp turn on the dirt road throwing gravel into the trees, Maddy says, "There aren't even any cars up here. There's nothing up here."

"Don't you think so too, Rayanne?" Gramma says, ignoring everyone else. "Don't you think it's too hot to go any farther? We've been going now for hours. By the time we get where he's going it'll be time to turn around and go home."

"Oh, Mother," says Rayanne. "It can't be too much farther. Can it, Charlie?"

She knows there's no stopping Charlie and while she wouldn't just tell him to stop anywhere, she wishes he would. She wishes they'd never even started this trip to a picnic place only Charlie knows about and especially with the girls who'd rather be back in town with their friends, flirting in the mall, doing whatever it is they do there. And her mother has always hated picnics. It's because she doesn't like getting her hair blown around and because she hates sitting on the ground even if it is on a blanket because there are any manner of bugs and things that can crawl on you.

She can hear her mother saying it, heard her say it the moment Charlie suggested they do it. She thinks Charlie's idea to go on the picnic is all just to irritate her mother and the girls. It's always that way, Charlie refusing to go to a beach like any normal person and, instead, driving them off into the hills where he says there's a little creek and Saskatoon berries big as plums.

The two girls lean over the front seat and both of them start talking at the same time, saying things like: "Where are we going, Dad? Why don't we stop, Dad? I'm tired, Dad. Mom, make Dad stop so we can get out."

"You girls sit back there and be quiet," Charlie says. "Rayanne, keep those girls quiet. It's getting so noisy in here I can't even think." He makes the car swerve on the narrow dirt road and hears Rayanne take a breath and pull the girls down onto the back seat. "You see," he says. Gramma's hand is holding tight to the door handle, her long thin fingers white and hard on the metal. "You better not hold too hard to that handle, Gramma, or the door'll fly open and you'll be gone. You know your seat belt's broke."

"Oh," says Gramma, "Oh."

"That's better," Charlie says. "Now all of you settle down cause we'll be there soon. There's no good places anywhere without having to drive a ways. And you'll really like this place. It's really great. There are Saskatoons big as plums where we're going. Big as plums."

He swerves the car again pretending to miss a rock on the road and spraying gravel into a bank of dusty grass. He sees Gramma grab hold of the door handle again.

"Watch it," he says. "You'll fly right out and that'll be it. You'll hit those rocks out there and there won't be enough left of you to put in a garbage bag."

Gramma lets go the handle and flutters her hands in her lap.

Rayanne says, "Charlie, now you stop that. You're scaring Mother half to death." She leans forward over Charmaine who is singing a song about some kind of heartbreak and touches her mother on the shoulder. "Now you know Charlie's just teasing," she says.

"I just wish we'd stop," says Gramma, shaking off her daughter's hand. "I hate picnics anyway. All those bugs and things. And my hair blows," she says. "You know how I hate it when my hair blows all over. And I hate these hills. If we were gonna go somewhere, why not where other people go? Or just stay home. We could've done that. Now we're miles from nowhere. I'll bet he doesn't know where he's going. Do you," she says to Charlie. "You don't, do you."

Gramma plucks at the blanket. "And I want to sit in back now. There's no seat belt here. None at all. I could be killed. This's the death seat. Your father always said that."

"Now, Mother," Rayanne says, "you know you can't bear sitting with the girls," hearing the same old whine she's been hearing ever since Charlie started this whole thing and hearing it even before that, all her life the same steady whining complaint. Nothing right, ever. No wonder her father just gave up the ghost that time.

"Charlie," she says, "aren't we just about there yet?"

"It's not far now," says Charlie. "Dammit, Maddy," he yells, and then to Rayanne, "Can't you keep her down. She's pulling at me. If you don't keep her down, Rayanne, I swear this car will just go right over the cliff and into the canyon."

"Oh," Gramma says. "Oh."

"It's a heartache, nothing but a heartache," sings Charmaine and Maddy joins in.

"What'er you saying, you girls?" Charlie asks. He's feeling better now. The old lady's upset, good and mad, but he isn't going to let that wreck the day. "What's that word you're singing, Maddy? Is that heartache or heartbreak? Is that some teenage song or what? Sounds country to me."

Charmaine and Maddy don't answer him, they just keep singing, so Charlie joins in and sings along without knowing the words. What he doesn't know he fakes, the girls know that and it doesn't bother them. Charlie's been doing it since they were little kids. Sometimes he sings heartache but mostly he sings heartbreak. In the middle of the song he stops singing and says to Rayanne, "Do you think they mean break like broken or brake like trying to stop?"

"What do you mean?" Rayanne asks.

"I wish we were there," says Gramma. "This whole thing is just crazy, that's what it is. I hate picnics." She is picking at the blanket beside her, plucking little wool balls off and throwing them nervously onto the floor.

"Is it break or brake?"

"Charlie," says Rayanne, "you stop now."

"I don't know," Maddy says from the back and then she yells, "Quit that," because Charmaine is poking her from behind Rayanne who is leaning forward again over the front seat. Rayanne's saying, "This'd be a good place maybe, don't you think, Charlie?"

"Hell no," says Charlie. "There's no water here or nothing. We're going to a creek I used to know. It's back here a ways is all. There's an old shack there I used to camp in when I was a kid. Used to be good fishing back in here. And Saskatoons. Saskatoons big as plums."

The car shudders up a low grade of washboard, the tires bouncing and skittering sideways on the loose gravel. Rayanne is bounced forward and she grabs her husband's shoulder, trying to brace herself on him. Charlie slips the steering wheel back and forth, holding the car on the road. "Hang on, Rayanne," he says, laughing.

"Oh my," says Gramma, "we'll die out here, I know it," and when no one answers her, she says, "I don't know why I came."

"Whoooeee," says Charlie to that, "can you feel her jump?"

"Charlie," Rayanne says, half-way over the seat. "Charlie!"

Charlie pushes down on the gas pedal and the car lifts forward hard over the crest going thirty-five clicks, the rear wheels churning gravel as Charlie accelerates, the road suddenly falling away into a much steeper hill on the other side.

Rayanne yells, "Look out, Charlie!"

What Charlie says is, "Shit." The word comes out in a bite from between his teeth as he cuts the wheel hard to the left and hits the brakes, the car twisting sideways on the narrow road and skidding with the front fender on Charlie's side aiming at the rock slide, the boulders and dirt coming up on them fast.

"Hang on!" Charlie says, the car skittering like a huge black bug down the road and coming to a stop with a thud as it bounces lightly against the rocks on the passenger side. Dust settles around them in a bright falling shower, fluffing into the open windows and making them cough.

"Jesus Christ," says Charlie, opening his door, getting out and then pulling open the back door. "Rayanne, you all right? Maddy? Charmaine?"

Charmaine appears first, clambering out on her knees so that

Charlie has to catch her. As he lifts her to her feet he sees through the dust Rayanne and Maddy and he reaches in and pulls them out, both of them coughing, Maddy almost choking. He grabs Rayanne and holds her by the shoulders. "You all right?"

"Yes," says Rayanne, her hand in her hair, pushing it back from her eyes.

"Jesus," says Charlie and he starts to laugh. "That was a close one," he says.

"Oh, Charlie," says Rayanne, touching first Maddy and then Charmaine. "You're all right," she says, "you're all right. Now Maddy, don't you start crying. You're okay. We're all okay," she says and wraps her arms around her youngest, patting the thin shoulders and starting to laugh along with Charlie's grin.

Charlie's got his arm around Charmaine and he's telling her not to worry. "C'mon, it's just an accident is all. It's no big deal, Charmaine. Nobody's hurt."

"I guess not," says Charmaine, looking at her mother and sister. Then she says, "Gramma. Where's Gramma?"

"Shit," says Charlie, dropping his arm off his daughter's shoulders and turning back into the car, leaning in the front door and waving his hand against the last of the dust still settling on the seat and the body half in and half out. "Gramma," he says. "You okay?"

He reaches down and takes her arm. She's on the side that hit the rocks and he can see the tumbled yellow wall of gravel, earth and stone past her through the window. "Gramma?" he asks, this time a little worried like he's not sure she's okay after all.

Rayanne tries to push around Charlie. She knows he's as likely to hurt her as help her. "Mom," she cries, "Gramma? Is she okay?" she shouts in Charlie's ear.

"I think so," says Charlie, "I don't know. She's probably just shaken up a bit. Get back outa the way and quit pushing me. There's only enough room in here for one."

"It's my mother, not yours," Rayanne says and hits Charlie a hard one on the back with her fist. "You don't even like her. Now get outa the way." When Charlie doesn't, she hits him again, this time harder, aiming where she thinks his kidney might be. She knows that's his weak spot. He's told her often enough. "Charlie," she says, "get out of there. Lemme in."

"Just a gawdamned minute, Rayanne, Jesus. And quit, for Christ's sake, hitting me. That hurts."

"It's supposed to," says Rayanne. "You think I don't know where your kidneys are?"

"You and that gawdamned course," Charlie says, grunting as he tries to lever Gramma's arm out from under her. "Who ever told you you needed to learn that stuff."

"Is she gonna be okay?" asks Charmaine from behind them both and then Maddy with a nervous cry, "Gramma? Gramma?"

"She's breathing I think," says Charlie. "Now back off a bit Rayanne and I'll pull her out. She's probably just banged up a bit, knocked her wind out or something. I'll get her out," he says, starting to cough. "You open the trunk and get out the cooler. I think a little drink'd probably help her. It'd help me for sure."

When Rayanne doesn't move, he kicks a bit with his left leg, catching her on the knee. "Rayanne, move, I got her, I tell you, I got her."

Rayanne climbs off Charlie's legs, punching him one more time for good measure, and grabs his belt, half-pulling Charlie as he backs out. Gramma comes with him, Charlie's arm under Gramma's arm, hooked there in her armpit. "I got her," he says to Rayanne. "For Christ's sake, I got her. Leggo my belt."

"Charlie Nickel," Rayanne says as she lets go of his belt, "if you've killed my mother I swear I'll do more than that to you."

"Is she dead?" wails Maddy and Charmaine hits her on the arm. "Oh, Maddy," she says, disgusted, "of course she's okay. Dad wouldn't kill Gramma. Would you, Dad? Would you?"

By this time Charlie's got Gramma under both arms and is pulling her out of the car. "Jesus, she's heavy," he says, giving a last pull so that her legs come out, falling off the edge of the seat and hitting the ground with the heels. "I almost dropped her," he says to no one in particular.

"You better not," says Rayanne, coming around Charlie and helping him drag Gramma over to the side of the road, Gramma's heels cutting two narrow furrows in the dust. "She's breathing, I think," says Rayanne. "I'm pretty sure she's breathing."

"I'll get the cooler," says Charlie. "Christ," he says to himself as he pulls open the trunk, "it wasn't much more than a bump was all. You'd think she could handle something like that."

He reaches into the trunk, throws off the coats and towels and blankets and lifts out the blue cooler with the food in it. Behind the cooler, wedged in against the spare tire is the Thermos jug with water in it. Charlie grabs it and heads back over to where Rayanne is, her mother's head in her lap, her left hand with the rings on it above Gramma's face, fanning hard. "She's okay," she says to Maddy, who's standing over them both and crying. "Stop that crying, Maddy. You'll scare Gramma, I swear you will. Charmaine? Get Maddy a drink outa that jug as soon as your Dad gets one for Gramma. Gramma?" she asks. "Wake up," she says and pats her mother's face, Charlie trying to get around her hand so he can pour some cold water into Gramma's mouth which is sagged open a bit on one side.

"Just hold her easy," says Charlie. "I'll pour a bit in her mouth there. That'll revive her."

"Be careful," says Rayanne.

"Oh for God's sake," says Charlie. "Of course I'll be careful. Why wouldn't I be?" He gives Rayanne a good stare to let her know he knows what he's doing. As he does this Gramma lifts her arm and swings it, catching Charlie on the side of the head.

"You sumofabitch," Gramma says and she swings her arm back and catches him on the other side, banging him hard on the cheek with her bony fist.

"Gramma?" asks Rayanne.

"He tried to kill me," says Gramma, kicking out with her leg as Charlie falls back. "I swear he did it on purpose too. I swear he did."

Charlie's sitting flat in the dirt with his legs outspread and his hand on his jaw.

"There was no call to hit me," he says.

"And I ain't heavy," Gramma says.

"You wait, Charlie," says Rayanne. "You'll get more than hit when I get up."

"It was just an accident," says Charlie. "Just a bump was all."

"You gimme some water," says Gramma. "You, not him. He don't even like me," she says to Rayanne. "Lemme up, I want to see if anything's broken. Lemme up, I say."

"You stay down a bit," says Rayanne in her soothing voice, trying to quiet Gramma. "Charmaine, pour Gramma a cup of water. The cup's over there where Charlie threw it."

"Threw it," says Charlie. "It was her. She knocked it clear out of my hand."

Rayanne says, "Charmaine?"

"Christ," Charlie says. "You can't win for trying." He gets up and brushes himself off. "I'm going to look at the car."

Rayanne says nothing to that and Charlie says, "I'm the one got her out, remember?"

"You're the one tried to kill us all," says Rayanne, "that's who you are. Got her out, huh? Almost killed her more likely."

Charlie goes over to the car and climbs around to the passenger side to see what damage there is. As he does, Charmaine passes Gramma a cup of water and Gramma sips at it, her head still resting in the crook of her daughter's arm. "I coulda died," she says after a drink.

"Now, now," says Rayanne. "Charlie wouldn't try to kill you, you know that."

"Huh," says Gramma.

"You were catnapping, weren't you," Rayanne says in a whisper and winks down at her.

"What if I was," says Gramma. "He deserved it, thinking it was him killed his own mother-in-law."

"What am I going to do with you two?"

"Nothing to do," says Gramma. She looks at Rayanne hard. "And I ain't heavy, no matter what he says."

"There was nothing to her," says Charlie. "Just moving a few of those big rocks from the edge was all. More'n enough room to get by."

"I'm not talking about it," says Rayanne. "If we go back and there's another slide or something and we can't get through or anything, then it's you's going to walk a hundred miles back to town." As she says this she's spreading a blanket under the shade of a poplar tree by the creek. "Charmaine? Maddy. You get over to the car and bring the rest of the stuff. And as for you, Charlie Nickel, don't you even mention what happened anymore. We're lucky to be alive, isn't that right, Gramma?"

Gramma is sitting on a boulder waiting for the blanket to get laid. "I hurt all over my side. I just know I'll be stiff and sore for a week." She gets up and steps over onto the blanket, bends down and straightens a few wrinkles, then sits. "I'm lucky to be alive is what." She ties a babushka around her thin grey hair, knotting it hard at the back. "And you know my hair will be a mess by the time we get home."

"Now Gramma," says Rayanne. "We're alive and that's the main thing." She stands up from the pile of towels and extra blankets and puts her hands on her hips. "This is a nice place after all," she says. "Real nice."

"I told you," says Charlie. He's back from a pine grove with an armful of dry branches. "Lots of this," he says. He looks around. "It hasn't changed one bit," he says. "You could swear it was twenty years ago and I was fourteen again, hiking up here with my brothers."

"Huh," says Gramma.

Rayanne puts her hand up beside her mouth and calls to the girls. "Charmaine? You and Maddy don't go too far, you hear. This's wild country up here. It ain't town. There's bears and everything."

"Yes, Mother," Charmaine calls back and then to Maddy who's walking beside her, "Bears, oh, really. There's no bears around here. There's nothing around here." Maddy says, "That's for sure. I wish we were back in town. I wish we were at the mall. There's nothing to do up here except listen to them or look at scenery."

By this time Charlie's gathered some rocks and put them in a circle and he's arranging sticks for a fire. While he's doing this he's talking to Gramma. "Now, Gramma, I know you were scared. We all were. But look at the fun side of it. It was an adventure, right? And you're okay."

"I'm still not talking to you," she says.

"You got quite a punch for an old lady," Charlie says.

"Huh."

Charlie laughs then. "Damn near knocked me out."

When Gramma doesn't answer, Charlie reaches out and pokes her in the short ribs. "C'mon," he says.

"Don't you do that," says Gramma.

"Well," Charlie says, and he starts tickling her harder, Gramma starting to laugh in spite of herself. "Stop that," she says. "That's the place I hurt," but she starts giggling anyway.

"See," says Charlie. "See."

"Never you mind," says Gramma, puffing a bit and trying to ward Charlie off. "I'm still not forgiving you for trying to murder me. And," she adds, "I ain't heavy. You ain't half the man you pretend to be. You couldn't lift a feather without it feeling like it was a hammer."

"Now it's murder?" says Charlie, making a feint at Gramma's side.

"Now, don't," says Gramma.

"Huh," says Charlie. "Huh," and then he grins his grin and

Gramma laughs a little, grudging it but still laughing.

"You two made up?"

"Rayanne, your Gramma and me can't stay mad at each other long, isn't that right?"

"Huh," says Gramma.

"Lookit the car," says Rayanne. "That side's sure crumpled up."

"It's not so it can't drive," says Charlie. "I pulled the fender out off the tire and that was her. She'll get us home okay. A little body work and she'll be good as new."

"I just don't know," says Rayanne, taking the bottle of beer Charlie hands her.

"Don't know what?"

"I don't know."

Gramma cuts in with, "Well I do. Charlie, you're a born crazy, you are. You know that?"

"Hey," says Charlie. "I wouldn't want to compare too hard between you and me. Anyway, where I am there's always excitement. You want a beer, Gramma. It's Old Style."

"Well, maybe one," she says. "You know my bladder," she says.

"Never met it," Charlie says deadpan and he and Gramma start to laugh.

While they're laughing and kidding each other, Rayanne looks off down the creek to where the girls went walking. It's open country and she can see a long way except for the occasional grove of alders and poplars, solitary pines and the occasional rise of rough ground, yellow boulders sprawled in the bunched grass. The sun is reaching noon and it's hot, but there's a coolness coming off the creek. She gets up, leaving Charlie with the making of his fire, her mother lying down now, resting at last, her half-full bottle of beer poked into the sandy dirt by the blanket.

At the creek side Rayanne kneels in the grass and sand and lifts cold water to her face and neck. She knows what happened back up the road was crazy, but everyone's all right. It's just Charlie and his ways and there's nothing she can do about that. She's tried often enough, more back when they were first married in Kamloops fifteen years ago, but it never worked. I've got me a crazy man for a husband and the girls got a crazy man for a father, she says to herself. And then there's Gramma who's crazier than all of us put together.

She lifts another palmful of water to her cheek and lets it

dribble down her front, the coolness sliding under her blouse and across the top of her breasts. Looking up the creek she watches where the creek curves out from around a broken outcrop of yellowed stone. Past the stone she can see the cabin Charlie pointed out when they got there. It was almost tumbled down, the porch tilting toward the creek, the shingles and shakes mostly gone from the roof. She wondered who might've built it, wondered if maybe some woman lived there with kids and all, some man like Charlie building it for her up here in the hills where they were going to make their lives.

"What you thinking?" asks Charlie, squatting down beside her and putting his hand lightly on her neck under her short hair.

"Nothing," says Rayanne. "Just thinking about that cabin. Wondering if maybe there was a family lived there once. You know."

"It was deserted back when I first came up here, though it was in better shape back then than now," Charlie says. "Don't know who lived there. I always thought it was some kind of lonely old man. Some guy who wanted to live far away from everybody."

"Funny, I kinda thought a woman might've lived there. Still, this's a pretty place," Rayanne says, putting up her hand to touch Charlie's. "It was a good idea after all. You know, coming here."

"Sorry I almost killed Gramma," Charlie says.

She knows he's mostly joking.

"She was just fooling you anyway," she says. "She was mad and wanted to scare you into thinking she was dead."

"Gramma's as crazy as the rest of us."

"Not as much as you."

"That's probably true." Then he says, "Hey, I think I'll go round up the girls. You get the hot dogs and stuff out. We'll be back in a little bit. They're not gone far, not around here. Just fooling around down the creek. There's deep pools down there clear as light with trout in them, or at least there used to be. The girls are probably there poking sticks at the fish, wishing they'd jump out all by themselves and get caught."

"Okay," she says, and she puts up her arm and pulls Charlie's face down to hers and kisses him hard. "I love you, Charlie Nickel. You know that?"

"I believe it," says Charlie, and he drops his hand to her bare shoulder.

"Now you go on before that gives you any ideas. Just cause

Gramma's sleeping and the kids are gone. This's still a family picnic, you know."

"I remember some picnics," Charlie says. "So do you."

"Get out of here," says Rayanne.

She watches him walk through the short grass by the creekside, his long legs and high straight back, and for a moment imagines him naked, his wide shoulders and his arms. He'll pick up a stick, she thinks, and as she thinks it, he does, like a deer snatching grass or a child finding whatever rock there is to hold or throw. Now he'll wave it around like he always does on these crazy picnics when he's gone on his own, so much a boy he must be a man, risking as he does for what there is of joy in every day.

She remembers him saying once he lived with her day to day and that was all. She remembers herself crying out something like, "But I thought we lived forever."

Something like that.

"Each day," is what Charlie'd said to her. "It's not like there's ever a tomorrow. There's this day and my loving you so hard sometimes I break right up inside, I ache so bad. If I had to think of tomorrow, I'd die, I surely would."

As he passes out of sight behind the first poplar grove she thinks him coming upon the girls, Maddy probably hung out on a branch over a deep pool and staring down into the dark, and Charmaine, already coming on to her womanhood, her periods started that spring, quieter, sitting on a boulder by the shallows and watching her sister still mostly child and remembering nothing of her own childhood, having gone past it in March.

He'll come up on them quiet, is what Rayanne thinks, and not to scare them, but to simply watch his daughters for a moment, that wonder in him at what he has made out of me.

She turns to the creek and lets her hands and wrists rest under the water, the coolness taking her blood. She glances once at Gramma, the old woman's snoring familiar, almost peaceful out in the open land.

This is a good place, Rayanne thinks, was and is, moving her hands in the water slowly, the current sliding around her skin. Tiny fingerlings nibble at her fingertips, thin branches of rainbow already growing on their silver sides. She stares up the creek at the cabin and, shaking her hands, the water drops flittering in a fine spray, she stands and moves up the creek's bank, the long brushes of grass bouncing gently against her thighs, spraying them with pollen.

This could've been my home a hundred years ago, Rayanne thinks. Even a thousand years ago. I could've lived here with some man like Charlie. A good man. It's got that look. It feels like it must've been a happy place.

She gazes across the creek at the cabin in the small meadow, tiny blue butterflies jigging in the sun, hectic and harried like butterflies always seem to be, going nowhere in their crazy flights. The creek is wide here with gravel shallows and a single deep pool caught in a curve with a low bank covered in what looks like buttercups. A path is there, still worn into the ground.

It's where she must've come for water, Rayanne thinks. Every morning, maybe, or at night just as the sun was going down. Yes, she thinks, it would have been at night so there'd be water for morning coffee, porridge and things like that, and she imagines a slender woman with a bucket walking up the path toward the cabin, the setting sun a flame in the far sky.

What man there is will be coming soon, she thinks. Out of the hills with maybe a deer he's killed or a brace of grouse like my father used to bring home. Willow grouse and blue. They always looked so, if you touched them, they'd break; so soft, all clamped within their feathers that to touch them was to think of air and sky and willow breaks with the world a fluster of startled wings. The drumming in spring, she remembers that, the male cupping his wings around the air and the female, quiet, seeming not to watch, but always knowing he's there. Look at me, he says, look at me, and her pretending not to look like females do the whole world over, that male strutting which is only need, that nothing which is men in their wanting, and she feels Charlie for a moment inside her, that filling of her, that going deep.

Sitting down on the grass, Rayanne takes off her running shoes and socks, rolls up her jeans and wades into the creek, riffles of water circling around her ankles like delicate chains. She steps lightly around the few large boulders, all water-smooth and bubbling, and keeping below the deep pool, wades to the other bank, pulling herself up by the thick twined eelgrass. She turns for a moment and looks back at where she was. The other side of the creek looks different now, she thinks. It's like whoever was there is gone.

She glances down the creek but she can't see where the blanket is spread, can't see her mother or Charlie. He must be still looking for the girls ... the thought of him slipping past her even as it comes.

Shoes and socks hanging from her hand, she walks the bank to where the path had been such a long time ago and, stepping on it, stands very still for a minute, the soles of her feet feeling their way into the ground almost as if there were footprints made for her there, the woman that was and is.

She turns then, and moves toward the cabin as if she's been doing it all her life.

If my hands had a bucket, Rayanne thinks, I'd be carrying it right now. I'd be swinging it, thinking of the man who lives here with me. It'd be light with love, she thinks. Maybe I'd be almost pregnant for the first time, and Rayanne touches her belly lightly with her fingertips. It's like there's a life in there now, a tiny thing smaller than a rainbow minnow, some child growing there, sleeping in the deep sweet waters. Like Charmaine, but it's not Charmaine and it's not Maddy. It's nobody or somebody, just there, in me, she thinks, like it was from nowhere.

She swings her hand but no water spills.

As she climbs to the worn porch and crosses over into the cool room, the door swings closed behind her on its one good hinge and she stands in the darkness, alone, a thousand filaments of light streaming through nail-holes and cracks in an intricate web. There are old blankets nailed to the windows stopping everything but what she sees. She walks into the web, not looking at the stove, the bed, the table with its one broken chair, and turns around in the many lights. Her hand rises to her chest and rests there on the top button, within her a chain of children binding her together, and then her hand falls away, sliding down the warm cotton, thin licks of light touching her, flickering over her arms and shoulders like tiny bird mouths.

Somewhere in her she thinks of a movie she saw once where there was a dancehall with a shining globe of mirrored light sending shafts of brightness among the dancers, and then Rayanne starts to move around the room, her feet finding their way on the dusty floor, her body moving slowly to some kind of music she can hear inside her.

I am what is beautiful, she thinks, and knows it's a beauty she's never thought of before because she's never been beautiful, ever. But this is, she says to herself, still moving. This is what beauty is, and her arms raise and her hands move among the lights and the dust as she turns there in a dance.

"Maddy, now don't you wake Gramma, you hear?" says Charlie, grabbing at her as she starts to run toward the blanket. "You too, Charmaine. The two of you just get quiet. Your Gramma almost died, or at least she thinks she did. She needs her sleep now," he says, looking down at Gramma who's staring through closed eyes straight into the great boughs of the poplar above her, the leaves showering her in cool shadows, and snoring like there's no tomorrow.

"Stop it," says Maddy, starting to giggle.

"It wasn't me," says Charmaine, almost hissing it. "It's you trying to make me giggle so I'll get in trouble."

"I swear, you wake your Gramma up and you'll spend the rest of the day in the back seat of the car," says Charlie, but he's starting to giggle too. "Now, you two quit it or else."

"Where's Mom?"

Charlie looks around a second or two. "Well, I don't know, right off. The point is, you two get some comic books outa the car and settle down for a minute. I'll find your mother. Once she's back we'll eat. Dogs with everything, and I mean everything on them. Chips and all. Home-made green-tomato relish, onions, mustard, everything. Okay?" He looks at them a moment. "And you stay here with Gramma. Don't go wandering off."

And Maddy and Charmaine head to the car as Charlie looks down one time at Gramma just to be sure she's really still alive.

I wouldn't kill you for the world, he says to himself, liking her beyond her complaints, her loneliness, her age. It's called being old is what it is. And tougher than hell, he adds, thinking of her whapping him in the jaw. At the same time, bouncing around in a car when you're seventy-odd, is hard. Hell, he thinks to himself, I hope I'm as tough in thirty years.

Gramma stirs in her sleep and he wonders for a moment what she might be dreaming, thinking that seventy years plus of living must give her a lot to choose from, but looking at her snoring there he knows there's no telling. Nobody knows another person's dreams, he thinks, only maybe your own and then not always.

I know where she is, thinks Charlie. It's where I'd of gone.

He walks the bank of the creek, high scudding clouds slipping across the sun, their shadows moving in swift waves across the high hills beyond the cabin. The coolness slips over his skin for a moment or two and then it's gone, the sun hotter when it returns, a quick burning to it as it flicks his skin. He pulls his shirt over his head and throws it over a branch of a Saskatoon bush, his hand stripping blue berries as it comes away. He puts a handful in his mouth and takes another for Rayanne. She never saw this bush, he thinks. If she had she'd still be here.

At the creek he stops at the same spot Rayanne did and does the same as she, taking off his shoes and socks and rolling up his pants. He lays his shoes and socks on the sand and steps into the deep footprints she left and then out of them into the sudden sharp chill of the water. He doesn't look at the cabin. He knows she's in there in the cool and dark.

For a moment he remembers sleeping in there when he was still a boy, the old spring bed and the woodstove, and wonders if those things are still there, but where would they have gone? Nobody would take them. An old rusted bed and stove, a rickety table, stuff like that. It was a prospector's cabin, he thought, or a trapper's. Somebody like that. Somebody alone.

Climbing up the bank, he slips for a moment, his feet sliding on the wet clay back down into the water, but then he gets a purchase on a jut of rock and heaves himself up into the grass, still holding the berries, their small blue fragile in his hand. His pants are wet above the knees but he doesn't care. He gets up and walks through the grass toward the cabin.

Looking at it you'd think no one was inside, but someone is. Rayanne's there.

He stops on the porch, feeling the warm grey wood through the soles of his feet. The door's closed and he reaches out, taking the handle in his hand and swinging it wide.

"Hey, Rayanne, honey," he says. "I'm home," and stops and looks at what he sees in the many lights, the door pulling shut behind him, his hand coming away and going to her, feeling ahead of him like a blind man must feel in a place he knows, his hand reaching out to touch what is there, in the cup of his palm blue berries big as plums.

Gramma opens her eyes into the moving shadows of the tree far above and for a moment she doesn't know where she is. It's a panicky feeling and she lifts her hand to her mouth, making sure her teeth are still there and haven't fallen out while she was sleeping. She's still half in her dream where she's been arguing with her husband about flowers and how he always thought they were a waste of time, especially the ones she planted in among the vegetables, an argument she's had with him before and while she thinks she won the argument one more time, she's not sure. Her eyes find themselves in the wind and the leaves and she mutters, "What are you doing coming back all the time?"

"What's that, Gramma?" asks Charmaine.

"What's what?" she asks, rolling over on her side and pushing herself up so she's sitting. Her hands go to her babushka and she pushes a stray wisp of hair up under it.

"Who's back?"

"Nobody. Me, I guess," Gramma says. "I don't know. I was dreaming was all. How long was I sleeping?"

"Forever," says Maddy. She pokes the dirt with a stick, flicking sand over at Charmaine. "I'm going up there," she says, "if they don't come soon. I'm hungry."

"Up where?"

"Where they went. Up there at that cabin," she says, pointing up the creek. "They've been there for a long time."

Gramma looks up the hill at the cabin in the distance. For a moment it reminds of her of a place she used to live when she was first married, a cabin much like it up on the North Thompson after the war. She stares up the hill. They'd been happy there. It was before the kids started to come, the bunch of them with Rayanne at the end, the last one, an accident like all the rest. It was a long time ago, before the arguing, before so many things.

"Well, I'm going," Maddy says. "This isn't much of a picnic with them going away and leaving us here," and she gets up, throwing her stick at the creek.

Gramma pokes at her hair. "Maddy," she says, her voice sharp, stopping Maddy two feet from the blanket. "You just stay. What you're going to do is go over there where your Dad was collecting branches and get some more. We'll get this fire going for them. Charmaine, you take that knife there and cut some alder sticks for the dogs."

"But Dad always does that."

"Well then, we'll surprise him, won't we?"

"But it isn't fair," says Maddy.

"Shush," says Gramma. "Go do as I tell you. Sometimes your

Mom and Dad need some time to themselves."

Charmaine looks up then, the knife in her hand, in her eyes a little fish-look there and gone as fast as it comes.

"Go do," says Gramma. "You, Maddy. Charmaine?"

"Yes," says Charmaine, putting her hand on her sister's arm in a way that makes Maddy stop and look at her, unsure of what such a touch might mean.

"This has been a day," says Charlie.

Gramma is sitting in the back now with the girls, Rayanne in front with Charlie. Gramma is sleeping, her head back on the seat, snoring, and Maddy is reading a comic book, her shoulder tucked under her grandmother's arm. She is following the endless story of Archie and Veronica, in her mind wanting to be Veronica and not Betty who never wins anything, least of all Archie. Maddy thinks of her own blonde hair and is sure somehow her life will probably be the same.

"I think we must've worn her completely out," says Charlie.

"She's not so young anymore," Rayanne says.

Charmaine is singing to herself, a whispering song. Charlie has told them to be extra-quiet and they mostly are. Charmaine doesn't look anywhere in particular, the hills sliding away from her, the car moving them all steadily home.

"It's a heartache," she sings.

"What's that?" asks Charlie, his voice low. "Is that that same song you were singing before? It sounds the same," and he turns to Rayanne beside him, putting his hand on her thigh. "Is that ache or break?" he asks.

Charmaine doesn't say anything. She's looking down into her folded hands. She sings as her mother turns toward her father, Rayanne's hand covering Charlie's.

"Ache," says Rayanne. "It's heartache, you know that."

Rayanne stares out the window and sees the whole land passing through her reflection, trees and sky and clouds. While she watches the light flow soft and warm around her, Charlie joins Charmaine, singing quietly with his daughter as he steers the car between rocks and ruts, the road curling and curving as he takes them all down out of the high hills.

Lightning Strikes

Brian Burke

A CLOUDBURST LOOMS – cumulonimbus massed over the city, tracking northward to shadow the University bus. The embedded convective cloud thickens and spreads, plunging this campus into premature dusk with slanted shafts of rust-coloured rain. I remember everything I ever learned about the weather.

So cross the open playing field and the oval track from the bus stop and head for the tallest building and the best vantage point from which to watch. Hear first then smell the searing hiss of ozone, and sense the crackle of scorched grass, the air so static-filled my hair tingles, caught as I am between a seething sky and the bristling, smoking earth. And then me, the conductive material linking two oppositely charged bodies.

The foreign pyrotechnics here in the heavy east are different from the faint flushes of lightning over the cool inlet back home, the rain forest and the luminous ribbons that flutter along mountain ridges. But that's all nostalgia and not really how it was or could ever be. That's all geography, from textbooks, carefully worded to say nothing about proximity.

My mother lies on her side, curled around her own clenched fist, which she clutches to her stomach. She keeps her face turned away, but I'm waiting in the doorway to her room, one tentative hand on the glass doorknob, the other on the jamb, because she calls me to her. Despite her position in the unmade bed I can still see the bruises over her eyes, along her cheekbones. She makes no attempt to hide from me the welts on her back and shoulders, raw seams on her skin running beneath the thin straps of an old slip she wears, angry weals like the kind left on white flesh by leeches from the lake. And the backs of her thighs, lumpy like the bread dough she pummels with those fists and rolls into lard-smeared baking tins.

She sniffles and wipes her bloody nose on the green bedspread.

"So get a clean glass," she says, swinging her pallid legs around and sitting up. She places her yellowed feet on the floor amid shards of broken glass. She wears a pair of my father's diamond socks to keep her feet warm, and she keeps a bottle of his whisky under the bed. It's this she's reaching for, one strap falling loose and revealing vivid red lashes across her sallow chest, and on that single withered breast a brutal rash I later come to recognize as a series of fresh cigarette burns.

One great truth has always sustained me. If my father taught me anything he taught me that women won't run away.

"What are you afraid of?" my father asks hunched over. He discovers me hiding in my closet, because if I open my eyes and lightning flashes I might see it, and if I take my fingers out of my ears and thunder cracks I might hear it.

His ruddy, insistent face, the ever-present beads of alcohol sweat that glisten on his high, slick forehead, that coat his protruding upper lip with an oily sheen, demands an answer.

"The thunder," I say, lying like any other frightened eight-year-old.

He laughs, a thin, whining sound. "There's no thunder," he says and touches my hair, unaware that my stomach's churning, that my guts are in a vicious knot. "Go outside," he booms, "and see if some lightning hit a tree or set the old garage on fire. Then you go and sit there. Go on. Lightning never strikes the same place twice. You remember that."

Probably there's no reason to fear him, although nothing he ever says convinces me that I'm safe, that he won't one day come after me. But he has other ways: on camping trips he likes to tell ghost stories in the tent at night. Pitch dark and he'll say, "Make sure you don't sleep too close to the tent pole, there. Lightning might hit it. You never know." Only once do I ever glimpse a sheet of silver lightning through the blue canvas. It renders the sky membranous, exposing the ripe veins. "Was that thunder?" he'll say at the dinner table, cocking his head in an exaggerated tilt, and cupping an ear. Or, "We sure could use a good thunderstorm. To clear the air." Then he watches while the paralysis that grips me takes hold and spreads, thickens. There is never the need to beat or mark my flesh.

"Where's he going?" kids at school ask whenever thunder chases me from the classroom. A single flash or just a dimming of the overhead lights, the roar of a jet, the rumble of another class being marched down the school corridor, any of these send me rushing home in cringing humiliation to see if she's okay.

"He's afraid," someone always shouts. Whispering starts, nervous, excited.

"There he goes again!" they shriek as I run, disgraced, bowels gurgling, breath sour with panic and coming in short sharp pants.

Often she forces me to return in the afternoon, steeped in my shame. Only during the summer holidays is occasional comfort derived from one of these degrading bouts of hysteria. While neighbours and kids on my block revert to normal activity after a heavy thundershower, come out again on the steaming streets or chatter on their verandas, I wait quaking in the profound silence that follows a summer squall. Is it over? Is it really over? Storms have been known to backtrack. It's much like the fabled quiet *before* a storm, but more conclusive, final.

When he beats her she rewards herself with a hot bath in Epsom salts. He brings her Five-Star whisky in a cheap champagne glass, to drink while her bruises soak. He places the plastic radio angled on the edge of the tub, and he plugs it in, while I do homework and wait for the radio to drop.

Twelve years old, I stand in short centre field hoping Ross will pitch this guy low and away, like we planned before the game. But Ross comes in over the plate and the batter just misses his pitch, sending a weak line drive right at me, instead of lifting a high flyball over the fence for a home run. No need for me to even move. Just reach up with my glove and pluck the dying ball out of the air.

"Nice catch," Ross calls from the pitcher's mound. He knows

it was close. The coach will wonder why I'm playing so shallow.

From centre field I can see the flow of the game. Everything is always in front of me. From the outfield I can pretend this park doesn't belong to this school, this town, this age.

When Ross strikes out the second batter on three straight pitches, the infield begins to chatter. "Hey, hey! Hey batter!"

Clouds surround me. Somehow they swing around from behind, anvil-headed thunderclouds, top-heavy with black bursting underbellies. It could be too late already.

To my right, the outfielder chants, "Two four six eight nine, batter looks like Frankenstein!"

That weak liner came from the bat of their best hitter. I should have been deeper. It's easier to run in than back to make a catch. Keep the ball in front of you. But I lucked out. Ross and I both committed mental errors. He gets the pitch in and up and I misplay the hitter. Yet we escaped unscathed. If the hitter gets hold of one … But then I see those clouds, black and boiling up with summer static. Sharp slanted rays of the fast-disappearing sun create planes of deepening black and downward fans of sudden rain.

Ross runs the next hitter to a full count then loses him. He walks a second man on four pitches.

The left- and right-fielders talk it up, calling encouragement. "This one swings like a rusty gate!" They expect me to start stuff like that. The centre-fielder is supposed to be in charge. The infield tries to rattle the batter as he steps into the box and taps the plate. "Hey! Hey! Batter! Swing!"

Two runners on but I still play tight. If one gets by me it's good for two, maybe three runs. I don't see lightning but thunder breaks and rumbles overhead. Parents stir on the sidelines. They move their lawn chairs back and send their smaller kids to the cars while I drift further out in centre field, deeper with each pitch, away from them all, hoping no one will notice. I try not to look up and pray in my head that I won't see a flash.

The batter shifts his grip and wriggles his feet in the dirt. He's nervous and fouls off another pitch.

I stare straight ahead. My chest constricts, leaving me breathless; my buttocks clench in cold fear. Off to the side I sense a flash, a cool whiff on the periphery of my eye. I'm sure I see one. Why is Ross playing around with this guy? Why doesn't he finish him off?

The hitter strikes out with runners on first and second,

releasing me. He throws his bat down in the on-deck circle.

My cheering teammates run in. Without looking back up or to the sides, I float off the field, past the row of trees and the school. Far enough away from the game I break into a panicky trot, finally racing home to hide in my bedroom with my fielder's mitt still clutched on my left hand.

Desert them. My teammates. In the middle of an inning. Before my turn at bat.

Pull the drapes and close my door and wonder how long before I jam my fingers in my ears and crawl into bed. How long before I squeeze my eyes shut. I never should have been playing in so tight: it's starting to affect my game.

Sixteen, and I steal my father's Plymouth on a regular basis. He's too drunk every Friday to notice. I join the wrestling matches at the local drive-in theatre, fumbling with my ashen girlfriend, the two of us sipping from a bottle of lemon gin, that trusted pantie remover, so legend has it, in the girls' locker room as well as the boys'. On-screen Godzilla fries half of Tokyo with his breath while Japanese scientists bombard him with electronic shockwaves. He eats the stuff, growing stronger on the fumes.

Sinewy tendrils of heat-lightning flicker in the distance. Too far off to worry about yet, but I'm more relieved than disappointed when I give up trying to render the girl naked and drive her home. We paw each other briefly in front of her house, both of us sweaty and frustrated, then she rushes inside.

At my place my father sprawls unconscious in the kitchen. I step carefully around a shattered whisky bottle; splinters of glass still glint in his headwound. My mother's jaw is broken and three of her teeth lie on the floor, snapped off like Chicklets, like tossed white dice.

Sweep the glass and drive her to the Emergency Ward where they wire her mouth shut.

While she sleeps I stand guard. My bleeding father can stitch himself up. I take the long, curved carving knife and bury its steel blade in the kitchen wall, surprising myself by not killing him.

June. The end of school. The last summer before college in the fall. He purchases a lightning rod, then shares a twenty-sixer of Five-Star with her and offers me the plastic star from the front of the bottle. I used to wear them stuck on my shirt, my puny chest plastered with a half dozen or more sheriff's badges. My galaxy of stars.

Dad – for that's who he is, despite the cruelty, the rancid breath, the constant sweats, the incoherent rages and tirades, and I'm as dependent on his disturbed fatherhood as were any of the early-sixties television kids on their domesticated, well-meaning Pops – Dad swings an old wooden ladder to the eavestrough and climbs to the roof, breaking first the bottom rung. He clambers up the shingled slope, scrambling on his hands and knees, the prized lightning rod clutched like a freedom flag in one hand.

"Watch this," he shouts, tickled with his own ludicrous image. "Look at me, college boy."

My inebriated mother watches from our overgrown front lawn. She's giddy and holding on to what's left of the Five-Star. "You know your father," she apologizes.

The father I am guilty of knowing straps the lightning rod to our red brick chimney. Miraculously, he doesn't fall and break his grimy neck, but he does manage to mangle the TV antenna. With a high, girlish giggle he slides down the roof on his rump, and makes it down the ladder with only a couple of clumsy missteps. Back on solid ground again the father who knows best around our place stumbles to his knees, wheezing and choking on his own laughter.

"If we don't get hit now," he claims, and struggles to his uncooperative feet to brush at his scuffed knees, "then there's no God. How about them apples?" he says smiling at me, challenging the skinny kid who graduated on the honour roll, who looks more like his mother than his dad. Where TV fathers bumble, he stumbles and staggers; where they recover their good-citizen balance and the graces of their neighbours in the final fading few minutes of the show, he trips over his own feet on his own front lawn.

Summer jobs take me to small towns and hot climates in the interior of the province. Between my turbulent first and second semesters, when I am placed on probation for excessive absences from class, lightning sets a nearby barn ablaze roasting alive the pigs penned inside. For days the bitter air reeks of their electrocution and bacon.

Driving a local girl's rust-encrusted Chrysler, a real boat, I'm momentarily blinded when a towering bolt with a dozen crackling rootlets strikes the white line down the middle of the highway that winds out of town. In our darkened room, rented for the night, she wants the curtains open so she can watch. Electrical storms excite her. Furious sheets ignite the skyline and sizzle overhead, all flashing at once. Multiple cannonshots crash and pound our small motel. While I will my eyes shut and my ears plugged, she lies nude, entranced. The thunderclaps are deafening. The storm grinds on for hours. When she sleeps *I* cover her, drawing the curtains closed and remaining awake until the danger passes minutes before daybreak. It's safe again. She'll never know how close she came.

The fourth doctor I see in six months is more impatient than the others. He's not a fan of phobias, and not the least impressed with mine, despite its persistence. He is also not overly excited about putting in time working for campus student health services.

He shakes his head at all I say, sucking in smoke from the cigarette drooping from his bottom lip.

Between years two and three I eat lunches parked in a shiny black Bronco owned by the foreman of a reforestation crew. I've grown bolder away from the charged atmosphere of home.

Here, thundershowers sweep the eastern slopes of the Rockies. Alternating patterns of light and shadow flow along the low hills.

My mother has been hospitalized, my father finally jailed. She is treated to electroshock therapy. He's doped, stupefied by narcotics, given jolts of aversion therapy. The juice only sustains him. The bastard loves it. I can only wonder if this long-overdue breakdown is caused by my absence. Without me there does he pursue her harder?

But my mother always takes the path of least resistance.

Third year and I transfer out-of-province.

Lightning strikes dilapidated barns, cows grazing in the field, golfers slicing along fairways, boats floating on lakes, people getting in and out of cars, children hiding under smouldering trees and a man in the United States a total of five times until he takes to his car one afternoon to escape the onslaught of a storm, drives across the stippled countryside, stops and gets out at what he considers a safe distance and is struck by a rogue bolt a sixth time, and killed.

Ripley's Believe It or Not contends that another man, exiting from a small stone church, is hit by lightning that first strikes the piked steeple then bounces off to burn all the clothes from his body. He's found unconscious and naked but unharmed except for a seared ring of scar tissue left around his neck by the gold crucifix he wears. Believe it or not.

Before beginning classes my final year I go to the Graduate Student Lounge where they are supposed to refuse me service at the bar: I do not join the graduate elite for another year yet. The air outside carries the acrid sting of burnt ozone, and the Grad Lounge is located on the top of a fourteen-storey highrise of offices.

Women here see me as something of a prodigy, so young, and they volunteer to buy me drinks. They inquire into my nonexistent thesis and are informed that various psychology tests maintain that phobias are used to express feelings too complex and frightening to put into words, and that they only occasionally respond to conventional forms of therapy. Struck inarticulate like that, I am assured seduction.

My last undergraduate year crawls by. A fifth psychiatrist hypnotizes me.

"Forget the past," he says. "We can change your life starting right today." I flash back instantly to my leaving home two years ago. The loaded plane holds on the tarmac as late-summer lightning streaks across the horizon. The pilot receives clearance from the shrouded tower. I close my eyes; it's planes and flying these fellow passengers will think I'm afraid of, and I smile to myself and listen to the sibilant whoosh down the runway as we're sucked off the ground by a vacuum our own momentum creates in front of us, so I believe. Engines roaring defiantly, we angle up through the thunderheads.

This fifth shrink, a coffee-guzzler who's applied for jobs at every hospital in the country and several abroad, tells me while I'm in a trance to think of something likable when there's a storm. "Think of sex," he advises me.

He then takes me on a trial run. In my head, clouds appear; they build into murky thunderclouds. Fork lightning bursts across the sky, followed almost instantly by sledge-hammer thunder. On my own I toss in hurricane-force winds – thinking, what the hell – to blow the downpour across my brain like bullets, to uproot trees and flatten houses. In this tempest he tells me to imagine women I have loved.

Graduate school embraces me within its enclave. To earn living expenses that summer I accept a night job in Calgary hammering together prefab trusses for the housing boom. A savage scrawl, seen through the dirt-streaked window of the washroom where I extract long slivers of wood from my greasy hands, signals the eruption simmering all afternoon and evening.

The guys eat their eight-o'clock lunches outside in the yard.

"Not yet," says Len, not the foreman and not the oldest, but everyone's choice as leader. His return to his press signals the end of coffee breaks. When he rolls closed the brown paper bag he carries his tuna fish sandwiches in each day, we follow him back to work.

"Not yet," he says again. I listen and hear a rising steady roar I don't recognize.

Lightning dings the transformer in the yard. The real foreman, an unpopular hireling from an outside competitor, dressed in oilskins and a yellow slicker, eats his lunch exiled to his forklift. He parks beneath the transformer seconds before it's blasted into flame. Sparks shower down onto his bloated body. The raingear makes him appear inflated. The lights inside the shop sputter, then die. He races from his forklift as thunder cascades over his head. The night crew convulses into laughter. Len too. And me. The machines, fed by electricity, go down for the remainder of the shift.

"Now!" shouts Len, scooping up his lunch bag and Thermos bottle. We all rush inside, squeezing through the doorway just in time.

The incessant roar grows louder as a volley of hailstones arrives from two blocks away where it has been drumming on rooftops. A torrent of ice ricochets off cars and lumber. Small pellets skip through the open door, their velocity shooting them against the far concrete wall as they invade the plant.

When the squall line passes over, we lean out behind Len and silently witness the pulverized ice in the yard, the sun's reappearance below the ragged edge of the cold front, and an eerie green light. Feeble lightning flicks, followed long seconds later by the reassuring lull of soft, distant thunder and an impossible rainbow.

The atmosphere in the lecture hall sparks with the whiplash of bottled tension. This is it, my last exam. It's like a death in the family. You won't have to deal with it anymore. Like a dead parent, it won't be there when you go home at night.

The place is full of nail-biters; but I met a girl last night. She takes me home. We drink red wine and sleep on her white couch. Afterward, a peal of thunder awakens me, starts me to my feet.

Better judgement counsels me to accept a job in the psychology department of another university, in order to leave a girlfriend I'm close to living with. This morning the sun's barely visible through a thick haze. It soon disappears behind a darkening bank of cloud.

The dead humidity has me praying for it.

I can't spend another night in her apartment. We draw too close; too close. The fan I bought for her room proves a great success, blowing over us while we undress, evaporating our perspiration. Her fine body warm against me; but it's a warmth I find strangely cooling. The fan just keeps me awake all night.

I wish I could know I won't hit her. I wish I could know that she will leave me if I do.

Lightning finally strikes the playing field, the oval track, the parking lot below. Another rattling bolt, it seems to me, jolts the flagpole. My tingling hair still bristles, even here inside where the air hums. So how can I stand so calmly at this window, my shoulder braced against the frame, my eyes sparkling as I blink them clear, while the Psych Lab vibrates and trembles, shaken by sonic blasts of radiant thunder?

Light casts odd shadows in the east. Release is a relief.

What a mismatch they were: him flushed and florid, her so anemic. What could possibly have linked them? Opposites attract, years of schooling have taught me. Lightning never strikes twice. Me, the Educated Man, forever apologizing to each new woman for crimes committed against the last.

The power kicks off, knocked out. The intense blackness fades to a dull ray in a deluge of pelting rain, as the tides shift.

My mother lies buried, the only real shock being that she died what they call a natural death.

My father has remarried.

Pilot

William Klebeck

It is a cloudy April morning and the forecast is rain. I'm out in the stubble field waiting for Lee the cropduster to make his pass. Nearby, my young son boots around hardened clumps of dirt turned up by the cultivator last fall. He's excited by the prospect of seeing the plane.

The rest of my family, my wife and daughter, my sister and her husband, are huddled back by the quonset, out of the chill wind. Hands in her jacket pockets, my mother is standing further back, conversing with the minister.

Lee's Pawnee aircraft appears over the western horizon, at first a dark moving speck above the distant tree line. The whine of the spray plane's engine builds as he approaches. My family walks out to join my son and me in the field.

Soaring past overhead Lee salutes us from the cockpit. He makes a wide banking turn way out east over Paulson's summerfallow and comes in low towards us, so low it seems the front wheels of the Pawnee should kick up gravel on the grid road at our field's edge.

The side window of the cockpit is slid back and Lee's holding a plastic bag outside the plane. A thin sprinkle of grey-white dust trails out of the bag as the plane skims over the field past us. When he's a couple of hundred yards away, before he can empty it, the bag blows out of his hand and drops, still weighted, to the ground.

Let us pray, says the minister. I watch the nose of the Pawnee lift up, the plane speed away skyward, before I bow my head. I did not shed any tears when my father died last November, not at the memorial service, not afterward.

The minister offers us some reassuring words. Lee makes one more fly past, tipping his wings. We all wave at him. He's going to drive back to join us for lunch. I tell everyone I'll meet them at the farmhouse in a little while.

As I walk across the dry furrowed land, my breathing becomes quick, deeply drawn. I pick up the plastic bag that contains the remains of my father. In a few minutes I will broadcast the rest of his ashes over our field, as he asked, but now I stand here, under the heavy sky, tears wetting my grown-man cheeks.

Before dawn today, back and forth, my line, my way is fixed by the long light of the tractor's high beams piercing the morning dark. Floodlights mounted on the top of the cab illuminate the red frame cultivator sunk into, pulled through, ripping up the ground behind. Back and forth, yesterday's bad news repeated every half hour on the radio, I work the land. Outside the cab the darkness thins, lifts. The large sky, lit by the rising sun, overwhelms the near horizon. At the edge of the field, in our yardsite, the steel quonset gleams.

Broad daylight I drive straight into this pothole. Drawn down by the heavier load, the tractor's engine labours. Behind me, the tandem wheels of the deep tillage push up balls of mud. The moist ground draws the forty-two broad steel shovels down deeper into it. My drive wheels, losing traction, begin to spin.

I can hear you. The best way to get out of a pothole is not to get into one. And now I can see you, leaning back there against the driver's door of your old '73 rust-spotted yellow half-ton parked just off the worked part of the field. Pulled down low on your forehead, a cap with OPRYLAND stencilled on the front. Arms crossed in front of you, workboot heels shoved into the earth, you're grinning as I spin my wheels, shaking your head.

You get a guy out here who's a couple years out of high school, and he's never lost or fought for anything, and he goes by the book and tells me what to do. The assistant loans manager in the credit union these days is a rosy-cheeked young guy named BROCK PETERSON, if the black-and-white nameplate on his glass-top desk is correct. He sits with my file, my whole history, open in front of him, tilting back in his cushioned swivel chair, fingering the perfect knot in his paisley tie all the time I'm explaining my situation.

The credit union's been debiting my operating line-of-credit to make the payments on the mortgage I took out to buy the Murdoch land in '84, at $80,000 a quarter, so now I'm already up to my authorized limit. I need an extension this spring to cover some of my costs, seed and fertilizer, spray and fuel, until I can sell the rest of my grain.

He asks how much grain I have on hand, how many acres I plan on seeding this year. When I tell him, he murmurs something about their land loan being undersecured. You want some more credit, Mr. Landis, he says.

Follow the breadcrumbs, boy, I want to say. But I don't, I just nod my head. That's why I'm here.

I'm sorry. This kid snaps his stylish green suspender straps and flips the cover of my file closed. I'm just doing my job, he says.

My son, Calvin, older now. He's fiddling with the radio in the half-ton on our way back from town. Driving past Hurrell's land, Rudneski's land, our land, I tell him where we're driving, seventy years ago, was mostly bush, like right over there on his side of the road. Then Ukrainians, Icelanders, settlers like his grandfather came out here, got a quarter section of bush land, one hundred sixty acres of hard work. The homestead. And they sawed down trees, used teams of horses for pulling out roots and rocks. They cleared small fields out of this land, and just look how thick that bush is.

But, as usual, Calvin's not listening. He's too busy bopping to the pop music blaring out of the radio. He's a smart kid, though, wants to go to university when he graduates high school. He wants to became an aerospace engineer. The future's out there, he says sometimes, pointing up.

It is one of those rare, perfect harvest nights in late August, cloudless but warm, windy enough to keep the dew off the wheat swathes. It's past midnight and the grain is nowhere near tough yet. We should be able to combine all night.

In the middle of the field, wearing only a short-sleeve shirt, I'm lying on my back on the roof of the three-ton truck. Above me, against an endless purple backdrop, stars winking beyond, fistfuls of colour are continuously opening up, extending long nimble fingers of red and green and pink across the dark sky. It's as if the northern sky is being played by a grand pianist and I'm so capti-vated by the performance I don't even notice the floodlights of the combine blinking on and off until it's almost adjacent to where I'm parked in the field.

What the heck – he shouldn't have the hopper full yet. He just unloaded the last one into the back of the truck less than ten minutes ago.

I slide down over the windshield onto the hood, then swing around the open door onto the seat behind the steering wheel. When I pull up underneath the auger of the combine, my father is standing on the platform just outside the cab, leaning against the railing. No grain is visible at the top of the hopper.

That usually means breakdown.

I wait in the truck as he clambers slowly down the ladder and opens the passenger door before stepping off the combine onto the running board of the truck. There's a wince on his face when he sits down on the bench seat. He lifts, with both hands, his stiffened right leg into the truck behind him.

I think I got to go home, son, he says. For the past few days he's been quietly complaining about pain in his back and today, at supper, he mentioned his leg was, for some reason, starting to swell up.

I can run the combine for a while, I say, if you want to take a rest.

My father straightens his back, lifting himself off the seat. I don't think I can even drive the truck, he says, rubbing his knee.

I'll shut the combine down, I say.

After I dump the wheat in the hopper into the truck, I idle the diesel engine for a few minutes before pulling the Stop button and canceling all the lights. I drive the half full three-ton across the field, slowing down near his yellow half-ton parked near the main road.

Just go, my father says. We can pick up my truck tomorrow.

With the northern lights in the dark sky flashing above us, I drive my father the ten miles down the main road home from what we call the South Half.

A farmer should go out of his way a considerable distance not to drive his tractor into a pothole. I can hear you.

Now you're taking off your cap, your greasy finger adding another dark smudge to the underside of the peak. You pass your other hand back over your head, pressing down the thin strands of grey hair remaining. You're still grinning, rubbing it in.

When your drive wheels begin to slip, gear down.

Geared down, my wheels are still spinning, flinging clumps of mud back behind me. I know. The tractor has power enough to propel itself and pull its load through the field, providing it has traction, providing its drive wheels don't slip.

One of the proudest days of my life starts out like most other days in late July. It's the end of the crop year and we're hauling grain, scrambling to deliver all of last year's crop to the elevator before the initial price drops again on August 1st. It's hot, seems like it's always the hottest day of the year when we haul barley, and that morning it's so windy when we park down near the row of granaries and both open the doors at the same time, my permit book blows off the dash of the big truck.

Like all other days before he got sick, my father climbs inside the bins when they're almost empty to help me shovel the grain out of the corners, Despite his age, breathing heavily in the air thick with disturbed dust, he scoops just about as many shovelfuls of barley into the hungry auger as I do.

But after we put the last load on the three-ton that afternoon, I tell him to go on up to the house. I'll take the load to town. I hop into the driver's seat of the truck but before I drive off to the elevator I watch my father, his legs slightly bowed, the back of his workshirt darkened with sweat, make his way slowly up the hill to the old house.

After making the delivery to the elevator, I take the Wheat Pool cheque, the proceeds from the sale of all my grain that day, to the credit union.

I remember nine years ago, after I proposed to Cheryl. I was just a kid with long hair and dirty jeans, standing around outside on the sidewalk for a while, hesitating, before I finally took the big step and opened the glass entrance door. I walked right up to the counter and told one of the tellers I'd come in to see about a loan to buy some land.

She led me down the hallway and showed me the open door to the manager's office. Ed Florie was still around then, sitting behind a desk messy with lots of loose papers and thick file-folders. He was a working man's banker. His sportcoat was hung over the back of his chair and his long shirt sleeves were rolled up to the elbow. He looked up when the teller said there was a young gentleman here wanting to discuss some business with him.

Sure, sure, he said, gesturing for me to sit down.

I told him I'd been working on the farm with my father the past three years, since leaving high school, and I was thinking about getting married. I thought it was time to strike out on my own. I told him I had a handshake deal with Big Jim Hafford to buy a good half-section of land a couple miles up the road from our farm. I hoped they could help me out.

Sounds good to me, Ed said, and started filling out my loan application right then. When he passed the form across the desk for my signature, he said, Just have your father come in, co-sign, and the funds will be ready when you need them.

Just like that, I was a farmer.

Now, when I get back out to the farm after doing my business in town, I stop by the two-storey house before going home to our newer three-bedroom bungalow on the other side of the yard. As soon as I step into the porch, I smell boiled cabbage. My mother's making cabbage rolls. I hear steaks sizzling in a frypan on the stove in the kitchen.

I take my boots off in the porch, spilling a few kernels of wheat out on the worn remnant welcome mat and walk into the living room.

With his feet up, my father's sitting in his favourite chair, the recliner that has one padded arm beaten out of shape, pounded pulpy by his right fist when he gets excited watching the Saskatch-ewan Roughriders. He's still got his work clothes on.

I sit down on the chesterfield near him.

Dad, I say.

His grey eyes shift from the weather on TV to me.

I paid off the loan on the Hafford land. I dig in my shirt pocket for the paper I got from the credit union today. Here's the guarantee you signed for me.

He doesn't say anything. The lines in his face, on his high forehead, at the corners of his eyes, do not relax, nor do they become more pronounced. He just takes out of my hand the paper that bears his fading signature.

From the kitchen my mother yells, Soup's on.

You hungry, son? my father asks. I felt proud, simply asked to dinner.

When we were first married Cheryl used to stick our unpaid bills on the fridge with small, brightly coloured magnets the shape of vegetables. Not any more.

One day this spring Ray Tamblyn drives into the yard in his bulk-fuel truck. Our family has dealt with his family for more than twenty years. Calvin and I are down by the shed, changing over to shovels from spikes on the cultivator. Tamblyn drags the hose out from underneath the truck and climbs up on the small wooden ladder leaning against the steel stand. We walk over as he fills my five-hundred-gallon galvanized tank with diesel.

Just come from Dave Hunter's, Tamblyn says, standing above us. Dave Hunter's a farmer down the road. He summerfallows, doesn't use much fertilizer or chemical because he believes it's bad for the land. Tamblyn says, Hunter went to a lawyer yesterday who charged him three hundred bucks to tell him he should give his land to the bank.

Not much surprises me these days.

Tamblyn climbs down the ladder when the tank is full. As he folds up the heavy hose, I start to write out a cheque. Tamblyn slams shut the metal door below his truck tank and stands up to face me.

Shell's putting the pressure on me to come up myself with the bills over ninety days, he says. I got to deal with you on a cash basis. I'm sorry, Emery, he says to me in front of my son.

I go up to the house to get some of the twenties Cheryl and I keep in the drawer in the night-table in our bedroom. On my way through the kitchen, my shoulder brushes against the fridge. My daughter's latest crayon colouring flutters to the linoleum floor.

Unhitched, without a load, you can sometimes pull yourself out. In neutral, idling, I open the door of the cab and hop down three steps onto the field. The tractor's duel drive wheels are buried in mud to the hub. The heels of my cowboy boots sink inches into the moist ground when I walk around the tractor and rip out the hydraulic hoses, pull the pin on the cultivator.

Back inside the cab, wiping oil off my hands with a rag, I see you, with your cap on, getting into your half-ton truck.

I let the clutch out slowly, ease up the throttle. If the drive wheels grips gradually, gain some traction in solid ground beneath the mud, I'll get out of here on my own. But as the engine gains power I can feel the rubber tire lugs underneath me tearing deeper into the wet earth.

I kick the clutch in, stopping all motion, and turn, in the tractor cab, in the driver's seat, toward you. But you're gone. Your departure today, in the old yellow truck, leaves no trail of dust whatsoever.

I climb down out of the stuck tractor. I know. Another power unit, another tractor hitched in front, will get me out. This time, as soon as my feet hit the ground, I break into a run. Across our field, across the dark, soft, tilled land I worked once more this morning, I run for home. In our yardsite the steel quonset reflects the sun. A jet stream streaks the blue sky.

Exit Pursued by Bear

Mark A. Jarman

W E'RE HUNTING IN honeyed light, moving inside a circle of mountains; precambrian valleys eat into each other under the caves and treed ridges. "You think a cougar killed it?" asks Neon. "Maybe we'll see a cougar. Let's go back and get my camera."

We've been walking the eastern slopes and whale-shaped foothills of Beauty Creek; Neon and an ex-player from the Calgary Flames fan out ahead of me while I study their ears, while I think about Waitress X's slow voice and the low sound of my father's voice, for I have just learned my father's liver is cancerous, a tumour laid like a butterfly over three of four sections. There's no telling how long he has, how long our family has. It'll be like a grin with one tooth gone. We stumble onto an elk dead under a cliff. Parts are missing. If a cougar did it, Neon definitely wants his zoom lens, wants a good shot of the cat. This light is perfect, he says, so we walk back down to the red 4 x 4 to grab Neon's Russian camera, then climb once more uphill to the kill, our rifles loaded just in case.

Weird noises rise now in the pretty alpine meadow: yellow wildflowers, scarlet rosehips, a butter-coloured grizzly feeding on the elk's hindquarters, snapping out bits and shaking its head. We back up pronto as the grizzly rears on dark legs, making more strange noises, jaw doing something I've never seen before, its flat nose up sniffing for us. And then it charges, galloping faster than I've seen any creature run, a cross between a horse and a wild dog at full bore, crazy grace and a hump of muscle like a ball. We cannot get away and start alternating shots. Metal hits it. I shoot, Neon shoots, going for the chest, trying to break down the shoulders. The other guy shoots, our guns noisy, echoing as percussion off the stunted pines, the cliff, a blackpowder smell sharp up my nose. I don't bother with the grizzly's head, its skull is too thick; I keep my shots low. The bear's tiny eyes seem half crossed, teeth snapping. Shots hit the ragged fur like ink, bloodspots blooming deep in the thick fall coat, but the grizzly won't go down, it wants to get at us. I shoot, he shoots; gun butt killing my shoulder, the bear still charging with these weird canine noises, big obvious holes in it but charging, and I'm thinking now of five claws mauling my eyes, my vulnerable liver, yellow teeth clamping my skull like a soft apple. We blast away; this part seems to go on forever. One of the grizzly's legs is clearly ruined but it's still charging. And then the bear staggers and slumps on its huge face, slides, then tumbles downhill right past us and it's over, dark gums and scarred ears stopping a couple yards beyond the toe of my boot. My ears ring, I'm deaf and stunned. The grizzly's ears remind me of a cat's; they're chewed up at the edges. The bear stinks and its face seems two feet across. Its curving incisors, the colour of a daylight moon, are long, long as my fingers.

In these same golden mountains where our blonde grizzly lies twitching, Marilyn Monroe once asked my father to take a snapshot of her and Joe DiMaggio. Joe and Marilyn were sitting on a railing, looking at Mt. Edith Cavell and Honeymoon Lake. This is before Joe's temper, before he hired the detective to follow her. There is a gap between his front teeth. There are peaks and satellite peaks, older rocks thrust over new. "That prick wouldn't drop," Neon says, "shot that prick six times, prick didn't know it was dead." The sky comes back in focus, birds return to their flowers' tiny hearts and organs. Neon keeps talking, pacing, calling the grizzly names. Everything I do seems at the wrong shutter speed, and the bear is shrinking into autumn's earth and yellowed grass, sienna spruce needles and synclinal rock. One shot in my chamber, none in Neon's rifle. If we'd been one yard closer it would have hit us, eaten us. It didn't know it was dead. It misunderstood.

I have that sense of adrenaline and admiration and failure after a fight with someone you like, someone you find had a bum hand or shoulder. I feel obscene. I have to sit on the ground while Neon takes dozens of pictures, a photo opportunity, the Russian camera's antique motor growling like a nest of wasps. I believe polar bears' livers are poisonous; I wonder if it's the same with grizzly livers? Who will get the scarred coat? The paws? Sometimes you find a dead bear and that's all that's chopped off: the hands and feet. A delicacy for some.

Marilyn Monroe was filming *River of No Return* between Jasper and Banff. In the movie she plays a saloon singer with red shoes and a fall in her hair. Robert Mitchum is in the picture. It's a bad movie: Otto Preminger must have owed someone. I caught it once on Siesta Cinema on Channel 3, back when there were only two channels. I remember she posed dramatically on a raft as it swept down a seething river and those pesky natives tore at her blouse. Did they use a double on the distant shots? Fake scenery? Is this what would drive her to dye her hair the colour of honey? To make it so much fake scenery? My father was the only person who didn't know who the blonde woman was. They were parked in a viewpoint west of the highway, little more than a dirt track in the 1950s. My father stood tall and polite in a white cotton suitcoat, a relic of Oxford and the war years in Ceylon with the Royal Navy. "Would you be so kind…?" Marilyn asks, not finishing her sentence. My mother does not approve; Joe and Marilyn are not yet married and though there is a pretense of separate hotels, my mother believes Joe is sneaking over to Marilyn's room at the Jasper Park Lodge. My mother's Bible says for women to adorn themselves in modest apparel, with shamefacedness and sobriety; not with braided hair, or gold, or pearls, or costly array. The river is braided: on its gravel bed it separates and rejoins, separates and rejoins, over and over as the river moves toward the railroad yards of Jasper, and the Arctic Ocean.

In the movie everyone is chasing something and no one returns. Marilyn finally wins the widower sodbuster's heart, ditches her symbolic red shoes and joins his family. My father took two pictures and put the small camera back in Marilyn's hand. Don't you know who that was, they said, don't you know? It didn't matter to him who they were. They're just people. Joe and Marilyn looked childishly happy, teeth evident. The earth is fairly new, the future bright and harmless as mountains, sordid affairs banished, behind us. I wonder now if my father ever had an affair; did he ever have his Waitress X? My father converted from Church of England to Catholicism to marry my mother, a war bride, to start a family.

Back then everyone would go see the bears feed at the dump. They built bleachers. The bears open and close their mouths. Late in the day the light is perfect, like reddish oxide and downfolded quartzite.

Marilyn Monroe talks to my father, sleeps with Joe DiMaggio, and makes her bad movie. Late in the day you park your huge American car on the tender alpine plants and climb into the bleachers set up by the park rangers. My father drove a tiny Ford Prefect. All of us took our places. All of us, Marilyn Monroe, my father, me, two years old and asleep, will dwell in this light forever. Barbiturates and detectives, carcinomas and my motorcycle crash wait in different rooms down the hall. Like the grizzly I will shoot in these mountains, we don't know yet that we're dead. The bears file in like a vaudeville troupe. All the men wear charcoal hats. My father never wears a hat.

The bears put on a show by simply showing up and eating our garbage, like sin eaters; Joe and Marilyn put on a show, smiling like shy honeymooners, just ordinary folks. The crowd eats it up. A man approaches with a Brownie box camera but he doesn't want Marilyn; he wants a bear. His blonde child has honey placed on his palm, a photo opportunity. Just in case there's trouble he has a pistol tucked in his baggy wool pants. You're not supposed to have a gun in the park. The bears work their jaws peacefully, hunched in a private circle like a family playing Scrabble. When they are born they weigh half a pound. The father pushes his child. Go on, the father says, go on. Then they turn.

The Sound He Made

Richard Cumyn

THIS DOPE ADDICT friend of mine, I had not seen him since the fall, heard that I had a kid and got hold of my phone number from my mother. Gayle and I were in a bachelor apartment in Lowertown then, subletting off a guy who moved back into his old house while his father wintered in Florida. Gayle was using the electric breast pump we were renting because the baby was not latching on properly. The first thing he said when I picked up the phone, he could hear the machine sucking in the background, was, "What is this, Hill, I dial into an obscene call?"

I knew it was him right off. We had not seen each other for about eight months, not since the time he showed up at Miller House on a Thursday pub night and shared a cigarette with Gayle as we sat together at a table and watched student teachers dance to the Village People. The music was pretty lame. That was before I got Gayle to quit smoking.

Bam was what we called him from the time he collided with this white Citroen while riding his bike. It was the sound he made, like a gun going off, as he bounced off the hood. He didn't ask for his own cig, just kept sharing with Gayle like they were doing a private number together. He explained his nickname for her, rolled up his pant leg to show her the L-shaped scar in his calf where his front mud guard had gouged out enough meat to make a Big Mac. His words. I don't know what I did. I think I just looked away.

His real name is Mitchell O'Day. We met the summer we were

twelve years old and going to the same summer day camp, the one run by the civil service recreational association down on Riverside Drive. His father and my mother both worked at Supply and Services but didn't know each other. Due to the accident, Bam missed the middle session of the camp. When he started going again, he was supposed to be using a crutch but he always ditched it in this hollow tree in Vincent Massey Park first thing in the morning.

Early August sometime and we had been riding our bikes after dark, a bunch of us. Only one guy had a headlight, the kind that generates its own power against the front tire, but he never used it because he said it only slowed him down. Bam hit that Citroen like a gun going off. The driver didn't even stick around to see if he was all right. The guy with the headlight and I ran to get Bam's father. We were in his street, a dead end, just a couple of houses away, actually.

Last time we saw each other I had told him to find the nearest slimy rock and climb under it. I guess that's what happens. A crowd of student teachers were doing the body language to "YMCA." It was a real education living there in residence that year with those teachers-to-be. It made me think seriously about home schooling but only in the abstract. Gayle and I had only made love the once. Bam didn't even know we were interested in each other and we had no idea how quickly things would progress. He must have had a feeling about us, though. It's not something you can hide very well. It just wasn't anything we had told anyone yet. As far as he was concerned, Gayle was just this very self-assured, sophisticated-acting honey sitting at the same table as he was. She was somebody to share a smoke with, bounce a few of his moves off of. I sat there smiling at his whole act.

He bled one bucket of blood. The bike had been run over, that was obvious from the way the frame was now operating in two planes instead of just one. Bam's father came running out with this sofa cushion in his hand, the first thing he had grabbed. Bam was sitting up hugging his knee to his chest. The whole pant leg of his jeans was soaked. Mr. O'Day stood there with this puzzled look on his face, turning the cushion over and over in his hands like he was trying to figure out some way to stop the bleeding. Then he saw the wrecked bike in the middle of the street and he started yelling at the rest of us. That was how he dealt with it. His son had totalled his new BMX that had cost about two hundred dollars.

They were playing "Macho Man" for about the fifth time when one of the real idiots in our building, this nut who had decided to become a teacher after eighteen years of being an appliance salesman at Sear's, brought his Volkswagen into the building. He must have got all his buddies to help lift it up the stairs. We heard the motor running and turned around to look where people were pointing at the cafeteria windows behind us and there he was driving backward and forward in the hallway. Two student constables went out to try to stop him but couldn't really do anything except look stern and shake their heads the way their parents might in the same situation.

This was too much for Bam. He'd been working in the mail room of the Empire Life Insurance Company since high school and I could tell it was getting to him, draining him somehow. He wasn't even supposed to be with us. He'd just taken off at noon, driven all the way down, about a two hour drive, with no intention of making it back in time for work in the morning. "You got me for the whole fucking *fin de siécle*, Hill," he said. He meant the weekend but he actually went back home that same night.

Gayle was being too cool about him being there. I wanted her to give me a sign that it was time to head up for the night but she kept touching his arm when she spoke to him. When Bam saw the VW Bug outside the pub doors, he downed the last of his beer and Gayle's, too, and grabbed her by the hand. She laughed and almost stumbled trying to keep up. They ran out the door together and I went out behind them along with most of the rest of the pub.

We heard that the ex-salesman killed himself just before graduation. Not many people knew about it. They were all out trying to get hired. He was making this show of weaving close to the people in line who were waiting to get into the pub, making them think he was going to hit them. He skidded to a stop in front of Gayle and Bam. She was still holding onto his hand. In reflex she turned and buried her face in his chest.

It's hard to knew what made Bam do what he did next. He has this streak in him. It made me think about him getting that Citroen driver back only a week after the accident. I don't even remember the asshole's name, only that he lived on Bam's street right where it ended, owned a chain of drycleaning outlets, and drove the only car of its make in the neighbourhood. Someone we knew said it was considered France's Rolls Royce. The guy wasn't really that old, forty maybe. He lived all alone in this huge house. Every Sunday morning he washed his car. He loved that funny looking car, we could tell by the way he buffed it dry with a chamois before he waxed it. We played ball in the park at the other end of the street and every Sunday a stream of sudsy water ran down and soaked the area around first base. Bam would look up the street at the source of the stream and yell, "Frog Face!" He knew the guy could hear him.

The name Frog Face started back in the winter. Any time we had a road hockey game going and the Citroen guy was coming home after work, instead of slowing down to give us time to move the nets over to the curb, he honked the horn impatiently to let us know that he had no intention of slowing down. The first player to see one always called, "Car!" any normal time and that meant one thing. Bam was the one who first yelled "Frog Face!" at the Citroen and we knew that meant get out of the way as fast as humanly possible. We all began saying it. That was when it started between them. That was before Bam got his nickname.

Bam still had his stitches when he fixed that fucker's wagon but good. He never told Mr. O'Day who the driver was. He never even mentioned the car. The story he told his father, the one he made me and the other guys swear we'd stick to, was that old lady Billingham's yappy terrier had run out in front of him and he had to stop so quickly that he went right up over the handlebars. The next question was how had he bent the frame all to ratshit if all he had done was flip over the bars and how'd his leg get so cut up by the fender? Bam said it just did, he didn't know exactly how. It just did. His father let it be.

The phrase Frog Face was all Bam, even when we started saying it and fitting it into dirty songs. He had nothing against the French but he had a powerful hate on for that drycleaner who washed his car so devotedly every Sunday. Even after we stopped playing road hockey and took to the ball diamond round about the first of June, whenever he saw the Citroen he yelled the insult loud enough the guy would have had to be deaf not to hear. When he drove past, he looked straight at us like he was trying to burn a hole right through our eyes. He would have killed us if he'd been able to get away with it, that was the message. He would have killed us, not despite but because we were children. He was an adult who lived across a gulf none of us could conceive of spanning. Ever.

The guy knew us to see us, we'd yelled Frog Face and splattered his car with dirty salt slush enough as he drove by. But he didn't know Bam's cousin, Henry, who was our age and lived on the other side of the city. Henry was over visiting with his little brother, Justin, the Sunday Bam got the guy back for running over his bike. I was in on it but never told anyone I knew a thing about it, not even after the shit called the police and made our fathers bring us down to the station to answer questions about it. Bam shouldn't even have been walking around, the risk of popping his stitches was still too great. But Henry's family was over visiting and it was this lush midsummer morning that made me think that it had to have always been that bright. At no time could it have been dark night. Bam had money from his paper route, five dollars, which Henry said he would split with Justin but we knew otherwise. We wouldn't have shared it either.

I would have done exactly what Bam did if I'd had the guts. It's what I was thinking when Bam lifted Gayle onto the roof of the Volkswagen: I wish I had thought of doing it first. It was such a commanding gesture. He put his two hands around her waist that she had been so proud of, barely 22 inches before I got her pregnant. She used to be proud of the fact that I could almost encircle her waist with my two hands. He boosted her up onto the roof of that car as if she was queen of the parade and he was king and this wasn't a car being driven inside a college residence by a drunken student teacher but the lead car in a grand football parade. Bam looked up at her, at his handiwork, this queen enthroned, and beamed. He opened himself all the way up smiling.

Gayle didn't know what to think, that was clear from her face. She gave me this pleading look as if to say, Who is this person you say is your best friend since you were kids? Who is he that he looks so pleased with himself? Not, Get me down from here. She was fully capable of sliding off quickly without much problem, although sometimes I think about her being up there and four weeks pregnant and neither of us knowing a thing about it. That was how green we were.

No, she stayed up there of her own volition but her look was full of these questions I knew she was demanding I answer. Explain Bam before another second passes, for one thing. That would have been something if I'd been able to do it. Explain Bam. That's a good one.

The guy who drove the Citroen, he might have been thinking

the same kind of thing. He had no proof it was Bam who did that number on his baby, but a person would have to be a moron not to make the connection. You try to run over a kid out riding his bike at night and a week later the paint on one side of your car is burned off? It doesn't take genius.

Little Justin set up the distraction which wasn't difficult because he had no clue what was going on. I mean the kid was all of three years old. He loved to do just about anything there was to do with Henry and the little squirt loved to draw on things most of all. Bam gave Henry the fiver and a Coke bottle full of sulphuric acid that he'd funnelled from Mr. O'Day's basement workshop where he did plate metal etchings as a hobby.

"Don't get it on your skin," he told Henry, "and don't let Justin drink any."

Henry tapped his shoe in the stream of soapy water coming down the street and said, "What do you think I am, a moron?" Then he and Justin started hand-in-hand up toward the big house at the top of the street. Bam and I hid in Mrs. Billingham's cedar hedge where we took turns peeking through my father's field glasses.

I saw Henry bend down and whisper something in Justin's ear. If the guy saw them, he wasn't paying any attention to them. The little pecker scooted around to the side the man wasn't washing and began to go at the car with his coloured sidewalk chalk. Bam kept grabbing the binoculars from me. When I looked again, Henry had walked a way back down the street and doubled back giving Justin time to draw one hell of a surreal mural on the driver's door, the wet colours smeared all over the place.

Then Henry walked up behind the guy, who was down in a crouch doing a hubcap. We got the full report.

He said, "Hey mister, have you seen my little brother around here?"

"No, I haven't," said the man without looking up. I imagine him thinking, Leave me alone, you little peckerhead, this is the only day of the week I have to relax.

Then he noticed the little pair of feet under the car and the sound of creative humming. "What the…?"

I saw him come around the front of the car, where he saw Justin making his masterpiece, and bring his hand up to his forehead. Next thing, he hauled the garden hose around to that side and started hosing the colours off. Justin began to cry. The guy finished spraying, then crouched down so that he was level with the boy, trying to console him, but that only made Justin cry harder. We couldn't see Henry who was around the other side of the car but we knew what he was doing.

What was it about Bam and cars? The guy driving the Volks-wagen, the drunk, reached one hand up through his open window and grabbed hold of Gayle's leg, at the same time throwing the car into reverse. This was getting to be too much. I yelled for him to stop. Gayle was screaming at me. I looked at Bam who was laughing while he unbuttoned his shirt. The car shot forward, toward us again and Bam stepped in front of it. The guy slammed on the brakes hard, leaving rubber a good thirty feet past where Bam sidestepped it. When the car stopped, Gayle kept going, rolling down the windshield and hood and onto the floor like some crash test dummy without its seat belt. Bam was still laughing. I ran to Gayle, got her to her feet. She was shaken and crying but unhurt.

Bam said to Gayle, "You have just experienced the ultimate rush, my dear."

I told him to shut the fuck up. Then I walked back to the car and kicked the guy's door in, I was so mad. When he heard the sound he roused himself and hung his head out the window. I'd put a sizeable dent in the middle of the door panel. He got out to inspect it. Someone said later that he had been drinking since early that morning. He'd got his first practice teaching report back and had received unsatisfactory ratings in all five evaluation criteria. The third day in the school he had put some punk up against a locker and started cuffing him in the head. The principal had advised him not to come back to that particular high school to teach.

He ran his fingers along the dent where I'd cracked the paint. I was ready for him to come over and pound me out. The engine was still running, it sounded like a rattling little tank. Someone told him to turn it the fuck off, he was going to asphyxiate us all, but he left it running. He walked around to the other side and hauled back and kicked the passenger door with the flat of his foot.

"There," he managed to say. "Equilibrium."

He actually stayed at the college longer than we did although, like us, he didn't graduate. He was directing the annual drama department production that year, Agatha Christie's *Mousetrap*. He put so much time into the play that he did nothing else. None of his media labs got done, none of his lessons were prepared. We heard that the play was a big hit, though.

Slowly and deliberately, the way people will when they are trying to sound sober, he said, "If someone will help me, I will remove this vehicle from the premises," as if the whole lot of us had just finished dress rehearsal and he was putting the wraps on it, the final word. "If some of you would step forward …" He was swaying forward and back. "If someone could just …" He dropped off, losing his thought.

"It's all right, Bud," said Bam. "Don't worry. We'll help you."

About twenty of them lifted the Volkswagen down the stairs and out of the building for him. Though he hadn't damaged anything, he had to pay a fine for the violation. I was still angry at Bam for the way he scared Gayle and I told him so when he came back inside. He looked at me like I was crazy.

"You haven't got the hots for that one, do you? Her ass is too big. She's a cow."

I told him to find the rock he'd crawled out from and slide back under. I told him I never wanted to see his ugly face again. I could have killed the son of a bitch. Gayle never knew what he said.

"He's just like that," I said after he'd gone. "One minute he has plans with you and the next he's out thumbing his way across the country."

Gayle said, "I noticed he limps. Is that from the accident?" Jesus, after terrifying her half to death, he still had her conned! I could have killed him.

The Citroen guy lost the skin off his right hand up to the middle of the arm and paint off the driver's side of his car. By the time he realized what had happened, Henry and Justin were gone and we made sure they stayed out of sight until it was time for them to leave. He came around that evening, his hand bandaged, asking if we'd seen two boys that fit their description. He let us know by the way he looked at us that he knew what was going on. In September he put his house on the market and moved away.

He was out to kill Bam that midsummer night, though. The car's got those headlights that wrap around flush with the nose of the car. Bam knew it right away, even in the dark.

"Look," he said, "it's old Frog Face."

He stopped his bike smack in the middle of the street.

"Car!" he called, the way we did in the winter.

Instead of swerving around him, the guy stopped inches from Bam's wheel

"Get out of the way, please," said the driver in this voice, this fatigued, condescending, hateful voice.

"Go around, Frog Face," Bam said. I couldn't believe it.

"Move your ass, kid, or I'll run it over."

"Go ahead."

The guy considered this for a minute and then backed down the street all the way to the park where we played ball. At first I thought he was going to turn around but he stopped, still pointed toward us.

"What's he doing? What's Frog Face doing, Hill?"

I said, "How should I know?"

Then the Citroen's high beams flipped on and he started cruising up toward us, not really giving it much gas, just letting the car find its own way up.

"He's not stopping," I said, squinting, from the curb. "Better get out of the way, Mitch." What did I know?

He stood up on his pedals, balancing, waiting. Then he released his brake and, still standing, began to roll down toward the car. Though he didn't pedal, he was picking up momentum faster than the car. The collision was stupid, just a stupid, avoidable thing. When Bam hit, he had lifted his front wheel right off the ground. I couldn't see all that well in the dark but the way it looked, he was as bent on attacking the Citroen as Frog Face was determined to roll unimpeded up that hill into his own driveway. It sounded like a gun shot. Bam hit, slicing his leg open on his own fender, and somersaulted the length of the car over its roof. The car kept on going straight, running over the bike on its slow, relentless march home.

When Bam arrived, Gayle was having a bath and the baby was asleep. He had three studs in his ear, big deliberate holes in the knees of his jeans. His Converse sneakers were two different colours, one red, one green. Port and starboard, he said. He was drunk. He dangled a champagne bottle by its neck.

"Where's this kid?" he said.

I told him the baby was in its cradle in the bedroom. When he opened the bottle, the cork flew across the room and hit our one and only print, a Bateman cougar, cracking the glass. I came back from the kitchen with two juice glasses. He filled mine to overflowing and took a chug from the bottle. Some of the carbonation back-fired through his nose and he started laughing and sputtering.

He talked about what he was doing, working for a record distributor now. He had a company car, free concert tickets any time he wanted them, an expense account. He was making more money than his father.

"Most of it goes up my nose," he said.

For some reason he got to talking about this story his father had told him. Mr. O'Day used to work for a mining exploration company. Much of the electromagnetic work was done in the winter when they could get out onto the frozen lakes. It was tricky, though, getting up there. They had to wait until freeze-up to be sure it was safe enough to land the planes on the ice. Mr. O'Day was the leader of a group of eight men prepared to establish a base and run tests right through until spring thaw. His men were eager to get in there and start banking their isolation pay which would begin to be deposited the day they set up camp. The problem was that there had been a series of short freezes and thaws that fall and the ice was what they called candling. Mr. O'Day thought it wouldn't hold a plane. He stepped out onto the ice and showed them by ramming his axe handle down through the first crust. He wanted to wait another week.

The other men were not willing to wait. Mr. O'Day was replaced as leader. He was told that the plane was flying that day. He could come with them or stay. He thought about his wife and new baby that he had left so far away at home. If he had been single, he told his son, he would have risked it. They could probably run the plane on its skis as close to the shore as possible. If it started to go through the ice, the worst that would happen would be that they'd get wet and cold wading through the shallows. The balance was tipped, though, by the fact that he had two people back home depending on him. He decided to forfeit the isolation pay and stay put. There was nothing for him to do up there and so they shipped him home.

The plane landed safely and the crew had a successful winter. Their tests indicated the presence of a substantial ore body beneath the lake, what would become a lucrative mine. The man who took over from Mr. O'Day as crew foreman that winter went on to become a vice-president of the company.

"He said to me, he said, 'Mitchell, the night I drove you to the hospital, I was as frightened and angry as I have ever been in my life. I sat in that waiting room with your mother for five hours while they reattached the muscles and nerves in your leg and I wept. Like a little baby. Boy, it was as much for me as it was for you that I cried.' Doesn't that beat all, Hill?" said Bam.

I could hear Gayle's light splashing sound coming from the bathroom and I knew she could hear us. When she takes a bath, she likes to let hot water from the sponge dribble down onto her face and chest. Bam talked and drank until the bottle was empty. I had the one glassful. Then the baby woke up hungry.

"I just fed him twenty minutes ago," I said.

I got a bottle of breast milk from the fridge and heated it up in a pan of water. Bam stood in the doorway of the kitchen and watched.

"You got it under control, don't you, Bud?" he said.

I had the kid on one shoulder and I was swaying from side to side, trying to calm him down while the milk warmed.

"I'll be on my way, then," he said.

"Thanks for dropping by," I said.

"Is that all, Hill?"

"I guess it is."

"So you went ahead and married her."

"That's what people do."

"Frog Face," he said.

When she heard the door close, Gayle said, "Come in here. You have to see this."

I opened the bathroom door. The water was level with the top of the tub. Her breasts floated on the surface.

"Watch this," she said. The baby had stopped crying for the moment and was rooting at my shoulder. Gayle lifted her breasts and twin jets of milk spurted out. "As soon as your friend came in, this started to happen. I was listening to you talk and these started going crazy. Look at this water now." It was all cloudy.

"I thought you were going to say, 'As soon as the baby started crying'."

"No, it was as soon as I heard his voice."

"Why didn't you get out and say hello?"

"I don't know why. I was starting to flow. It was nice. I didn't want to move."

"He drank an entire bottle of champagne himself. He looks ... not so great."

"Then I'm glad I didn't get out. Here, hand him to me," she said.

"In the bath?"

"It's warm. Take his sleeper and diaper off." I undressed him and passed him down to her. "There. It's nice," she said.

It took a while for him to stop crying again. On the best of days he doesn't enjoy his bath in the little plastic tub we fill up on the kitchen table. Gayle played with him until he got used to the feel of the water. She held him so that he was half-floating, half lying on her stomach. Her milk was flowing so freely now that it was no effort at all for him to suck. They looked like sea mammals lying in the shallows, all sleek and pink.

"I'm glad I only listened and didn't come out," she said. "He is your best friend. I like to think about you having a best friend. Does it make you sad?"

I said, "Yes. Yes, I guess it does. He came over because he had heard about the baby."

"We'll see him again," she said. "What was that bang I heard earlier?" I told her about the picture.

When he had drunk his fill the baby fell asleep. The three of us stayed like that for a long time, me on the toilet seat, Gayle and the baby floating together in the steamy water. I didn't want to move.

A Dream of a World Without Women

Lee Gowan

WAKE TO THE smell of wax. Something greater than me rolls me across the hardwood living-room floor and into a collision with the wall. When I open my eyes a rolling bottle bounces off my forehead and I lie awhile, safe inside my skull, before I look again. There's the couch across the room where I passed out. Something presses me against the wall. I lift my head. Debris – beer bottles, mounds of cigarette butts and ash, the plastic head of a doll, his one eye open, staring – has collected, with me, along the baseboard. And that pressure, still a ghost pushing. Something greater than myself.

Gravity.

"My God. The house."

The doll doesn't answer.

The floor slopes up to the opposite wall. Dad's very particular about his floors: he likes them level. I shake my head, trying to realign my middle ear. The furniture's still in place, as though Dad nailed it to the floor, but the house is definitely listing, and the remains of the party have gathered against this lowest wall. Clambering to my feet, I stumble through the bottles and climb the floor into the dining room. The frilly plates and crystal glasses Mother left stand displayed in the china cabinet. I pass through the kitchen and the sunporch, using the empty coathooks for support, to the front door.

Stepping outside, I recognize the pasture, the barbed wire fence I helped build, the reddish-brown gravel, the clump of trees on the horizon. I'm at the top of the hill at the edge of the valley above where my father's house stands on a rise beside the river – or rather, where his house stood. Now it leans on the grid road, half-a-mile from home. Or rather, from foundation.

Party par tee par tea part e parrr teee parrrr teeeee

If I run as fast as I can to the lip of the valley, and if I don't look behind me once, the house will be back there where it belongs. Home will be in its proper place. This is only a dream. What has happened could not happen. Yellow sparks spin into my vision, but I don't stop running.

The foundation is empty. I turn. The house leans like a ship beginning to sink into the prairie. I puke in the ditch, wishing I were dead.

Harmon and Michael

Back at the house, I climb the stairs to their bedrooms, searching for remains – *no no God not dead not dead please not dead* – digging for them in a pile of fifty years of *National Geographic* in the corner of Harmon's room, digging until I collapse in a heap of glossy geography, New Guinea tribesman under my elbow, Oklahoma school teacher under my heel.

"It's all over."

What really horrifies me is that this is not the end; their deaths don't matter to the world carrying on through its paces like one of those Goddamned joggers in the city who've invented a way to make their hearts, for a few minutes a day, beat fast enough that they won't keel over and die at forty-five, and what does their meaningless expenditure of energy create except worn-out shoes and the extra few grey years and the extra few brown feet of sewage they'll drop for the rivers to wash away? The world will wind on down as though nothing had happened, until even I will be convinced that all of this was only natural – God's way.

A noise comes from a long way off: the purr of machine. My ears buzzing? I shake my head but the purr continues, gradually intensifying into the growl of my father's '52 Case. Scrambling to my feet, I stumble through the *Geographics*, descend the staircase, ascend the floor, until I'm outside in the breeze, sprinting once more toward the lip of the valley. An unsummoned image of my father driving the tractor slows me to a walk.

The tractor bursts through the horizon. Michael drives and Harmon, pale, sits on the fender. They drag a flatdeck trailer up after them. When they reach me, they stop.

"What're you smilin' about?" Harmon shouts over the grumble of the engine. "Your dad'll be home for supper. What's he gonna say when he finds the house up here?"

I don't answer. Michael spits. "Party's over," he says.

Once I had a mother, a great fat woman who jiggled when she walked and seldom spoke. I had a sister too, but mother was always hungry, and, though we lived on a ranch, there was never enough meat in the house.

"So what are we gonna do?" I ask. They don't answer. "What the hell *can* we do?"

"It's under control," Michael assures me, pushing the clutch lever ahead until the wheels begin to turn. When they reach the house he steers into the ditch and cranks it back toward me, then backs the flatdeck against the house before he kills the engine.

"Impossible," I say. "You'll never get it on there."

"Just watch," Harmon says. He jumps from the tractor and Michael hands him down two jacks, then jumps down himself with two more.

"That'll never work," I warn them as they start to jack up the low side of the house, Harmon at one corner and Michael at the other. "It can't work. How can it work?"

"Four jacks beat a full house," Harmon says. He leans his weight on the jack handle and the house inches higher.

"Is there anything left to drink?" Michael asks as he works the jack up another notch.

"No! There's nothing left, not even a house, except the one you're jacking off the ground here that'll fall – either the jacks'll tip or the house'll split in two.."

"Got a better idea?" Michael asks.

"Kill ourselves. Run away to Asia. Take a picture and sell it to *Better Homes and Gardens*."

"Do you want to help?" Harmon asks.

"I want to yell help! Wanting to is a long way from helping in a hopeless situation." Harmon ignores me. He knows I hate it when he ignores me. "Whaddaya want me to do?" I ask. Harmon pauses his jacking to lean on the handle and look at me. Alcohol pours off him in the form of sweat. I ought to collect a glass for Michael.

"Pray," he says. "You're the one who should pray."

I don't know what to say. Is he making fun of me?

"Pray?"

Harmon strains down on the handle again. The house creeps higher, to level and then past. "You'd be better at it than we are," Harmon says. "That's all I mean." They stop jacking. The side of the house resting against the road is the low side now; the south side is three-and-a-half feet off the ground, balanced on two flimsy looking jacks. Michael picks up his second jack and carries it to the other side of the house. I follow.

"I spoze you think I should pray too," I say to him. I know they're making fun of me.

"Can't hurt," Michael says with a straight face.

Can't hurt? As though he had ever explored a fraction of the possibilities of pain. I drop to my knees, pound them into the earth, and stare down at the crested wheatgrass. If they want a prayer, I'll give them a prayer. They're grunting, fighting the jacks, about to raise the house completely from the earth; I anticipate the crack of walls splitting or crash when the jacks topple. And I pray. I do my part to make the house fly.

"Oh Holy Father, oh Father who created this earth and then created man to destroy it oh great magician oh ruler of the universe and of man and woman and dog and rock and fish and ditch wheat oh Lord with your ridiculous rules your Law of the Arbitrary oh snidely sardonic sarcastic Father who sends His sons to be slaughtered in His name and to rape His daughters in His name and then turns on them all His children with His sneering scolding judging eyes and blames all of the bombs and burnt babies on us oh Father who enslaves us with His greasy guilt that only He can wash away if we pay Him enough if we can kill enough to pay Him oh Father who murdered our Mother long ago and for a long time we pretended we didn't notice so as not to arouse Your anger oh Father who killed our Mother and set us down here to kill Yours oh Father oh Father oh Father oh Father who gave us this world oh sweet father who made the water and the tree and the bark and the beetles under the bark and the woodpecker beating through the bark to eat the beetles under the bark and the porcupine eating the bark oh Father who made the beast and the breast and the hips and the soft skin of the thighs oh Father who we love and whom we hate oh Father if You are there if You are listening Father who built us with all care out of clay or ape or slime oh Father who created us and therefore must love us even though You have denied us You bastard have said to us You don't care have told us You don't care a bit for us have wiped Your hands clean like a butcher wiping away the blood of an animal oh Father please Father please help us oh Father please help us oh Father please Father please help us oh Father please help us please help us please Father please help us please Father please help us please Father please Father please Father please love us Father only love us Father, please!"

I scream the last over the growling of the tractor, my hands on the earth and my eyes closed. The tractor engine relaxes to an idle. I'm afraid to open my eyes. When I dare, I see the flatdeck under the house. Michael and Harmon lower the house until it rests on the flatdeck. Harmon turns to where I sit watching.

"Good prayer," Harmon says. Michael nods his head.

My sister, Angela, was the rebellious one. She walked halfway round the world, and her legs never once got tired. The amazing thing about her was her breasts. I thought so, at least, but apparently they were not all that unusual.

They bind the house to the flatdeck using ropes and nails. I help tie the ropes and hammer nails, toenailing the floor joists to the beams of the flatdeck. My aim is bad though, and I bend the nails as often as I drive them cleanly.

"We'll never get it out of the ditch," I predict, remembering a crooked rack of strawbales I built which tumbled me, riding atop the load, as Dad pulled it home. I felt it sway too hard and had to climb onto the side of the stack as it fell – a surfer riding a wave of straw – in order to avoid ending up under the bales. I succeeded in that, at least, emerging unscathed when the straw settled. Broken bales lay strewn about me. We reloaded those that were still whole. My father didn't speak. Neither do Harmon or Michael. They're tired of my pessimism, but I tell them once more anyway, "It's gonna tip for sure when you try an' get it on the road."

Michael eases the clutch-stick ahead and the gears mesh as smoothly as can be managed with the old Case. The house jerks forward, boards yawning as the wheels roll through ditch holes.

Harmon walks beside, as if he doesn't realize that the house could collapse on him, or as though he planned to catch it if it did. Michael feeds the tractor more gas, and cranks the wheel to turn up the incline onto the road. The house moans, leaning ditchward, the nails screaming as their hold slips on the wood, and the house lists, wailing, bangs level and the balance shifts backways onto the road, sways hard, skeleton shifting, nails straining the other direction, and then it begins to swing the opposite way again, then reverses its course more gently, then more gently still. In the ditch Harmon and I jump in circles, hugging, howling in celebration, while Michael drives with one hand on the wheel and one arm raising a clenched fist.

I love women. But it must be admitted that if they are only equal then nothing has been lost without them. It's basic math.

At the lip of the valley, Michael stops the tractor to test the brakes. "Take it real slow," I say. "Don't get goin' too fast or them brakes'll never hold."

"Suuure," Michael says, and jerks the clutch ahead. The house leaps forward, then slows again as it dives into the valley.

"Asshole," I say.

Harmon and I climb through the fence into the pasture. We'll cross the river at the rapids, where the bulls cross, and meet Michael and the house at the foundation. The tractor chuffs hard, holding the house back. We run down the first steep incline, then walk slowly down the slower grade.

"I dreamed I was walking here last night," Harmon says, looking over his shoulder to check the tractor and the house as he speaks, "and I didn't know what I was doing here and then this helicopter flew over and I started running because, all of a sudden, I knew you'd done something terrible and the guys in the helicopter were looking for you."

"Me?"

"Yeah. You did something terrible and the helicopter and a hundred-and-fifty policemen with rifles and dogs were searching for you. You know how you just know that kind of stuff all of a sudden in dreams? It's like, as soon as you think something could happen in a dream, it does happen."

"Looking for me? What did I do?"

I detect the manifestation of my own greatness. I hope

Harmon hasn't mistaken me for my father. We look somewhat alike, only I am younger.

"I wasn't sure at first. I remember I was walking at the top of the hill, where the house was when we found it this morning, and all of a sudden I got really scared. I didn't know what the hell I was doing here, but I knew something bad was happening, and then all of a sudden this helicopter flew over. I started running down the hill right here and when I came into this draw your dad was sitting over there waiting for me, and he caught me and threw me on the ground and stepped on my throat and asked me where you were. I told him I didn't know and I said, 'What'd he do? What'd he do?'"

"What'd I do?"

Harmon looks at the ground.

"You died."

Lichen crunches under our feet – the only sound except the steady growl of the tractor.

"I wonder what that means?" I say, stopping to pull a cactus out of my sock. It catches my finger and I have to pull it off with the other hand.

"And then I woke up," Harmon says.

I nod. "Dreams." Harmon nods. We turn to look at the house; the tractor engine works easier now. It's half way down the hill, through the level grade, then plunging into another steep descent.

A sports car, white with black flames on the sides, speeds by the driveway. It brakes, fishtails on the gravel, then onto the bridge where it stops on the asphalt. The tires spin smoke and the car fires onto the grid, roaring up the hill towards the tractor. Michael brakes on the incline.

"Keep going," I shout. "They'll get out of your way."

Michael either doesn't hear me or ignores me.

The car barely stops in time to avoid colliding with the tractor. Three figures get out of the car and approach Michael.

"Who the hell are they?" I ask.

"Friends," Harmon says.

"What do they want?"

Harmon shrugs.

Michael gets off the tractor and all three follow him back to the house.

"The stupid ass. The brakes'll never hold," I shout.

The four climb up onto the flatdeck and enter the house. Harmon starts running and I follow, trying to keep up, but

Harmon was always faster. The tractor sits there with all that weight behind, pushing.

Harmon and I stop running to watch the house plow the car off the road and gain speed on down the hill and across the bridge, shaking like a localized moveable earthquake. The ditch yawns, anticipates its return.

"It'll stop now," Harmon says, "It'll slow down and stop."

At the driveway it makes a neat right turn, wrong turn, and crosses the ditch on the approach into the north pasture. It teeters along the edge of the cutbank, above the creek, rolling toward my father's poplar grove – all those rows of trees he planted on the corner of one of his fields – rumbling as it accelerates. And for all my listening, I don't hear one scream. Why don't they scream?

The house disappears over another hill.

Harmon and I are knocked on our bums by the explosion. The white cloud rises, billowing from the funnel of its own force, and then graceful plumes of ribbons float out from the smoke: blue and green and red and yellow remnants of the cloud, drifting down to earth. I can't move. That was Michael.

I try to cry but can only sit wide-eyed, amazed at the power in my father's house. This is unbelievable. This is impossible. When I consider it all, nothing that's happened today could be real. There is no power so great as the one I'm dreaming. None of today could be true.

Harmon stares at the ribbons of flotsam wafting to earth. I stand and pull him to his feet.

"Don't worry," I say. "This didn't happen. It couldn't happen. We've been dreaming all along. It was a nightmare. Don't worry."

Harmon nods his head, staring at the ribbons falling.

"I'll show you," I say. "I'll show you it was a dream."

I grab Harmon's hand and lead him to the road, over the bridge, across the approach to the north pasture and along the trail running above the cutbank that leads to the grove.

"I'll prove it was just a dream."

"I believe you," Harmon says, catching a red ribbon that loops down from the sky.

"Drop that! If it wasn't a dream the house would have ended up down there." I point over the edge of the cutbank to the river. "If it wasn't a dream the house would have never been off its foundation in the first place. How could the house get up there?" Harmon shrugs and drops his red ribbon. "It has to have been a dream. I'll show you it didn't happen." My logic has almost convinced me. We approach the edge of the hill where the house went over, and I try not to imagine rubble.

First, we see a neat pile of fresh yellow two-by-fours; then, a clean square of concrete. Michael carries a stud, walking behind Dad, who marches, with nails in one hand and a hammer in the other, across the foundation.

"Oh shit," I say.

Dad's muttering to himself: "Stupid damn kids don't have enough brains or ambition to grow moss but they manage to destroy a man's house. It's enough to make you wonder. No respect for anything. With all the things I've done for them this is what I get for thanks. Bring me a stud!"

Michael brings one of the two-by-fours and holds it in place while Dad nails it to the plate. "Get another," Dad orders and starts mumbling again: "What in hell did I do to deserve this. Worked hard all my life. In my day you didn't get away without hard work. Did everything I could for them. That was my mistake, I guess. My own damn fault for givin' them what they should've had to work for. Couldn't expect them to be anything else but a bunch of drunken, swearin', dirty-minded fools." And with that, he finally glares at me.

What can I say? Excuse me? I run down the hill shrieking, "You asshole! You're the one who killed our mother!"

"I what?" he cries indignantly. "Like hell I did. If anybody killed her she killed herself. Wouldn't walk to the other end of the yard if she could get the truck started and she never stopped eating until she was so big you couldn't walk around her. You must remember her: how could you forget anything that big?"

But I can't, even though I'm the oldest and she had to still be around when I was two when Michael was born. All I remember is what Harmon has told me. That, and the other part, about how she was murdered, which I found written in a leather-bound book that was hidden in a crawl space behind the linen closet, about how I'd once had an older sister named Angela, but my father had cooked her and served her to my mother, telling her it was roast pig, and when my mother had finished her meal my father had told her the truth, and she threw up all her insides and died.

"The thing is," Dad says, turning for a moment to Michael, as though for confirmation, before he looks back at me, "the body's a machine. Now you know very well that a machine could run forever if it was taken care of – if someone adds oil and looks after it and doesn't put anything in it that could hurt it. Well, if you don't go puttin' drugs and booze and forty-pounds-of-food-a-day into your body then there's no reason it shouldn't last forever. The only reason it doesn't last forever is that something in the body's been programmed to make it break down. Built-in obsolescence."

"So God's no better than General Motors," I say.

He sneers at blasphemy. "I guess He figured if He didn't do that the world'd be overrun with people. He never figured that so many'd be out to kill themselves." With that he goes back to his hammering nails.

"Well, you won't have to worry about watchin' me kill myself anymore, cause I'm leavin'."

When the nail's in, and a moment later the echo of the last blow returns, he looks up at me, his eyes so fierce with anger that I can almost see tears. "I don't care," he says. "I couldn't care less," and he turns his attention back to the next stud. Then I turn and, without a goodbye for Michael, walk back up the hill to where Harmon still stands.

"Don't listen to him," Harmon says, grabbing my arm. "He doesn't mean it." But I keep walking. For a moment Harmon follows and then he bends and picks a green ribbon from the lichen and stuffs it into my shirt pocket.

"Keep this," he says. "Maybe someday it'll mean something."

When I wake up, everything is fine. There is even a woman lying next to me in bed. And I think, what a nasty bit of work that was. So I wake her up to tell her.

Biographical Notes

BONNIE BURNARD is the author of *Casino* (nominated for the 1994 Giller Prize) and *Women of Influence* (winner of the Commonwealth Best First Book Award). She edited an anthology of love stories titled *The Old Dance* (Coteau 1986). After residing in Saskatchewan for several years, she recently returned to live in southern Ontario.

LAURIE BLOCK is a poet, storyteller and child care consultant in Winnipeg. His poetry chapbook, *Governing Bodies*, was published in 1988 by Turnstone Press. "Duets in the Dust" is his first published fiction.

BRIAN BURKE has had more than forty stories and two hundred poems published in literary journals in Canada, the USA, the UK, New Zealand, Australia and other countries. His chapbook, *margaret atwood island*, was published by above/ground press in 1994. He lives in Vancouver.

WARREN CARIOU is writing a thesis on the poetry and art of William Blake at the University of Toronto. He was raised on a farm near Meadow Lake, Sask., and has worked as a construction labourer, technical writer, and political adviser.

RICHARD CUMYN's first collection of short stories, *The Limit of Delta Y Over Delta X*, was published in 1994 by Goose Lane Editions. His stories have been published in magazines and in *The Journey Prize Anthology VI* and *The Grand-Slam Book of Canadian Baseball Writing*. He lives in Halifax with his wife and two daughters.

LARRY GASPER is a Regina writer of speculative and mainstream fiction. He is working on a collection of interconnected short stories, of which "Princes-In-Waiting" is the first to be published.

GRAEME GIBSON is the author of five books, most recently *Gentleman Death* (McClelland & Stewart, 1994). He is active in writers' organizations and has been writer in residence at the universities of Waterloo and Ottawa. He was appointed Member of The Order of Canada in 1992.

CURTIS GILLESPIE has had fiction and non-fiction published in such magazines as *Malahat Review*, *Fiddlehead* and *Western Living*. He is program manager for Catholic Social Services in Edmonton.

LEE GOWAN's collection of short stories, *Going to Cuba* (Fifth

House), was published in 1990. He wrote the screenplay for "Paris or Somewhere" (Credo, Real Eye Media), released in 1995. He works as a sessional lecturer, library clerk, and installation officer in Swift Current, Sask.

DAVID HENDERSON is from Vancouver (via Boston and San Francisco) and now lives in the Ottawa area. He has published many works of short fiction and poetry and was a finalist in the 1994 League of Canadian Poets National Poetry Contest.

GREG HOLLINGSHEAD teaches at the University of Alberta. His book of short stories, *White Buick*, won the 1993 Georges Bugnet Award and his novel, *Spin Dry*, won the 1993 Howard O'Hagan Award. *The Roaring Girl*, his new collection of short fiction, is to be published in fall, 1995.

MARK ANTHONY JARMAN's books include *Dancing Nightly in the Tavern* (short stories) and *Killing the Swan* (poetry and photographs). "Exit Pursued by Bear" is excerpted from a novel to be published by Douglas & McIntyre. Jarman is a graduate of the Iowa Writers' Workshop now teaching at the University of Victoria.

DON KERR's most recent book of poetry is *In the City of our Fathers* (Coteau). He has just completed a play, "Lanc," about a Lancaster bombing raid over Germany. He teaches English at the University of Saskatchewan and is working on a book of poetry and prose on cinema.

WILLIAM KLEBECK's short stories have been collected in *Where the Rain Ends* (Thistledown, 1990). His work has also appeared in *Grain*, *NeWest Review* and other magazines and anthologies. He lives in Wynyard, Sask.

PATRICK LANE has published twenty-one volumes of poetry over the past thirty years. His collection of short stories, *How Do You Spell Beautiful* (Fifth House), was published in 1992. He received the 1979 Governor General's Award for poetry for *Poems, New & Selected*, and the 1988 CAA Award for his *Selected poems*. He lives in Saanichton, BC

EDWARD O. PHILLIPS is the author of six novels, including *Sunday's Child* (1981) and *Buried on Sunday* (1986), which won the Arthur Ellis Award. Before he began writing he was a painter and teacher of English and visual arts in Montreal.

CRAIG PIPRELL was a writing instructor at the University of Victoria who also wrote fiction, drama and historical pieces. His work has appeared in several magazines, including *CRASH, And Yet,* and *Seventh Wave,* and in the anthology *Nothing North of Disneyland.* He died in 1994.

WILLIAM ROBERTSON is a writer living in Saskatoon. He enjoys hunting, fishing, cooking, music and books. He is the author of *Standing on Our Own Two Feet* (Coteau, 1986), *Adult Language Warning* (1991), and *k.d. lang: Carrying the Torch* (1992).

LEON ROOKE now lives in Eden Mills, Ont., after several decades in Victoria. He has published three novels and thirteen collections of stories, the latest being *Who Do You Love* and *The Happiness of Others.* His novel, *Shakespeare's Dog,* won the Governor General's Award for fiction in 1984.

MICHAELVSMITH is a young writer who has attended classes at the Sage Hill Writing Experience. He describes himself as a no-nonsense man from the industrial city of Cornwall, Ontario, "a poet and playwright and pansy."

BIRK SPROXTON sees himself as a prairie bird. He was born in Flin Flon and has studied and taught in the flatland cities of Regina and Winnipeg. He now roosts in Red Deer. He is the author of *The Hockey Fan Came Riding* (Red Deer College Press) and two other books. He flies across the west calling "Next year! Next year!"

RUDY WIEBE received the Governor General's Award for his most recent novel, *A Discovery of Strangers* (1994). He has written three short story collections and nine novels, including *Temptations of Big Bear,* winner of the Governor General's Award in 1973. Until recently he taught English and creative writing at the University of Alberta. He still lives in Edmonton, where he writes full-time.

About the artist

KAREN SCHOONOVER received her BFA in painting and ceramics from the University of Calgary in 1975. Her work has been exhibited extensively and is included in several public collections, including the Saskatchewan Arts Board, the Dunlop Art Gallery and the University of Saskatchewan. She is director/curator of the Rosemont Art Gallery in Regina.

Acknowledgements

Stories in this collection which have been previously published include: "Steady, Marcus, Steady," in *Prairie Fire* (Vol 14, No 3); "Princes-In-Waiting," in *Grain* (Spring '95); "Digs," in *Prairie Fire*; "Badlands," in *Quarry*; "Rose Cottage," in *The Malahat Review* (#102); "Blurred Edges," in *The Antigonish Review* (Winter 1985); "The Boy From Moogradi and the Woman with the Map to Kolooltopec," in *Ploughshares* (Emerson College, Boston, 1993); "The Redheaded Woman with the Black, Black Heart," in *Boundless Alberta* (NeWest Press) and broadcast on CBC Radio's "Alberta Anthology"; "Pancho Villa's Head," in *Canadian Fiction Magazine* and *87: Best Canadian Stories* (Oberon); "In the Ear of the Beholder," in *Canadian Fiction Magazine*; "Thin Branches of Rainbow," in *Grain*; "Lightning Strikes," in Matrix; "Pilot," in *Grain* (Spring 1992); "Exit Pursued by Bear," in *Queen's Quarterly*; "A Dream of a World Without Women," in *Prairie Fire*; "The Sound He Made" is reprinted from *The Limit of Delta Y Over Delta X* by permission of Goose Lane Editions. Copyright © Richard Cumyn, 1994. At the time "The Sound he Made" was selected for this anthology it had been published in *NeWest Review* and the *Journey Prize Anthology*.

Re: *In the Ear of the Beholder*

Excerpts from THE MIND OF NORMAN BETHUNE, copyright © 1979 by Roderick Stewart, used with the author's permission.

Excerpts from A GUN FOR SALE, by Graham Greene, used with the permission of the publisher, The Bodley Head.

DREAMS ON FIRE © Kathleen O'Brien. Quote used with permission of Harlequin Enterprises Limited.